Capricorn, Utopia & Days Gone By

Novellas *Volume II*

Jerry J.C. Veit

BLUEWOLF PUBLISHING
Waukesha, WI 53186

The Complete **Jerry J.C. Veit** Collection:

Apocalypsia
Into the Night
The Glass Demon
Capricorn
Days Gone By
Utopia
The Form

Library of Congress Control Number: 2022919603
ISBN 979-8-9871666-6-6

Books

Capricorn

The City is a Cancer. They are the Cure.

Contents

1

Capricorn, Montague, and the Demon

Save moderation for death. To live is to indulge. Do not be convinced that you are here to save the world; you are only here to best it. The conquering of achievement takes nothing more than a little greed and lust. Clever diversions and conundrums occupy brilliant minds are all juxtaposed together in a world fueled by deception. Do not be fooled into the belief that a hopeful mind will bring riches and success. Positivity can only lead to disappointment. Ambition can only award the brave the status of pariah. Don't look for divinity if you want to survive here. Become worse than the evilest of your foes and maybe when it meets you—it dares not attack. There are no consequences or punishments for the actions of others. There is no justice except for individual retaliation. The law is crafted at whim and all who oppose must suffer. That's all there is.

A war-torn city lies in shambles with no chance of ever being built up or repaired again. What it was is no longer relevant—it is now a place without order. A fierce storm produces sudden thunderclaps and heavy rain that cause the streets to become deserted this evening. Flickering neon lights reflect in the puddles of the flooding sidewalks and the gutters where debris prevents the sewers from redirecting the water. Some inhabitants find suitable and well-concealed shelters where they live unseen and only leave to gather much needed supplies and food. The more sinister roam freely. They congregate in bars to drink and gamble or prowl the city for unsuspecting victims to rob and rape. But one has never seen the city, never lived in it, and does not know anything about it. She was born in the sewers and for twenty-two years lived unnoticed.

Underneath this ruined city and through the zig-zagging corridors and drainpipes, if one should ever find the exact path, it will lead to a spacious room decorated with Persian rugs across the floor and red velvet drapes and various tapestries covering the gray stone walls. This room does not fit, not for the sewers, not even for this city. It resembles a room belonging to a castle of an aristocratic order who holds lavish parties and celebrates happily. It cannot exist during these hellish times.

In the middle of the room is a large king size bed with a red quilt and a multitude of pillows. The room is lit by several ornate standing candle holders and one hanging chandelier.

It's to be expected that the dark and damp environment will attract a multitude of bugs, but their existence is rarely accepted. A giant brown spider slowly crawls up one of the stone walls. It's a hunter of rats and may not harm a person, but its grotesque appearance is an unwelcoming presence here.

"Spiiiderrr, Spiiiderrr. Do you know what happens to those who enter my space without permission?"

The sound of a crossbow firing echoes followed by an arrow striking through the spider's abdomen. White guts ooze down the wall as the spider curls into a ball.

"Now you do."

The voice belongs to a girl named, Capricorn. She hangs upside down with her legs wrapped around a rafter and lets her arms dangle down while holding her pistol crossbow. She's barefoot and dressed in a white nightgown but shows little concern for her minimal attire. She slides off the rafter and then spins before landing on her feet. Her extended time in solitude has played havoc on her mind and has created illusions and fantastical expectations. Capricorn leaves her crossbow on the floor and then stands up straight. She raises her arms above her and starts to sway her body from side to side while wiggling her fingers.

"O' Gods and Goddesses both old and new. To the Muses, the Fates, the Graces, and the Furies. Can you hear me? Can you see me? My name is Capricorn." She waits for a response, but the room remains silent. She yells in annoyance. "Why do you ignore me?! Am I not still in your favor?" She spins across the floor, always swaying her body, always wiggling her fingers as if preforming a ritual dance. She looks up at the ceiling and suddenly becomes paranoid. She gasps as she looks around the room as if afraid. She drops to her knees and attempts to cover her upward view with her open hands in front of her eyes. "The yellow eyes are back—Always watching me. No, not you, leave me alone! I know you. You are nightmare coming to steal my sleep," she says and then runs to her bed and crawls under her covers.

She hides for about a minute before peeking out again. After a short moment she feels safe enough to toss the covers off and lies on top of the bed. She squirms, rolls, and turns on the bed while giggling. She kneels up and begins to sigh and moan as her hands run up her stomach to cup her breasts. "Now it is your turn to visit me, sensations, desires." She grabs a pillow and puts it in between her legs under her gown as she rubs herself against it and humps it as she clutches her fists around the quilt. After several moments she grabs the pillow and throws it away from her while yelling. "You will not have me!" She raises her hand and looks concerned at the blood on them. Her white gown also has blood stains just under her waist. She holds her bloody fingers above her as she inspects them. "I bleed again. Why do I bleed? I see no wound. Was I a bad person? Is this my prison? Is this punishment?!" She waits for an answer again but receives none. "Answer me! Why must I be abandoned here alone?!"

She becomes agitated and jumps out of bed in a fit of rage while screaming. She pulls pillows and blankets off the bed and tosses them around before tipping over some of the furniture pieces. After her outburst she falls to her knees and sobs. She lies on the floor and curls up into the fetal position before tugging on a nearby blanket and rolling herself up inside. Too tired to return to the bed, sleep finally finds her where she is. She has grown up in this room all alone, it is all that she knows.

It's still raining hard in this crumbling modern metropolis that fell into ruin and decay. Neglected, it became a victim to weather, fire and time itself. Trash and papers collect in the corner of a small alley between two brick buildings. Among them is a newspaper showing a picture of people holding torches and guns while fire engulfs a store in the background. The headline reads: Riot escalates into Civil War.

A scaly hand with long black fingernails pokes out of a black sleeve as it slaps against the brick wall of the corner building. This creature roams the night and hides entirely inside a black cape, with a large hood, to conceal its identity. It's referred to only as, the demon, and it talks in a deep growling tone.

"In the shadows I hide. On wind currents I glide. I am serrated inside." The demon darts its head up and to the sides as it catches the scent of its prey. The sound of a heartbeat from an unknown direction fills the air. The demon listens with interest. "One heartbeat in the still of night. Music to my ears." The demon hurries through the rain and around corners with speed and agility as it leaps over obstacles or pushes them out of the way with ease.

A man is walking sluggishly ahead. Drunk or drugged it matters not now. The demon quickly closes on the unsuspecting man and with one quick flash of claws blood gushes into the air. The man falls to the ground with nothing more than a faint moan escaping from his lips before expiring. The demon leans over its prey and begins to feast. It rips into the dead man's chest and snaps off rib bones and then tosses them away after scraping all the flesh and muscle from them. It claws deeper for the man's lungs and heart with a ravenous appetite, but an interruption comes from above.

Someone leaps off a fire escape and lands several feet from the demon. This man is also cloaked, but a human hand grasps the handle of a sword resting at his side. The demon turns its attention now to this new being as the man draws his black steel sword from its sheath. The demon roars and charges with swiping claws. The man holds his ground calmly and lands a swift kick to the demon's torso to force it back. With several quick swings the man attempts to land a devastating blow, however, the demon is a formidable foe and blocks or dodges every attack.

The rain blankets the two in a life and death struggle, but neither appears to be giving up nor tiring. Soaked clothes do not slow either down as their attacks slice through the large raindrops.

While many would avoid the demon, this man eagerly engages it with determined strikes. The demon finally lands a well-placed crushing punch to the man's shoulder blade. He falls to his knees with a grunt, but quickly swings his sword up above him. The sword cuts nothing but air and rain. The man stands up and looks around him, but the demon has swiftly retreated in an unknown direction.

At one time he embraced his birth-name of Montague, but now he has no need of it, there's no one left who knows him by it. He will come to be known by another—

Montague slowly approaches the victim lying in a pool of blood. The blood mixes with the rainwater as it streams down the street gutter. He looks down only for a moment before walking past him. "The city is a plague—and I am the penicillin," He gruffly announces. Montague sheaths his sword and then continues his stroll through the city. The rain doesn't seem to bother him as he ponders his recent observations. "Underneath the streetlights and the warm glow of the neon signs there is pain and destruction. There is anger and sorrow." Montague leaves the city behind him as he climbs the soaked grassy knoll at the city's outskirts. "Walk through the streets and you will hear crying, you will hear yelling, and the desperate calls filled with agony by the victims captured by predators. I looked into the eyes of this professional evil, and I did not escape unscathed. We who lack claws cannot live unseen by these natural born hunters. This city is a cancer—a concrete and steel jungle." Montague stands at the top of the hill looking down at the rolling hills of the countryside as the faint city lights are in the background behind him. The wind blows his hood off his head to reveal a face chiseled by the harshness of survival. His skin is rough, and his glare is focused. A deep scar runs over his left eye across his nose and ends at his upper lip. In between the lightning and thunder he yells into the storm. "Montague!! No, not anymore—I am the heretic."

The rain has finally stopped, but the ground is still soaked and flooded as night falls over the city. A woman is running through the street with her fist holding her coat closed over her chest. She hurries up the steps to an apartment, but as soon as she opens her door a figure grabs her from behind and forces her inside.

The woman screams as she's tossed to the floor. The man tears her coat off and then pulls down her pants. He holds her shoulder down with one hand and keeps his knees in between her legs as he attempts to expose himself.

Chance has put Montague here as well. He kicks the man off the woman and then pushes his sword through his sternum before he can react. The woman scurries to pull her pants back up and recomposes herself while watching Montague pull the sword from the dead thug. In a shaky voice she announces her gratitude, but Montague's response is his idea of advice. "Stay hidden or adapt." He did not save her, he killed someone he despised. He's not a hero, he's vengeance.

He exits the apartment and continues his walk in the dark streets without any further word or thought of the woman. Montague does not want the job to save others, he just happened to be there, and his desire to cull the city of all who occupy it is the only motivation he needs to step in on someone being attacked. "No one deserves a trial here. In this city if you aren't a victim, you're guilty."

Montague enters a decrypted warehouse that looks as if it may collapse at any moment. Debris, scattered wood planks, and metal rods are spread across the floor and several steady streams of rainwater continue to leak through the roof. It could pass as a large dumpster. It is a fine home for rats and an acceptable home for those who have no place else to go. Montague climbs a rusted metal staircase that squeaks and groans with every step. He continues across a catwalk that leads to a metal door. He takes out a keycard and swipes it on a device to open it. Perhaps he should have looked behind a stack of crates nearby first. A man steps out from behind them as soon as the door becomes unlocked and puts his pocketknife to Montague's throat while motioning him to walk inside.

"Alright, slowly, walk inside," the man commands. Montague cannot reach for his weapon and obeys the order for now. They enter the small maintenance closet that Montague calls home. An old mattress with a pillow and blanket is on the floor in one of the corners and a table with a supply of flashlights, first aid kits and knives is in another. Several boxes are neatly placed under the table that contain bags of food and bottles of water Montague scavenged or traded for. The man ignores Montague for a moment to take out his bag as he begins to toss Montague's food and supplies inside. Montague takes a step towards the table.

"Do you have children to feed?" he asks. The thief halts his actions to point his knife in Montague's face.

"What the fuck do you care?"

"I actually don't," he admits and then quickly snatches a hunting knife from the table to slit the robber's throat. He then pulls the man, who's clenching his neck and choking on his own blood, towards the railing of the elevated walkway before pushing him over. If the knife didn't kill him the thirty-foot fall did.

Montague stares at him expressionless as blood begins to spread around his body. He's emotionless as he glares at the corpse before returning to his room and lets the door close behind him. He lights a lantern, hanging on a hook, and then lies down on the mattress. He stares up at the ceiling for most of the night while surrounded by the dim glow until finally falling asleep. Society crafted a cold and desensitized heart out of Montague over the last several years. A young mind is filled with hope and wonder, but Montague misses neither; they never brought him anything good anyway. He only has one feeling now—distaste.

2
The Meeting

Capricorn is sleeping peacefully when shadows begin dancing on her face. The disturbance awakens her as she sits up with a jolt. She's surprised to see a woman clothed in a white gown with a white veil draping over the sides and back of her head. She holds a small bowl of fire in the palm of her hands while pacing in front of Capricorn's gaze.

"Do not be afraid, child," she begins.

"Who are you?"

"My name is Hestia."

"Hestia—?" Capricorn ponders the name for a moment. "I know you. You're the Goddess of the home?"

"Yes," Hestia answers with a smile.

"I have been trying to speak with you many times. Why do you never answer me?"

"Things are not as you believe them to be, little one. Your innocence allows our meeting for this one time only." Hestia strolls toward Capricorn while giving her a fond gaze. "I come with a warning, and a message. Both good and evil are coming. The first has done bad things but will not hurt you. The one who follows will. Go with your instincts, they will never lead you astray." Hestia begins to fade away as Capricorn shouts out.

"Wait! What does that mean? Don't leave me yet!" Capricorn awakes and sits up in bed while looking around the room, but she's alone. Was her encounter real, or nothing more than a dream?

The demon's domain resembles a crypt in the catacombs of a dungeon; lit by torches and populated with several iron barred prison cells. It was once a mid-size jailhouse but has since been claimed by the demon to house its damned captives. Within these walls suffering and anger endures to amplified and extreme measures. The stones are stained with blood and gore and the hallways are lined with maimed limbs that hang on hooks over pools of blood from the still dripping body parts. Naked corpses impaled through the rectum and protruding out of the victim's mouths occupy other areas. This is a place where death does not come quickly, prolonged torture and horror are experienced by all who are unfortunate to be a prisoner of the demon and its followers. The most corrupted human beings gladly stab and flay the captured men and women to the point of near death. They carryout unthinkable and horrific acts with no regret or hesitation. They sodomize the enslaved in dark corners and watch venomous insects and spiders crawl, bite, and sting with delight.

The demon strolls past each cell while peering inside. "My memory is enduring. I know of things that the world has forgotten. My joy is your pain. My life derives from death." The demon stops at one of the cells and grips one of the iron bars with its scaly hand. A lifeless body of a man covered in grime and clad in torn rags lies in a pool of dried blood. The demon continues its speech to his prisoners. "Deny the mind hope and bliss and visions of madness set in. Deny the body compassionate embrace and humanity dies. The mind refuses to live, and this body breathes no more. I am eternal." The demon opens the next cell door and approaches a man chained to the wall. The man hangs helplessly as horror robs him of his voice. "Bring me my enemies and slaughter them before me." With a snarl the demon's head, still hidden inside the hood, aligns with the man's neck. The man lets out a gurgled yelp only for a moment before his head falls and a river of blood runs down his body. The demon releases him and swallows the chunk he took from its victim's neck.

Meanwhile, at Montague's hideout. Montague is looking into his cracked mirror with a pail of water nearby and a razor to his cheek. He finishes a stroke and then shakes the razor in the water before returning to his face. He loathes his reflection and can't see anything other than the grotesque scar running the length of his face, but how it got there is only a partial memory. It starts with a room engulfed in fire. He can feel the heat of the flames and the smell of dense smoke to this day. He can hear the crackling of the building's framing before it begins to fall around him. He continues looking into the mirror and remembers the demon hunched over a woman who's face down on the floor as flames continue to climb the walls. The demon turns to notice its observer and leaps toward Montague while swiping its claws. Montague takes a deep breath and closes his eyes. He hasn't forgotten that day, but he cannot retrieve the entire memory. It's shattered bits and pieces hint at the true history he had with the demon, but what's remembered is quickly buried again. He finishes his shave and then dumps the water over the railing.

Not all the rainwater he catches is deemed drinkable. Many times, the water runs through rusted metal, insulation or rotting wood, but what cannot be consumed still has a use to bathe with. The luxury of warm water is no longer available, and all forms of soap is utilized, if discovered. This includes dish soap, livestock shampoo and industrial sanitizers. The skin is left dried out and prone to weeks of rashes, but any sort of hygiene is still a safeguard from illnesses caused by fecal waste and bacteria. This warehouse once supplied factories with cleaning solvents, lubes, and oils. It also still has a stockpile of floor and glass cleaners that Montague can rely on as a backup; however, these tend to cause sheafing, and the closest thing to lotion to relieve this comes in the form of food-grade machine grease. Luckily it has been some time since Montague had to rely on this method of washing. He dresses himself and grabs his cloak before leaving once again.

The street market acts as a trading post for the citizens of the city and is a high traffic location in the center of a large intersection. Tents, umbrellas, and booths are set up filled with both useful and useless products. The merchants either try to peddle their goods by calling attention to their offers or remain silent while on guard for potential thieves.

Montague finds comfort hiding under his cloak while in the

company of others. There's always a level of mystery and caution when dealing with one who cannot be completely identified. If, and when confronted the cloak acts as a degree of power, no one really knows what to expect from him. Some rather not take the chance and assume he is not to me trifled with, while others may look forward to the challenge. He isn't aware that he has been making a name for himself over the years. The people know his cloak and his sword, but they do not need to know his face. That will soon change; however, Montague's reputation is about to make him very well-known. He continues to make his way past displays while ignoring the merchants explaining how their products are a must have in times like these.

"Thief" someone cries out! A man sprints through the crowd with a jar under one of his arms, but he doesn't get far. A knife is hurled through the gawking crowd and lands swiftly into the bandit's back. He falls in front of Montague, who only takes his next step wider to walk over the corpse, otherwise, he remains unfazed about the situation. Montague justifies his actions as defiance to the locals who live among him. In reality, the city is corrupting him. He's being consumed by the wicked ideals that run rampant. He is overcome with hatred and disgust, he's cold and value others less and less. He is slowly being claimed by that which he hunts. He will argue that he stands in opposition to his surroundings, but he's closer to becoming one of the fold than he knows. Then again, sometimes it takes extreme suffering to find courage and hope.

Montague locates a man who's selling bottled water and approaches his stand. He picks up a bottle, uncaps it and then takes a whiff. Water is a dangerous product to buy. It can look clear and clean and can even taste pure on the first few sips. However, it is common for merchants to mix poison in water or process it through poor filtration that presents a breeding ground for bacteria. This will cause food poisoning or lead to a fever. With no doctors and clinics available the common flu can be a death sentence. Disease can claim more victims than any weapon that's wielded.

"It's fresh," the water merchant assures Montague.

"Where does it come from?"

"It's from the city's water supply, but we run it through our own purification filters too." Despite the lawlessness, people have still developed ingenious methods to survive. Being the first to ransack local hardware stores and stocking up on tools and other essentials help too. With so much already looted, and now hidden in secret areas around the city, the only two methods to attain goods are to barter or kill. Montague reaches into his pocket and takes out a flashlight. He turns it on and off several times to prove its operational.

"How many bottles for a working flashlight?"

"One thing for one thing."

"In that case this flashlight also has three batteries inside." The merchant seems a bit stunned that his hustle backfired.

"Fine, no more than three bottles for flashlight."

"Good enough," Montague agrees. He hands him the flashlight and then picks up and pockets his bottles of water. Nearby another merchant is calling attention to his stand.

"Come closer and gather 'round! Choose a girl for a minute or two!" Montague glances up at four women standing on a raised platform. From what he can tell they seem to be there by choice as they giggle and smile at the men cheering nearby. The women sway their hips provocatively and push their butts out to reveal their thongs. One of them goes a step further and unsnaps her bra to flash the crowd which gets a roaring reaction. The merchant continues his sale. "One beer or wine per minute or trade a gin, brandy whiskey or tequila and get a bit longer—that is if you can last." The merchant lets out a long raspy laugh. A few men raise their bottles of booze high above them and start to advance toward the merchant as he attempts to keep order. "First come, first serve, but don't worry. These little nymphos are always ready."

A display stand crashes to the ground and people start screaming from another area of the marketplace. Montague jolts his head in the opposite direction, toward the ruckus, just as a man soars over the crowd that's scrambling away. The man falls near Montague with a broken neck, but this attack reeks of a foe he knows all too well. Taking advantage of the distraction, and the fleeing masses, several men quickly grab the girls and start to run off as their pimp demands payment. "Payment upfront Goddammit!" Knowing the ilk of these men they have no intention of paying or ever releasing the women back, but that is not Montague's problem. He is about to have his hands full with another threat. Across the vacant lot stands the demon motionless and dead locked on Montague as if silently taunting him. The marketplace is only occupied by Montague and the demon, but around the perimeter are some merchants, who refuse to leave their goods. They remain ducked low in their stands while slightly peeking up to cure their curiosities.

The demon hunches over and places its hands on the ground followed by Montague slowly drawing his sword. The demon charges toward him on its hands and feet similar to a gorilla. Montague takes his stance and waits for the demon to come to him before the two meet in a frenzied battle. The demon's claws meet Montague's steel blade before the demon switches its attack to its second hand, but Montague dodges. Montague jabs his sword and then swings it upwards, but the demon avoids both attacks. It counters with a kick to Montague's ribs, but besides uttering a grunt, Montague ignores the sharp pain. He thrusts his sword through the demon's cloak and manages to graze its flesh. A drop of blood falls from Montague's sword as the demon takes note of it. They keep their eyes locked while slowly circling each other.

"Your strength is impressive. I never fought anyone like you before," the demon admits.

"You put me on this path," Montague responds. The demon's laugh is a deep rumbling one that vibrates in Montague's chest and echoes like thunder in his ears.

"You have no idea how much like me you really are. Join me and I will give you some of my power."

"I'm not after your power; I'm after your death."

"Fool, I am death."

The demon spins into a deadly combo of kicks and claw attacks, but Montague ducks, dodges and blocks them all. In the middle of the ordeal Montague swings his sword before backing away. The demon looks at its arm to find it bleeding through the sleeve.

"So, death can bleed—twice," Montague jokes.

"Naive and unwise. You will not survive your feud. You will not survive me."

The demon becomes enraged and roars with extreme energy before it picks up a metal pole embedded into a concrete block from a downed display stand. He lifts this heavy piece of debris and wields it with ease. Montague's slight victory has filled him with a false sense of confidence, and he decides to taunt his enemy further.

"What's the matter, a human too much for you?"

The demon brings the hulking concrete block down with incredible speed and slams it in front of Montague. The road cracks with every hit the demon makes as it seems to be doing so without end. These attacks are clearly not meant to hit Montague and he assumes they are meant to unnerve him, but little does he know he's being forced into a trap. The demon swings the pole where Montague is standing to send him into a dive and roll. His chosen escape route is where the demon wanted him to be.

"Last chance to take my offer," the demon warns. Montague is tired from the onslaught but remains steadfast.

"Take mine. And maybe Hell will be temporary."

"You shall see it first!" The demon smashes the block against the ground one last time. The cracking road creeps around a large perimeter with Montague in the middle. Montague looks around him as the ground breaks apart and then collapses. There's no time to escape—Montague falls into the darkness of the sewers.

Montague doesn't know how long he was unconscious, but as he peers up at the gaping hole above him, he can see the light is fading. He realizes he's trapped under a pile of concrete blocks and rubble and begins to squirm and crawl while groaning. His sore body is stiff and aches, but nothing appears to be broken. Montague struggles to free one of his arms so he can lift a chunk of concrete enough to squeeze his other arm out. He tosses or pushes the rubble away as he huffs and puffs as little by little, he becomes free. He's finally able to slide his legs out and becomes free from his captivity. He pulls off his hood and sits up to rest and regain his strength. He looks up again at the hole he fell through more than twelve feet above him. There's nothing to scale to get back up to the surface—at least not at this location. He'll have to find another way which means exploring the labyrinth-like sewers. He staggers to his feet and spots his sword a few steps away; he picks it up and sheaths it and then reaches into his pocket for a flashlight he had not yet traded away. He turns it on before advancing down the sewer corridor in search for his exit.

Montague ignores the rats scurrying around as he continues his search. He shines the light on the walls around him and ahead as he walks, but to his dismay he finds a dead-end. He wonders if he took a wrong turn somewhere, but any path he decides to take will always just be a guess. He looks through a grated cover over the end of a pipe and views the other side. Perhaps that will take him closer to a ladder to a manhole. He pulls and wiggles the grate, but a bolt seems to be holding it in shut. Montague looks around on the ground for something that may help him. He spots a rock of a suitable size and slams it several times on the bolt. The rusted bolt begins crumbling away until the grate slides to the ground. Montague holds his flashlight in front of him and crawls through the pipe. A swift kick knocks the latch loose on the grate on the other end allowing Montague to freely lift the hinged cover up. After he slides out of the pipe he is faced with more choices.

Three corridors branch off here and any one of them could lead to an exit or nowhere. From his viewpoint they all look the same and with a sigh decides to just pick the one to his right. This decision also appears to have a grim outlook as no ladders or stairs have been located yet. Several drainpipes line one side of the wall but climbing into one that doesn't clearly show the other side may not be the best path. To make matters worse Montague's flashlight begins to flicker. He looks at it and shakes it. "Oh, come on," he says with frustration. The light continues to flicker and dim. "Come the fuck on!" Navigating the sewers with a light is proving to be hard enough. Without one will surely mean his demise. Montague continues with a dimming light hoping to find his exit before the batteries die. He turns down another corridor, but his visibility has greatly diminished to just about two feet in front of him. A glimmer of hope enters Montague when he spots a metal contraption on the wall just ahead. He hurries toward it and discovers it is indeed a ladder. "Yes," he whispers ecstatically as he follows the ladder up with the last of his light; however, hope soon turns into despair. The ladder is missing its middle portion and the distance between the lower and upper ends cannot be scaled. "What the fuck—" Montague says in a low defeated tone. The flashlight slowly dims more before finally going dark. Montague tries to turn it on and off thinking that he can tap into some reserved juice that may still be in the batteries. The struggle is futile, the flashlight is dead. He loosens his grip on the light and lets it slip through his fingers into the stale water he's standing in. Montague has fought heartless criminals and survived multiple encounters with the demon, a feat that no one else can claim, but lost in the sewers is how Montague will perish. He glances ahead to take note of his own faint shadow on the sewer wall. *At least I will have company in my final moments*, he thinks. He stares at his shadow before he's able to think past his woes. "Shadow—" he whispers out loud. "How can there be a shadow unless there is light?" He looks behind him and notices a faint orange glow gleaming out of a large drainpipe in the wall. What other choice does he have but to pursue the origin of this mysterious light. Montague climbs inside the pipe and heads toward the light at the end of it.

Montague enters the room cautiously while taking in his surroundings in bewilderment. This is a comfortable shelter, and its occupants will undoubtedly be ready to defend it vigorously. At that moment a voice echoes through the room.

"Who are you?" Capricorn asks while staying hidden from view. Montague looks around the room and above him trying to pinpoint the voice but does not respond. "I asked you a question," Capricorn continues. Montague neither replies nor moves from his spot. Only his eyes scan the room for the owner of this voice. Just then, an arrow whizzes past him into the wall by his right ear. Montague freezes his glare on the arrow inches from his face. "Answer me or the next one will be embedded in your skull!" Capricorn warns. Montague decides introductions may be required at this point.

"I am the heretic."

"Is that a name?"

"It is who I am." Montague pauses before asking his question. "And who may I be speaking with?" Capricorn drops from the rafters right in front of Montague and raises her pistol crossbow to his neck.

"My name is Capricorn."

She takes several moments to study Montague's entire appearance with interest. She lifts her other arm and hesitates for a moment before tapping his shoulder. She quickly withdraws her hand and continues inspecting Montague. This is the first contact she's had with another person in her adult life, and the first time seeing a man. She glances down and notices his sword and slaps the sheath. "What is this?"

"It's my sword."

"What does it do?" she asks. Montague's response is simple and to the point.

"It kills." Capricorn gets close to his face to look him in the eyes and jerks her crossbow.

"I have something that kills also."

"I can see that."

"It is called a twang."

"That's a description of its sound; not its name," Montague corrects her in a sarcastic tone. Capricorn gently presses the arrow tip that's loaded in her bow against his neck.

"Are you renaming my things?!"

"No, it was named a long time ago."

"And what would you call this?"

"I would call that a crossbow." Capricorn retracts the bow from his neck and then holds it above her. She turns it at different angles while admiring it as if seeing it for the first time.

"A cross—bow?" She giggles then pauses before laughing again, but then becomes serious immediately after. She forces the bow back to Montague's neck with anger. "It's called a twang!!" Montague raises his arms with open palms.

"Alright, alright, it's a twang." Capricorn smiles feeling she has won the disagreement. She lowers her bow and leans her head close to Montague's face again. She takes in his smell and then puts her hand on his cheek. She smells around him and sniffs his hair. Montague remains still and silent unsure what this strange woman is doing.

"You have a smell about you."

"Do I?"

"Yes. It's unique." She reaches for Montague's sword, but Montague tries to stop her by placing his hand on the handle. Capricorn slaps his hand away and grabs the handle. She keeps her eyes fixated on his as she slowly withdraws his sword. She holds the point of his sword toward him with one hand and the crossbow fixed on him with the other as she slowly backs away from him. She never takes her eyes off him as she sets both weapons on her nightstand and then returns to Montague. She caresses his face with both hands and then lets them slide down his ribs. She puts her face closer to his and licks his cheek.

"I feel strange," she admits.

"You feel strange?"

"Shut up!" she shouts. She backs away and stares at him for a moment before yelling out and grabbing his cloak with both hands at his chest. She whirls him around and pushes him onto the bed and then jumps on top and straddles him. She calms down again and gazes at him with intensity. Montague looks up at her in utter bewilderment at her latest action. He knew something was off about this woman, but he did not expect to be thrown in bed. Capricorn glides her hands up his stomach and to his shoulders.

"You aren't quite like me," she observes.

"I'm a man—and you—you are a woman."

"What is this talk of man and woman?" Montague thinks for a moment. How does he explain what sets a man apart from a woman?

"It's complicated," he answers.

Capricorn lowers her head close to Montague's lips. Emotions, desires, and needs are all swirling together in a large ball of confusion for Capricorn. For Montague, he cannot deny his distance from others have created a void; a forgotten feeling that Capricorn is reminding him of. He does not plan it or has time to consider it when he lightly touches her lips with his. Capricorn backs away and looks at him for a moment. Neither have words to utter. They are completely entangled in each other's presence and the exploration of this moment. Capricorn lowers her head back and places her lips on his. Montague kisses her as she catches on and repeats his actions.

Capricorn's curious hands removes his cloak and shirt before tossing them to the floor. She unbuttons his pants and begins to slide them down, which soon joins his shirt on the floor. He allows Capricorn to take her time and lets her advance at her own pace. She puts her hands on Montague's chest and feels his heartbeat.

"Your heart is beating fast. Do I frighten you?"

"It's not fear," he replies softly. Capricorn removes her gown and allows Montague to slide his hands up her ribs and cup her breasts. She lets out a sigh and a moan as Montague gently pinches her nipples. She has waited long enough to take his briefs off. She removes them and slides her hand up his scrotum and then wraps her fingers around his erect penis. She rubs her vagina against him and is content feeling him pressed against her. Eventually his penis slides inside of her. She accepts this new feeling and thrusts back and forth slowly while he caresses her breasts and nipples. As the moments pass, she becomes more comfortable with him and the sensations she's feeling. She speeds up her motions as they let out moans of ecstasy. They kiss again as Montague holds her as she thrusts above him until he ejaculates. He lets out several grunts and sighs as his body jerks from his release. He lets his arms fall to the bed and Capricorn stops.

"What's wrong?" she asks. He smiles as he places his hand on her cheek.

"I just need time." She smiles and nudges her head against his hand. She pulls her covers over them and lies next to him in his embrace.

For the first time Montague has found a place that is not dark and cruel. He has found a person who is pure and innocent. This place is safe and warm, and the air feels light and inviting. Does the city call him back? Of, course it does. It is his purpose and his duty. It is what gives him meaning and a sense of accomplishment. Then again, does the city need him or does he need it? Can he return if he chooses to leave?

For Capricorn the fear of being alone again is a dreaded thought. The idea that this is just a dream, and she will awake to an empty room again haunts her. Her body needs another just as much as her mind does, but how will she cope after this experience if he is not here anymore. That cannot happen. She will not allow it. She needs to demand it.

"You cannot leave." Montague doesn't answer right away. He almost doesn't want to admit it.

"I have to." Capricorn pulls away and sits up while glaring at him. Her voice is strict but cannot hide the fear she feels.

"No, you can't. I don't want to go back to being alone."

"I will come back. I promise."

"Where is it that you must go?"

"To the city."

"What is this—city? The word means nothing to me."

"The city is above us. I must return to it. I have an obligation."

"To do what?"

"To kill those who have no reason to be alive."

"Who gave you this task?"

"Nobody."

"Then why is it yours?"

"Because there is no one else." Capricorn is not happy with his reasoning but becomes fixated on his scar instead. She assumes it has caused him much pain and just as the scar is still seen so is the pain still felt. Montague doesn't have to admit it or tell her, she can sense it. She gently rubs her finger the length of his scar.

"What is this?" she says compassionately and with concern. Montague seems ashamed of it and turns away.

"It's a scar. It was given to me by something which I've hunted my entire life. Something which I still hunt. I know it only as the demon." Capricorn gently guides his cheek back towards her.

"Will I like this city?"

"No, it is home to the lurid and the crude and a trap for those who are neither."

"I have never left this room. I was born here. I shared this space with another I called mother. She taught me many things. She told me about all the different deities and whom I should pray to for different things. But they never answer me when I call."

"It's mythology. It's only for entertainment." Capricorn ignores his response and continues.

"Mother, she would always make me feel better. My sweet Capricorn, my sweet Capricorn, that's what she used to say to me." Tears start to roll down her cheek. "One day her eyes closed, and she never opened them. I called to her, and she wouldn't answer. I don't know why." Capricorn cries as she remembers the memory as Montague listens showing empathy for the first time. He too has a memory of his mother, but it is clouded and skewed. "I could see her," Capricorn continues. "I could see her, but something told me she was no longer there. She left me." Montague brings her close and hugs her.

"It's okay, these things happen." Capricorn, comforted in his embrace, lies her head on his chest after wiping her tears away. Her thought returns to this city Montague seems so eager to return to despite his clear hatred for it.

"In this city—there are others?"

"Many others."

"I'm envious; all I hear is the loud hum of empty space."

"Solitude would be grand." Capricorn lifts her head and looks at Montague somewhat surprised at his response.

"Solitude is terrible!" Capricorn kneels upright on the bed and puts her hands on top of one another against the middle of her chest. Her voice is both angry and sad. "I am abandoned; denied my desires as if punished for some horrid act I did not commit!" Montague sits up and leans back against the headboard.

"I share in your emptiness. It's like my essence has been drained and my soul has surrendered. My skin is rough and bumpy; as if I'm in a permanent chill. My hair stands on edge; as if I'm in a constant state of fear. All that I am is a shell."

"Can you not stay with me? Can you not care for me?" Montague looks at Capricorn in silence for a moment, but his words seem to contradict his own heart.

"Love is not how the world works; it always has been and will always be war that shapes life. Every future generation is worse than the one that preceded it. In the end, all you have is your unrealistic dreams of a future you could only hope for as an imaginative child. The lucky die young—they never get to see the reality that exists around them." Capricorn slowly inches her way back towards Montague.

"Perhaps, you accept only what lies before you, but cannot discover how to make it more desirable." Capricorn lies down on her side facing away from Montague. He turns to look at his sword on the nightstand where Capricorn had placed their weapons. He then looks back at Capricorn as if silently making a choice. At this moment he cannot find a suitable response to Capricorn's statement. She has left him speechless. He gets close to her and puts his arm around her while resting his head on his other arm. Capricorn takes his hand and holds it tight as the two drift off to sleep.

3

This Cold Night

It's difficult to tell if morning has arrived with no natural sunlight or windows to the outside. Montague can't remember the last time he had such a peaceful and uninterrupted sleep, but as soon as Capricorn has awakened any hope to rest is futile.

"Wake up sleepy, wake up," she says while shaking his shoulders energetically. Montague slowly opens his eyes to see Capricorn swaying from side to side as she looks above her. She then drops to her knees and wiggles her fingers and arms above her head while leaning backwards. Montague is curious about her actions and keeps watching. She stands back up and twists and turns her body and swings her head from side to side and tossing her long hair around her. She is either dancing to music only she can hear or trying to get the attention of the Gods she believes are real. She jumps on the bed and rolls over Montague to the other side and then crawls back over Montague.

"Why are you so hyper?"

"What's that?"

"It means full of energy."

"I don't know. Why are you still in bed?" Capricorn grabs his hand and pulls him up. "Come," she insists.

Montague puts on his pants and follows Capricorn to where the room connects to a narrow hallway that leads to a large hole in the sewer wall. It looks as if it has been broken down deliberately by force with sledgehammers. Beyond this wall is a damp cavern with water dripping from the ceiling into small pools, and the walls are heavily covered with dark brown lichen. Capricorn breaks off a piece of this lichen and unexpectedly shoves it into Montague's mouth. Montague makes a disgusted look and pulls it out.

"Eat," she demands.

"You can eat this?"

"Yes, it's rock tripe. Look." Capricorn snaps another piece off the wall and eats it as proof that it's edible.

"Is this all you eat?"

"No, sometimes rats, but never spiders."

"Well, at least you've set your standards."

"I hate spiders. Yuck. Disgusting creatures." Montague can't help but smile as she kneels to sip the water from the pool.

"Where does this place take you?" Montague asks while looking further into the cave.

"I don't know," Capricorn answers with a shrug of her shoulders. "I never explored it," she admits.

This cave might lead back to the surface, but it also could make one who ventures into it become lost. A crash from the room interrupts Montague's thought and Capricorn jolts her head up from drinking. "Someone is here. Something not invited looms near." Montague puts his hand at his side and then looks down where his sword would have been if he had it.

"Dammit," he whispers. He glances at Capricorn and holds his open hand out towards her. "Stay here." Montague cautiously makes his way back to the room and peeks around the corner. He adjusts his gaze to the nightstand where Capricorn's crossbow still rests, but his sword is on the floor. He looks around the room and up into the rafters before stepping inside. He does not see anyone here, and wonders if the sword somehow just slid off. He heads to the nightstand while still looking around him just to be sure. He looks down at his sword and listens; nothing seems to indicate another presence. He reaches down and picks up his sword, but a slight creak above him makes him look up. The demon drops down from the rafters nearly on top of him. Montague rolls across the floor and out of the path of the demon's swiping claws. The demon speedily climbs up the wall and looks down at Montague without falling from its vertical position.

The candlelight shines on the face of the creature hiding inside the cloak. It has large bulging red eyes and a bat's nose. The demon opens its mouth to growl showing its long fangs and forked tongue. Montague stands back up with his sword ready.

"You are the essence of weakness, born out of misery. Off guard. Now perish," the demon says. It jumps toward Montague and attempts to wound him as Montague swings his blade hoping to do the same. Neither can leave a mark on the other as their fight takes them around the room. The demon tips over a standing candle holder as the fight continues, but Montague is too focused on the demon's movement to notice the tiny flame spreading across the rug. A quick swing of Montague's sword tears the demon's cloak, but it has failed to reach its skin. The demon climbs up the wall and onto a rafter before leaping onto another one. Montague has lost sight of it after the leap. It either vanished or is hiding in a darkened area. He slowly steps backwards while looking up until he bumps into the nightstand where Capricorn's crossbow used to be, but it is now missing.

"Capricorn—" he softly says to himself.

Crouching on one of the rafters Capricorn darts her eyes below her with her bow ready, but she's oblivious to the fact that the demon is carefully stalking her from behind. It walks upside down across the ceiling while making no sound. Capricorn remains focused below her as the demon gets ready to pounce. She's still unaware that it lurks right behind her. In a split second it leaps and collides into Capricorn. She screams and falls backwards toward the floor.

"Capricorn!" Montague drops his sword so he will be able to catch her in his arms. The demon takes the opportunity to attack and stampedes toward them while Montague is defenseless. Capricorn raises her crossbow, takes aim, and then fires at the demon. The demon is too close to avoid it and the arrow pierces its shoulder. It roars and flails around tipping over another standing candle holder. The fire from the first one has already begun to climb up one of the tapestries. The demon jumps over the flames spreading across the floor while still roaring. It finally retreats out of the pipe opening that Montague had first entered through. Montague unknowingly had led it here by leaving his scent as a tracker. Montague retrieves his sword and then picks up a pewter candelabra with two lit candles.

"Come on. We need to get out of here," he says in a tone that demands urgency. He runs to the bed and picks up the rest of his clothes as Capricorn looks at the fire engulfing her room with sadness and fear. Montague grabs her hand, but she pulls away.

"No, this is my home!"

"If we stay here, we will die."

"This is all that I know. This is all that I have," she cries.

"We do not have a choice." Montague reaches for her hand again and runs with her to the opening of the cave just as the rafters fall behind them. They take a few steps into the cave before Montague sets down the candelabra and puts the rest of his clothes on. Capricorn looks back at the faint orange glow flickering through the hole in the wall.

"Mother told me never to leave the room. It was not safe."

"She was right." Capricorn looks at her arm and notices that it's bleeding. She sets her crossbow down and licks her wound, but Montague gently lifts her up.

"I can take care of that."

"Where do I go now?"

"I have a place, but first we need to find our way out of here." Capricorn stays close to Montague as the two travel the only path the cave has given them. Capricorn snaps another piece of rock tripe from the cavern wall and eats it.

"I don't know how you can eat that," Montague says.

"I have always been eating it."

"Did you mother bring all that furniture into the sewers? Did she make that room?" Montague asks.

"I don't know. It was always that way to me, and I never thought to wonder what it was like before." Montague's curiosity is not answered, but it doesn't seem to matter now any way. The room is most likely nothing more than ash and dust now.

Montague helps Capricorn scale the rocks as they make their way to a ledge that arcs upwards. It's a glimmer of hope since up is exactly the direction they must go. When they near the top of the ledge light can be seen shining through a crevasse. It's not steep at all and can easily be reached, but where will they end up?

"That looks to be our way," Capricorn observes. Montague looks at Capricorn, in her white gown, and knows she needs to be a bit more inconspicuous.

"Yes, and you can't go out there dressed like that." He helps Capricorn into his cloak and pulls the hood out to cover her entire face and head. He also pulls the sleeves over her hands so no part of her can be identified. Montague blows out the candles and tosses the candelabra to the side. They scale the rocky wall toward the opening by grabbing onto protruding rocks and utilizing the narrow flat ledges to plan their ascent. Montague exits first and then pulls Capricorn up to the surface, which looks to be a small overgrown neighborhood park. Several benches covered in vines and a broken swing set is all that remains of what was once a happy place to visit. Montague takes a moment to get his bearings before he realizes where they are.

"Okay, we are on the other side of the commercial block. It's a little bit of a walk, but we should make it to my shelter, as long as we don't draw any attention." He turns to face Capricorn and holds her hands in his. "Do not take off your hood, do not talk, to not hold my hand or walk close to me. We have to look like two people no one wants to encounter." Montague pauses. "At least this damn scar is good for something. But you need to stay hidden."

"Are we playing a game?" Capricorn asks. Montague thinks for a moment, her child-like mannerisms may be how he can make her understand.

"Yes, a game. Sweet Capricorn is hiding, and she must not be seen or heard. Do you understand?" Capricorn nods her head.

Montague makes sure his sword is in clear view as the two walk the street occupied by once family-owned stores and consignment shops. They have all since been looted and now remain vacant and forgotten. A man with long hair and unruly facial hair takes notice of the two walking his way. Montague continues on his path, if he changes direction or slows his steps it will appear as weakness. The man takes a swig from his bottle of vodka and glares at them as they approach closer. He takes a step towards them, but Montague gives him a scowl that flares his scar out. The man takes a step back and continues his drinking without a word. There will be more people out when the sun goes down than there are now in mid-day. Many are still sleeping off their hangovers or scavenging. Only predators roam the city streets at night, all else stay well hidden.

Montague and Capricorn finally enter the warehouse. "Follow me and be careful," he says. They climb the rusted staircase and then make their way across the catwalk to the metal door. Montague takes out his keycard and pauses while looking at the stack of crates nearby. He draws his sword and quickly points it ahead of him as he sidesteps around the crates. No one is there this time. Montague swipes the card and then opens the door when the light turns green. He holds it open to let Capricorn in before making sure is shuts and locks. He gently puts his hands inside the hood and guides it back from Capricorn's head.

"Did I win?" She asks. Montague smiles.

"Yes." She looks around the small dark room and seems disappointed.

"Is this where you live?"

"Yeah, this is it." Capricorn is used to candles, rugs, tapestries and a big comfortable bed with pillows and covers. This room is dark, cold, and the mattress, on the floor, looks the farthest from comfortable.

"We were better off in the cave," she says softly. "I don't like it here."

"Neither do I," Montague agrees.

He sits Capricorn down in a chair near the first aid supplies and then kneels to clean her arm wound with a cotton swab. Capricorn watches him intensely as he wipes the dried blood away and then begins to wrap a cloth around her arm. He looks up at her and exchange smiles. "There you go. All better." Capricorn leans forward and kisses his cheek before wrapping her arms around him and putting her head on his chest. Montague embraces her and kisses the top of her head. Up until this very moment he hated everything about everyone. He leads her to the mattress and helps her lie down. "Rest here. It's not better than what you had, but it's all that I have."

"Where are you going?" she asks when she notices he's walking away.

"I'll just be right outside this door. I need to make sure it's safe and we were not followed."

For several moments Montague remains standing on the

catwalk while resting his elbows on the railing. He glances up though the warehouse windows and notice the setting sun casting a red and purple glow on the horizon. He then redirects his gaze below at two dogs searching for food. Hunger has made them mad and have driven them to hunt people. It is unwise to think they can be domesticated now; they will never again be considered pets. The door opens behind him, and Capricorn walks out with a blanket draping over her shoulders. He glances back and gives her a half smile before returning his eyes to the ground.

"Why are you still out here?"

"Just thinking I guess."

"Your room needs tapestries," Capricorn says while yawning. Montague chuckles.

"It needs a lot." Capricorn joins Montague at his side, but neither talks for a moment.

"This morning—what was that thing that ruined my room?" Capricorn finally asks.

"The demon." Montague answers plainly and without showing emotion.

"That's what you were talking about before?"

"Yes." Montague keeps a blank stare ahead of him and his voice is monotoned. "I was fourteen when I first saw it. I remember fire all around me. It killed my mother and then it came after me." Montague lightly touches his scar in remembrance of that night. "I have been surviving on my own ever since." Montague pauses, he doesn't know why he's opening up to Capricorn, but keeping these feelings inside for so long has taken its toll on his burdened heart. "I've ran into it so many times I've lost count. And every time it manages to escape. It cannot be killed. It is here to torment me."

"You dwell on all the times you couldn't kill it. You should remember all the times that it couldn't kill you," Capricorn points out. Montague turns to face her but becomes lost for words. All he can do is smile as his answer. How did a girl who had no interaction with others or experience with the world gain so much wisdom?

"Did the city always look like this?" she questions.

"No, but it might as well have been. I was just a child when the riots first broke out; my father was killed in them. I don't remember now what the spark was that ignited the flame. Most likely it was nothing more than a loose thread; a loose thread in which no one could negotiate a solution. They just kept pulling at it and pulling at it until a simple sewing needle could no longer repair the damage. The aftermath is the city we inhabit now—a city without order." Montague lightly caresses Capricorn's hand before she grasps it and holds it against her chest. "That's why your mother must have gone into the sewers when she was pregnant with you," Montague adds. "She wanted you to grow up without ever knowing this place. Without ever falling victim to it." Montague thinks out loud at how the city has affected him. "Even though I have survived it. I am still one of its casualties. I can never go back. My soul is tainted, my sense of wonder and hopeful dreaming has long been vanquished. All my aspirations have been diminished."

"I know you," Capricorn begins. "You hide behind a fake smile assuring yourself the world will never notice. You go to sleep at night and dream. And these dreams evolve during the day into a reality you can only wish was yours." Montague listens to her with all his attention. Capricorn pulls her hand away from his and then puts her fingers just inside her lips. She glances away for a moment and then back at Montague. "You wonder if you made a mistake somewhere in your not too distant past or perhaps paying for a sin committed in a not so distant life. You feel there is always something more you should be doing; someplace you should be going, but in the end, you can't bring yourself to walk ten feet from your door. You fear there's nothing in this world that's meant for you, or you fear when you do find it you won't be able to hold onto it. Maybe it won't be as pretty as it was when it was in your head. You feel like you need to do more, but you don't know where to start." Capricorn has stripped Montague's defenses away. His eyes show vulnerability, his hard face softened. "You believe you should have had it long ago, but the strange assumption that you never will see it is all you can think about. You want an answer from unconventional means. You need to be told beyond a shadow of a doubt. You want it so bad you can almost see it, but it's still too far away to touch. Yes, I know you because I know myself."

"You do have more wisdom than me," Montague says after a long pause.

The glow from the flashlight lanterns cast shadows of

Montague and Capricorn intertwined with one another. They kiss passionately before Montague works his lips to her neck. He strokes her cheek as he sucks on her neck before descending to her breasts and nibbling on her nipples. She presses his head against her bosom wanting him to continue what he started. He squeezes her breast with one hand as he shows each nipple the same amount of affection.

Montague kisses Capricorn's thigh while his hand massages the back of her opposite upper thigh. She rubs his head and relinquishes herself to the moment and the feelings that are born. Montague kisses around her belly button before working his way lower. Capricorn breathes heavier as she lets him indulge his fantasies. He licks her clitoris while inserting two fingers into her vagina. She moans and whimpers as he pleasures her. He inches his way back up and inserts his penis into her. She folds her arms around him and closes her eyes while tilting her head back as he thrusts faster. After he ejaculates, he slides next to her and the two remain embraced.

"I never knew being with someone could feel like this," Capricorn says.

"Me neither," Montague admits.

"You're better than a pillow," she confirms. Montague laughs.

"Well, I'm glad about that." Content in each other's embrace the two drift off to sleep as the soft light from the lanterns gently fade.

The next morning, Montague is dressing and equipping his sword when Capricorn awakes.

"What are you doing?" she asks.

"I need to make a run for food and supplies." Capricorn picks up her gown and stands up to put it on.

"I'll come with you." Montague knows she's far too innocent for this world and lightly brushes her cheek.

"No, the city isn't a safe place for a beautiful woman such as yourself. Besides that, the demon is still out there." Capricorn looks around the room before finding and picking up her crossbow.

"I won't let the enemies hurt you," she says as determined as she can be. Montague just smiles.

"Thank you, but it will be safer for you here." Capricorn frowns and then forces her leg in between his before tripping him and pinning him to the floor. She draws his sword and holds it to his neck while sitting on top of him.

"Perhaps you were under the illusion that I am unable to take care of myself." Capricorn keeps her eyes glued to him, but his silence is her answer. Her stern glare becomes a wide grin as she kisses him on the forehead before standing back up. Montague continues laying on the floor dumbfounded at what just happened.

"Come on, lazy," Capricorn playfully taunts. What choice does Montague have now but allow her to accompany him—with some precautions in place, of course.

As usual the street market has a decent crowd as the two make their way towards it. Capricorn is once again hidden under Montague's cloak as she listens to his advice about all things concerning this market.

"Half of everything here is stolen, some of it is handcrafted and the rest is junk. Don't listen to anyone who shouts about their merchandise. If it was indeed helpful there would be no need to call attention to it. Everyone is trying to take advantage of everyone else. You have to play the same game as your opponent and honor only exists with a hint of fear. Everything else comes with experience—of which I have ample." The first stand they pass is stocked with colorful fabrics and blankets. Capricorn forgets Montague's explanation and becomes distracted.

"Ooo, soft blankets," she says and starts to veer closer, but Montague takes her by the arm and steers her away.

"No soft blankets. Another rule of shopping is to know exactly what you want and need before arriving. Don't allow yourself to be misled and never drop your guard. No one is trustworthy here."

"I need pointy sticks for my twang," she says.

"Okay, that's good, but up here they are called arrows for a crossbow." Montague and Capricorn locate a booth with various knives and swords on display. Montague whispers to her before they reach the husky, bearded man behind the stand.

"Let me do all the talking." The man notices his customers and greets them warmly.

"Ah, finally people with intelligence. Walking around without a means to protect oneself is after all not too smart." Montague gives him a smirk before speaking.

"Would you by any chance have arrows for a crossbow?"

"Hmm, what kind of crossbow are we talking about?" Capricorn quickly takes out her crossbow and holds it up before slamming it on the stand. The merchant is taken by surprise by her rapid and aggressive action as he stands frozen in place. He finally becomes more intrigued with the bow and picks it up to admire it.

"Ah, a compound pistol crossbow. You don't see too many of these. Not cheap either." He sets the bow down and reaches below the stand before laying two handfuls of arrows on the stand. He picks one up and places it into the bow to discover it fits perfectly in the groove.

"Yes, these should do nicely. There's about forty here. How many do you need?

"All of them," Montague answers. The weapon merchant looks at Capricorn and then Montague.

"Does your companion not speak for himself?

"Quite a compliment actually. He only speaks to those he's about to kill." The merchant looks back at Capricorn and accompanies his sheepish smile with a small wave.

"My apologies, sir." He then turns his attention back to Montague.

"What do you offer for these many arrows?" Montague sets a hunting knife down in front of the merchant. The merchant inspects it in lengthy detail before turning his attention back to Montague.

"It's a good quality knife and all, but as you can see, I have plenty of knives and daggers." Montague thinks for a moment before taking his knife back and replacing it with a bottle of clear liquid.

"Perhaps some gin then?" The man picks up the bottle and swirls the liquid inside.

"This looks like water to me."

"I will allow you to try it." The merchant glances at Montague unsure of his sincerity before uncapping the bottle and taking a small sip. He takes a moment for the flavor to take its full lasting effect before nodding his head in acceptance.

"That is pretty good." He puts the cap back on and sets the bottle down. He strokes his beard for a moment while thinking. "I would say this gin is good for about twenty arrows." Capricorn abruptly turns her head to face Montague, but he has a response ready.

"That bottle of gin can either get you drunk or be traded for a woman." The man chuckles. Alcohol is the best form of currency throughout the city and where there's booze, there's women with no boundaries.

"Would you like a bag?" the merchant asks. The trade is a success.

Elsewhere, the demon's torture is continually ongoing from day and throughout the night; never halting and never lessening. Most tortures involve dismemberment or physically harming the body. Barbed chains are used as whips and victims die in a bloody mess with no feature remaining to identify them. Other tortures are meant to destroy the mind and make the victim hopeless and afraid. Since the body doesn't succumb to its injuries these tortures are endless.

A prison chamber holds a naked woman who's bound and gagged while bend over a metal table. A grisly man approaches her from behind and pulls down his pants. She whimpers only for a moment when he begins raping her. The woman does not utter so much as a mummer afterwards. She knows it will do her no good. Nothing she does will make her avoid this outcome. When the next man steps up to have his turn, she remains silent. She does not squirm or shed a tear; she has given into her fate.

Braziers line the sides of another room, which belongs exclusively to the demon. A man wearing an overcoat and a black mask on the left side of his face approaches and stands up-right and silent until he's addressed. He has assumed the name Diomedes and never once shared any other name to anyone else; however, the demon knows more about him than it will let on.

"Do you feel uncomfortable in this room, Diomedes?" the demon begins. "Does it bring back bad memories? After all it was fire that stole half your face."

"Fear does not own me," he answers gruffly.

"No, you join it. Assuming you will be safe as its ally." The demon extends its clawed hand out from its cloak and makes a fist that flexes all its blood vessels in its hand. It then continues to speak in a growling tone.

"Montague, the heretic, different, not in man, but in soul. What is it that men obsess? Power, riches, phallic urges. These are the motives that drive their actions. Prior to recently the heretic was driven only by hate and revenge. A drive that is slowly being replaced by the one named Capricorn." The demon raises its hand in front of him as he feels the air.

"I want to corrupt him. I can sense him. I know where he is." The demon points its long bony finger at Diomedes. "Gather your men." Diomedes bows his head before walking out of the room. The demon voices its evil idea to itself.

"Nothing corrupts a man with more authority than by hurting the one he loves."

Later that evening, the radiant glow of the full moon casts an ominous presence above the city. Capricorn and Montague are walking side by side on this windy night as Capricorn's cloak flaps in the wind.

"It's colder tonight," Capricorn states.

"We'll be back soon," Montague assures her.

"How did you find me in the sewers?" Montague thinks back before responding.

"I guess you can say I saw the light at the end of the tunnel."

"I hoped for someone like you for so long. I never gave up on that. Did you ever hope for me?" Montague stops walking and takes Capricorn's hands in his.

"I never had hope—until I looked into your eyes. In your eyes I can see the stars. In your eyes I can surrender my struggle."

"What have I done to earn such a reaction? I just exist," she replies, but Montague only smiles. He breaks his own rule by taking her by the hand as they enter the warehouse, but Montague's salvation is not to be so easily gained this cold night. Diomedies steps out in front of Montague and Capricorn before they reach the staircase. Montague cannot react in time before eight men step out from the shadows and surround them.

"Who are you hiding under that cloak?" Diomedes asks despite already knowing the answer. Montague puts his hand on the hilt of his sword resting at his side.

"If the answer is that important to you, then you'll find it in the afterlife." Diomedes laughs.

"Today, you learn defeat, tomorrow you learn regret, and the day after that you learn to die. Get him!"

The men draw their daggers and rush Montague and Capricorn. Montague too draws his sword and stabs one of his attackers while trying to avoid the weapons from the others.

Capricorn's crossbow pokes out of the long sleeve as she fires an arrow into one of the men's chest. She loads another one and takes aim and then pulls the trigger—the arrow borrows deep into a gang member's eye. The wounded man drops to the ground while screaming in agony. Montague slices a deep cut into the side of another man, but it's the last action he's allowed to make. With four men down, the remaining ones crowd around Montague and start to beat him. He does not have room to lift his arm or swing his sword and he cannot find an opening to break free. Montague collapses to the ground as one of the thugs stomps on his hand until his grip loosens; he then kicks the blade away from his reach. With Montague now disarmed the others feel more confident to punch and kick him repeatedly. Capricorn remains on the offence and shoots an arrow into one of the attacker's neck. With little time to reload and worrying for Montague's safety, she leaps onto someone's back and begins to choke him.

"Leave him alone!" she yells with a panicked voice. Montague is able to grab one of the assailants' ankle and then twists it to tackle him to the ground. He gains leverage over him and punches him hard under the jaw. Diomedes has been fully entertained by watching the entire onslaught play out. All his men are down and yet he's still smiling. He pulls Capricorn off the asphyxiating man and throws her to the ground forcibly. Just then the demon swoops down from an unknown height and grabs Capricorn. She kicks and squirms trying to free herself from its grasp, but its hold is too tight.

"Let me go!" she yells. The demon keeps its arm under her chin as it backs up with her in tow.

"Leave her be, demon! It's me you want," Montague taunts as soon as he returns to his feet.

"Yes, it is you who I want. And it is you that I will have," the demon laughs. Diomedes slams his fist suddenly into Montague's gut. He lets out a grunt before falling to his knees and holding his stomach.

"She now belongs to me," The demon continues. "If you want her you will have to submit to my servitude, otherwise, I'm sure I can find others that will be more than happy to accept such a prize." Montague bows his head and takes a few deep breaths. He then glares back up with a determined and focused demeanor. His words are clear and strong.

"I will destroy you, and all who stand by your side."

"You have damned her," the demon replies as it takes the victory during this encounter. A swift kick from Diomedes' boot into Montague's temple blurs his vision before everything fades to black. The last image he remembers is the demon carrying Capricorn away.

Several hours have passed, but for Montague it's only been a few seconds. He finally awakes from his unconsciousness with a jolt. He stands up bleeding and sore as he looks around with anxiety—he is alone. He sprints out of the warehouse while looking in all directions. In the street ahead lies a motionless body. Montague hurries toward it expecting his worst fears to become real. He reaches for it when he nears it to discover it's his cloak, but Capricorn isn't under it. This single item of clothing is all that is left to remind him of her. The strong wind bombards him as he yells into the night air.

"Capricorn!!"

Montague returns to his shelter, but rest isn't on his mind. He pockets several first aid kits and then places several knives and throwing daggers into his belt. He grabs two flashlights and then sharpens his sword. He slides several boxes out of the corner and then picks up a Kevlar vest hiding behind them. He puts the vest on followed by his shirt. Anything and everything that may be of some use he finds a way to attach to himself. He looks over at his cloak he had flung on the mattress. He picks it up and catches Capricorn's scent. He's not trying to hide anymore. He folds it and sets it back down. He advances toward the door and stands in the doorway to look back one last time. Here he makes a promise.

"I will not return—not without you." Montague has made his vow; he's going to war.

4

The Gargouille and the Hexagon of Light

The demon's line has been cast and its bait has been set. Montague will go mad, and Capricorn is a long way from the comfort of her pillows and tapestries. No one is ever the same after meeting the demon. It enlists the weak, tortures the brave and devours the lost. Diomedes has pledged his allegiance to the demon in the hope that the return will be power, and all his desires fulfilled. The demon makes many promises, and it will keep them; however, the turnout is never what men fathom in their minds. Rewards come at a cost, and once that cost is paid the reward somehow loses its enticing luster. It becomes stale, hollow, and meaningless. These lessons come too late for some, but there are times when they occur at just the right moment.

Capricorn is a captive of the demon now and finds herself in his domain. She sits on the cold hard floor of her prison cell while holding her knees. She has experienced a lot in a short time and is still trying to make sense of it. Her carefree and playful demeanor is slowly being replaced with an instinct to kill. Even the purest in this world forsakes innocence for survival.

Diomedes unlocks the door to her cell and ventures inside

along with two men. Capricorn intensely watches their movements without leaving her position. Diomedes keeps a straight and focused face, but his men smile and cackle as they admire Capricorn. Diomedes is only interested in completing his job and yearns for a larger reward than the little satisfying moments his men are happy with.

"Before we bruise that sweet body allow me to taste its raw nectar," one of his men says with a sinister grin. The other thug laughs, but Diomedes keeps his composure.

"If you think you can; go ahead and try," Diomedes replies and stands aside without the desire to interfere. The thug nears Capricorn while smirking as she slides herself across the floor away from him.

"Come here, bitch," the thug demands. He grabs her leg and pulls her towards him.

"Don't touch me," she screams out. He pulls on the gown to tear it at the shoulders and then hikes her gown up to expose her thighs and waist.

"Leave me alone!" Capricorn begs, but no one is listening, and no one cares. The man holds her down as he tries to lay on top of her while fumbling with his zipper. He has his pants nearly off as he tries to force her legs apart. Capricorn finds words to be of little use on this man. She leans up and delivers a quick jab to his throat before wrapping one arm around his neck and the other around the top of his head. With a quick jerk she snaps the man's neck, and he falls lifelessly beside her. The second man steps forward and slaps her across the face with the back of his hand.

"I told you. This animal cannot be tamed," Diomedes says.

"The heretic was able to," The man points out, but his response only succeeds in irritating the demon glaring into the prison cell from outside the bars.

"I do not want to hear that name!" it roars. "Self-acclaimed heretic. He knows what he needs to become to get her back. And then he will be just like me." The demon waves Diomedes to begin the beating. "Carry-on, her suffering will bring Montague close to me." Diomedes pulls a baton from his belt and advances towards the defenseless girl. There is nothing she can do to prevent it.

Capricorn wails and cries out with every strike. Diomedes beats her on the arms, ribs, legs, and back while the other man restrains her so she cannot protect herself. Diomedes and his man leave Capricorn battered and sobbing as they lock her cell once more before departing. How much abuse will Capricorn endure? How many times will others come? Will she be able to fight them all away? At least this incident is has ended.

Back in the city a new name is quickly becoming known. Montague gives in to his primal rage as he slaughters any foe who challenges him. He interrogates those who surrender or have lost the fight for any information regarding the demon's whereabouts. He bloodies his sword and hands without fear of consequences. He considers most of these men immoral, useless, and inconsiderate by nature. He kills them easily and freely without regret, hesitation, or honor; it's all justified in his mind. Blood splatters on his face as his rampage continues. He tosses his daggers one after the other at the enemies surrounding him before finishing off the rest with his sword. He threatens the last man harshly for information as two others run for their lives. The man is shaking with fear and bends to Montague's will.

"Who's the man that accompanies the demon?"

"I think his name is Diomedes," the defeated man replies.

"Who is he? What role does he play?"

"I don't know. They have a pact or something."

"Where do I find him?"

"I don't know where he stays." Montague grabs the man's collar and presses the tip of his sword against his neck. The man raises his arms and forces the rest of his words out. "Wait. I've seen him at the Neon Lights Club before. He might be there." Montague backs away from the man to look down the street. He knows of the place mentioned. It's the epicenter of debauchery where drinking, gambling, and whoring are commonplace.

"Who are you?" the man asks. Montague glares back at him. His voice closely resembles a growl that's similar to that of the demon's.

"I am the Heretic!" He pushes his sword through the man's heart and then slowly pulls it back out. He may have once let the man live for his reluctant aid, but there are no rules or codes to abide by now. No one else does, why should he? Montague is slowly becoming what he had sworn to defeat, and worst of all— it doesn't bother him.

The sun sets and the Neon Lights night club explodes with activity. It's highly active at night and always draws a large crowd.

The only thing everyone has in common here is the desire to get drunk and laid. The exterior of the club is lit with several neon light tubes from every color of the spectrum and neon signs. One sign flashes from a naked woman's back and butt to her front, showing her breasts and pubic area. Other signs are alcohol bottles and cocktail glasses. It's the only place in the city that's still lit by electricity on a regular basis. Flashing digital signs and billboards advertise booze, strippers, and gambling. This is the gathering place for all the degenerates of the city.

A group of hookers stand near the club's entrance while two others are already engaging in their decadent acts a few steps away. One of them is performing fellatio, while the other accepts sex from behind as she yells in ecstasy and begs for more. Montague ignores the transpiring events, as well as the smiles and kissing sounds the other whores make toward him.

The club is just as crowded inside as it is outside with nothing to hide. The saying, anything goes, never applied to a better place. The tables are being used for dice and card games while others are used for fornication, and in some cases for both. The interior is lit with the same neons and trance music pulsates throughout the joint. It's easy to become distracted in a place like this with the scantily clad girls and the shouts of joy or agony from the gamblers.

Montague scans the area and recognizes a man sitting at the bar. He was one of Diomedes' men who attacked him and Capricorn earlier and is now drinking heavily in hopes to numb the pain from his many bruises. Montague begins to advance towards him, but a woman intersects him and grabs his arm while rubbing his chest.

"Hey baby. I never saw you here before. Nice scar." She says seductively.

"Bug off, I'm looking for someone," he answers sternly.

"So am I. How would you like to call it a night?"

"How would you like to call on someone else?"

"Oh, come on honey. I do everything," she insists.

"Then go catch flies with your diseased snatch." The hooker utters a stunned gasp and then slaps him across the face before walking away brashly.

It's no secret that venereal disease runs rampant among the ranks of these club attendees, but no one ever considers the risk while here. With no way to combat outbreaks, the disease continues to spread or worsens. The laws of man may no longer apply, but the laws of nature cannot be avoided.

Montague continues toward the thug guzzling his liquor until he's standing directly behind him.

"Where's Diomedes?" he asks.

"He's not here," the drunk man answers without turning around.

"I didn't ask where he isn't. I asked where he is." The man stands up and then turns around barely able to keep his balance. By the looks of it he's been drinking for quite some time now.

"You got some big fuckin' balls walking in here and talking to me like this." He looks at Montague for a moment before recognizing him. "You—" The thug draws his dagger, but Montague punches him in the face. The other boozers nearby hurry out of the way as Montague smashes the man's head against the bar's surface several times. He tightens his grip around the man's neck while pinning his face against the bar's surface.

"Where is he!" The thug gasps for air as blood streams down his forehead. Montague loosens his grip and pulls him back up. "What have you done with Capricorn?" Montague continues.

"I don't remember," the man answers.

"You have a short memory. Unfortunately for you I do not." Before their conversation can continue a nearby man points to Montague after studying his face.

"I know you. You're the heretic."

Whispers start spreading through the crowd of onlookers. Whether he was expecting it or not, he now has an audience.

"I was told you spit out daggers and that you once killed three men from just sneezing; however, I do not believe these tales," the man admits. He draws his sword to challenge him, but Montague doesn't have time for this.

"Neither do I, but I heard you once ate a dagger." He flicks one of his throwing daggers into the assailant's mouth before another step can be taken or another word uttered. He then turns his attention back to the man he was interrogating. "Now, answer my question."

"I don't know where she is, I swear. Only the demon's elite are allowed to enter its domain."

"Where is it?"

"I never saw it. I'm telling the truth. Please, spare my life."

Montague relinquishes his grip on the man and turns around while trying to think what his next plan of action will be. The thug assumes he has the upper hand and pulls a knife out. Montague quickly draws his sword while spinning around. In a blink of an eye, he decapitates the man before he has a chance to raise his blade. The nearby crowd jumps back as some even manage to make sounds of disgust.

"Your request has been denied," he replies. For once the club is silent as everyone watches him calmly walk out. In his wake two men lie dead and soft voices echo behind him.

"That was the heretic demon."

It's been a long night of endless perseverance with Montague no closer to finding Capricorn than the moment he first started. It's nearly dawn when Montague finds himself beside a rocky waterfall fountain in a quaint park. He brings the gentle flowing water to his lips with his hand and drinks the cooling liquid. He doesn't question how the pump is still functioning. He's mentally and physically drained, but too angry and worried to rest. This short moment is all he's allowing himself to have. He closes his eyes to the sound of the steady flow of running water. In the moment of exhaustion sounds have a way of fading away and blending together. Voices from unknown sources play out in his mind as foreign thoughts he has no control of thinking.

"Who are you? Who were you? Who will you be? Montague? Heretic?" There is a pause before the next voice is a loud whisper in his ears. "DEMON?!"

Montague forces his eyes open with a gasp and looks around. He's startled to discover another man sitting on the opposite side of the waterfall. He was alone when he arrived, and his eyes were only closed for a moment. How did this man get so close without being heard? The man has one leg up to his chin while the other dangles over the edge of the stone circle he and Montague are sitting on. He lifts his head from his knee and at first glance appears to be elderly. His skin is wrinkled, pale and bumpy, his fingers are long, and his nails are unkempt. His ears are also pointed near the top and extend much higher than normal. This strange man lowers his raised leg and stands up before turning to face Montague. His face is rippled with long dark wrinkles and his eyes are sunken in. His nose looks more like a small snout and on top of his head are two little bumps that resemble tiny horns. He's dressed in a leather vest with metal studs and long black pants. Montague immediately stands up and draws his sword, but the man holds his hand out to halt his action.

"Is your first impression of everyone the same? A threat that deserves annihilation?" His voice is deep, but his tone is steady and calm.

"You are evil," Montague replies.

"Why, because of my appearance? I may look worse than you, but you are far worse than I." Montague lifts his sword with the tip pointing straight at him.

"I'm nothing like you."

"You do not know who you are. And one who does not know themselves shouldn't declare war on others." He takes a few steps closer to Montague. "I am the gargouille, and for many, many centuries, I have played the apotropaic role."

"You expect me to believe you are a protector? You are a monster."

"And what are you? Do you think you can save her by becoming that which basks in dread?" Montague slowly lowers his sword.

"How do you know my plight?"

"I am but a fading memory. The truth is I live inside everyone, but I'm not the only one. What part of you fears me, Montague? The pure—or the evil?"

"How do you know my name?"

"I already told you. I live inside of your mind—your soul. Now sheath your weapon and listen to me."

This creature has proven to know more about Montague than anyone could have known, and his curiosities get the better of him. Montague hesitates, but eventually obeys the gargouille's request.

"If you are trying to deceive me know that I can draw my sword just as fast," Montague warns.

"Your desire to save Capricorn is unmistakable; however, it is your methods that are questionable. You resign yourself to that power which you feel you can control, but the truth is the longer you hold on to it the more it becomes you. You can't fight for love with that much hate. Your path has become obstructed and only you can clear it. A word of caution though—the demon's blood flows within you, but you are not lost to it yet."

"What do you mean—the demon's blood?"

"I am only here to warn, not to reveal." Montague glances up as the morning sun peeks over the horizon. The gargouille gives him one last helpful hint. "Look for the hexagon of light for your path." Montague returns his gaze to the gargouille only to find he's no longer there. He scans the area around him, but there's no sign of the creature, until his sights fall on the top of the water fountain where a statue of a gargoyle rests. It is a detail he could have sworn was not there before, but can a statue come to life?

Capricorn's wounds still bleed, and her face, arms and legs are bruised. She sits with her back against the wall with her legs straight out and her hands in her lap. She hears footsteps echoing outside her cell as someone approaches. She watches to see who will appear this time. Diomedes? The demon? Perhaps another man thinking she will be too weak now to fight him off? To her surprise it is Montague.

She wants to jump up, but her body is too heavy and stiff to move. She smiles and waits for him to unlock her cage and take her away, but hurried footsteps of someone running draw closer. Montague turns around to block Diomedes' sword with his own. Capricorn cannot move or shout and feels helpless as she watches them fight. Montague proves to be the better swordsman and slashes Diomedes across the stomach and then stabs him through the chest. Diomedes falls to his knees and then slides backwards off his blade. Capricorn rejoices to herself. It's finally over. Montague stays focused on Diomedes far longer than is necessary. *Why is he not coming to me?* Capricorn ponders.

Montague draws his dagger and slits Diomedes' neck. Capricorn is taken back by this. He was already defeated did he have to be mutilated? Montague continues to stab his dagger all over Diomedes' dead body. *Is his hate for his enemy greater than his love for me?* Capricorn is perplexed at his actions, and tears begin to run down her cheeks. Montague pauses only to tilt Diomedes' head back before he takes a bite out of his neck. He turns back to Capricorn with red eyes and fangs and his face is covered in blood. She is horrified at this sight and knows he is lost to her.

"He can't save you. He couldn't even save himself," The demon says when it appears. He picks up Montague's sword and then decapitates him. The demon holds his severed head in front of the cell with blood dripping from the fresh wound before tossing it at Capricorn.

Capricorn finally finds her voice and screams. She opens her eyes to find herself in her cell, but Diomedes' corpse is not outside the bars and Montague's head isn't at her feet. Her heart is still thumping in her chest and dried tears are on her cheeks. Was it a dream, or was it a vision of things to come? *No, it is the demon's trick. To drive me mad by robbing me of sleep*, she thinks to herself.

Eerily reminiscent of her dream, Capricorn hears footsteps outside her prison. Her anxiety rises as the footsteps get louder. Diomedes eventually appears outside of her cell and takes a long silent stare before speaking.

"Do you think he will come for you?" Capricorn doesn't acknowledge his question; she keeps her head down while looking at the floor. "Why do you hold onto hope when it only brings you pain?"

It was a cruel trick. Nothing more than a false story, a hallucination of the mind, a mirage of the night, Capricorn assures herself before glancing up.

"I know myself; I know him, and I know you. Your words are empty. His heart beats within mine. My blood mixes with his. Our path is the same. And there's nothing you can do that will change that," Capricorn answers.

"Neither of you will survive, and I will be there to watch you take your last breath," Diomedes barks and then walks away hastily without waiting for her reply. Capricorn closes her eyes again. "I know you will find me. Because when I close my eyes, I can see you the way I remember you."

Montague continued his search and interrogations to another part of the city, but his goals remain out of reach. Without food and sleep his exhaustion shows on his face and in his steps, but his reputation has preceded him. None dare cross his path and run as soon as they notice him.

"It's the heretic!"

Montague glances at the people peeking out from darkened corners and windows or fleeing altogether but gives little feedback of the transpiring events. Everything throbs, from his eyes to his feet, he needs to rest again. Montague wanders into a courtyard enclosed by several buildings that was once a school of art and design. Several sculptures and art displays are all that remain from a forgotten admiration for the arts, music, and literature—aspiration is now dead. He falls heavy near a large abstract metal art sculpture in the center of the courtyard. He leans back and closes his eyes.

Capricorn—I'm afraid that I will be too late, Montague thinks. Capricorn appears in his mind's eye encased in light.

"Hold me in your heart and you cannot falter," she says. The demon appears and grabs her. Montague is made to watch as a rope is tightened around her neck, and she is dropped from a high branch to be mercilessly hung. Montague swings his sword to cut the rope, but the sword passes through the phantom cord. She dangles and squirms while kicking the air and gasping for air as she suffocates. Montague can't save her.

Montague awakes suddenly and instinctively swings his sword in front of him. It has pierced someone. He looks horrified at his sword embedded in Capricorn's stomach. She looks at him with tears in her eyes. "I was wrong to trust you," she says. Montague awakes from this second dream with a distraught shout. He jumps up and unsheathes his sword and then shouts again as insanity takes hold of him.

"Who are you who curses me with madness?! You exile me then criticize my hatred! I slay you!" A few straggling people nearby bolt as fast as they can. Montague slashes the metal sculpture viciously as if it were a beast. The sword clings every time it makes contact, but he doesn't stop. Something needs to be defeated before he can find peace. Some enemy nearby must die. Montague cannot find his foe, so he created one. After several strikes he collapses to his knees while taking time to catch his breath.

A tear streams down his face. It is the first time he has allowed himself to sob in years. Capricorn's arms appear from behind him as they wrap around his chest. Montague raises his hand to touch hers, but his hand falls over his heart instead. He lifts his head and discovers the sunlight shining through the metal sculpture creates the shape of a hexagon on the building in front of him. The hexagon of light, he whispers. This was the gargouille's message. If this is a coincidence it cannot be ignored, but what can be so important here, in a place that is no longer needed? Montague rises to his feet and sheathes his sword. He advances toward the double doors and pulls the handle. The door opens with ease and Montague ventures inside. What awaits him is not in this world and it cannot be found by any other who may follow. He has vanished from this realm and returning is not a guarantee.

5

The Seven Trials

The door vanishes as soon as it shuts behind Montague creating a seamless solid wall. The room is all white and lacks windows, doors, or any indication of an exit. White walls stand in between the white ceiling and white tiled floor making it difficult to tell if this room is endless or smaller than it seems. The only shape is that of a woman sitting in a chair in what could be the center. Other than his footsteps echoing with every step there are no sounds in this vast white space.

Montague reaches the woman sitting with one leg over the other and stands in front of her. She's wearing a white cloak with no hood and her hair is cut at shoulder length. She lifts her gaze from the open book in her lap and smiles before gently closing the cover.

"Welcome Montague. We've been waiting a long time to see you." The woman begins. "Please sit down." Montague looks around him but doesn't see another chair.

"There's no place to sit," he answers. The woman looks at him for a moment before speaking.

"Do you consider yourself above sitting on the floor, or do

you believe you shouldn't have to look up at me?"

"I didn't mean it like that." The woman remains focused on him in silence. Montague finally sighs and unstraps his sheathed sword to allow him to sit with crossed legs. He places his weapon beside him and then glances up at the women.

"What were you reading?" Montague asks.

"I'm reading about you, dear Montague." The woman turns to the back of the book and fans through the blank white pages so he can see. "But it's not yet finished." Montague has little interest in this woman's wordless novel and decides to speed the conversation forward.

"Where am I and how do find Capricorn?"

"I was about to explain both to you. Your manners are in dire need of being retaught," the woman scolds him.

"I'm sorry, but time is against Capricorn."

"You don't have to worry about time here. Your clock, for now, is paused."

"You're trying to tell me that time has stopped?"

"Time is merely a tool to ensure everything is balanced and happens in order. Otherwise, everything will take place all at once. These rooms have no reason for time."

"What do you mean by these rooms?"

"There you go again. Perhaps your greatest challenge will be to listen," she reprimands.

"I'm sorry."

"This is the first room of eight. All descending by the colors of the spectrum and the time of day. This room and the next will always be day. The next two are always afternoon, followed by evening and finally night. The first four rooms have female watchers; the last four are male. Capricorn is being held at the end. You are in the white room and my name is the lady in white."

"Did you pick that name yourself?" Montague says sarcastically. The woman uncrosses her legs and leans forward to look Montague in the eyes.

"Do you want to receive a slap in the mouth?"

"Look, I don't get why I have to go through all of this bullshit. Did the demon have to do all of this when he brought Capricorn here?" The lady in white slaps Montague's mouth with the back of her hand and then stands up. Montague taps his fingers on his bleeding lip and then looks up at the woman towering over him.

"You had a dream about Capricorn not too long ago, did you not?" Montague stares up at the woman unsure how she could have known that. "You say you want to save Capricorn, but wasn't it your blade that pierced her flesh? If you cannot save yourself, you will never save her."

"Pacifism and peace talks are useless in times like these. Violence is the only way to be granted a voice. I have done nothing out of the realm of what is expected from a man pushed to my position," Montague argues.

"You still don't get it, do you? You have to ask yourself how bad you want to save Capricorn. If you fail one room, you fail them all." The lady in white offers her hand to Montague; he accepts her aid and rises to his feet as she continues her explanation. "You are not allowed to enter the demon's domain without invitation. If you do receive an invitation, it's already too late for you to save Capricorn because you would be the same as her captives. That's why you must go through us to reach her. All these trials test who you are; not on your physical strength or your skill with a blade." She glances at his sword on the floor and waves her hand in the air to make it fade from view in that instant. "It is impossible to beat these trials by lying. Who you are is determined not by what you say, but by what you do. If you succeed you will reach Capricorn, if you fail you will die. Is she worth this risk?" Montague looks her in the eyes and answers promptly.

"Yes." A trap door on the floor opens and a red light shines up.

"Then your trial begins now. You may advance to the red room."

This room also has no windows or doors, and the walls and ceiling are bright red. A red plush carpet covers the floor, and the only piece of furniture is a red couch. A woman with long red hair and wearing a red dress struts toward Montague to welcome him to her domain.

"Welcome to the red room. My name is—"

"Let me guess. The lady in red," Montague interrupts. The woman giggles.

"It seems you have caught onto our naming pattern." The

lady in red puts an arm around Montague's shoulder and places her thumb from her other hand on his bleeding lip.

"Oh, you are hurt. Let me tend to this." The lady in red pulls him gently towards the couch.

"It's alright. It's not that bad," Montague replies.

"Nonsense, I insist. Now sit down." Montague is gently eased down into the soft cushions. A red handkerchief is pulled ever so slightly from her bosom as she leans forward to dab the cloth on his lip. She leans in closer and seductively slides her arms around his neck. Montague looks at her a little surprised, but he eventually finds his voice.

"Isn't there—umm—some trial I'm supposed to complete?"

"We have plenty of time for that. I just want to make sure that you are well rested—I can be very nurturing."

She straddles him and leans her chest against his chin. Montague leans his head back as she continues inching her head closer to his. "Did you like those women at the club Montague?"

"The whores?"

"Yes, all the men love them. Are you any different?"

"They are unclean."

"So, you have standards. Admirable. But isn't the urge to feel their insides more demanding than what may happen afterwards? You want to release. Why restrict yourself?"

"I do not like them."

"The body does not know what the eyes see, or the mind thinks. It will still feel good." She grinds her pelvis against him and lets her hands caress his head, shoulders, and chest. "Do you like me? I'm clean. I will hold you in my warmth. Do you prefer to take or be taken?" Montague's eyes become heavy as he struggles with maintaining his focus. There is a desire to give into her advances and a lapse in thought as to why he is here. "Do I interest you?"

"You are attractive," he admits. She lets most of her breasts show over the top of her dress as she continues her seduction.

"Do you know that smell is the most powerful of all the senses? It can linger in the air for miles. It can stay on your mind for days. It can numb and hypnotize. It's so powerful that even years later when it is remembered it immediately takes you back to the exact time and place where it was first experienced." Montague does not have the words to respond and offers no resistance to her advances. "Are you also aware that women have their own unique natural aroma? Most men mistake it for perfume. It draws you in, a spell that you can neither repel nor rebel. It flows through your bloodstream and invades your daydream. My trap has been sprung catching you dancing on my tongue." At this moment, he remembers holding his cloak to his nose after Capricorn had been wearing it. Her smell remained in the fabric and his nose can smell it now despite being no where near it. He remembers her smile, her voice, her touch. The lady in red parts her lips and draws closer to kiss Montague. He snaps out of his trance and gently pushes her shoulders away from him before she can make contact.

"What you say is true. It is why I'm here. You see, Capricorn has that very same effect on me. I'm sorry, but you can never take her place." The lady in red smiles.

"I wish I came across more men like you." She slides off Montague and readjusts her dress to be less revealing.

"You have passed your first trial. Your heart does indeed belong to Capricorn."

"Wait, all of that was just an act?" Montague asks somewhat annoyed.

"A test—and you have many more to go."

"How far would you have taken this if I did not resist?" Montague asks. She gives a monotoned reply with almost no expression.

"We would have done everything you wished for as long as you willed it. Anything your mind could conjure up in any style or position for as long as you could last. I will then have told you how you've failed, and my mantis form would take over to snip off your head." Montague almost regrets his question as shock prohibits him to respond. The woman smiles and continues in an upbeat and excited voice. "But you've passed—so congratulations." She points to the wall on the opposite side of the room as an orange, glowing doorway takes shape. "Continue now to the realm of the afternoon and the orange room."

The orange room, just as the ones before, is windowless and without doors and the walls, ceiling and floor all are matching in color. This room only consists of a dinner table set for two and a grand feast on top of an elegant orange tablecloth. A woman dressed in an orange apron stands from the head of the table to meet Montague as he approaches.

"Welcome Montague. Please sit, you must be hungry." Montague looks at the food on the table before redirecting his gaze to the woman.

"Is this a trick?"

"No, you haven't had anything to eat for almost two days. You need to eat."

"Thank you, but I will pass. I do not need to be distracted."

"Do you think acting a martyr role will impress me? How will you fight the demon without sufficient energy? Would you give it such an easy victory?" Montague can't deny the food looks and smells wonderful and his rumbling stomach finally convinces him to take a seat. The woman pours him a glass of water from a pitcher and then hands him a serving plate of chicken. Montague smiles and nods his thanks. He takes a drumstick and places it on his plate as the woman holds a bowl of buttered noodles near him. He drops a few spoonfuls on his plate and starts eating.

"Is everything to your liking?" the woman asks.

"Yes, thank you," Montague replies while nodding. He is then offered a plate of chocolate chip cookies.

"How about dessert?"

"Sure, thank you," he answers excitedly. This warm, soft, and gooey cookie is a treat not experienced since his childhood. Every bite reminds Montague of a time before pain, sorrow and hatred consumed him. A child's viewpoint of the world where anything is possible. An innocence where dreams are adventures and life are full of magic.

"I take it you like cookies."

"Yes, these are exceptional."

"Well, in my room there are no shortage of these."

"Can I have another one?"

"Of course, you may have as many as you like." Montague takes another cookie and starts nibbling. Freshly baked cookies will never be found among scavenged food. These are all gone from the world with no way to make more. Montague finds himself grabbing two more cookies before completely swallowing the one he had. Who can blame him? After this moment this delicacy will beyond his reach. One is lucky to find a can of condensed soup, but all forms of bakery are extinct.

"I think I'll just have one more, if that's alright?"

"Help yourself." Montague picks up another cookie but has lost count how many he's had. At this moment indulging his apatite is the only thing on his mind.

"Aren't you going to eat?" he asks noticing she has not taken anything for herself.

"No, I'm not hungry."

"Neither am I anymore, but these are just too good to pass up. It's almost like I'm—" Montague thinks for a moment before lowing his half-eaten cookie. "—Addicted to them." Montague becomes agitated and enraged at his realization. "You said you weren't trying to trick me."

"No, what you asked was if the food I was offering a trick. At the time of your arrival, you were indeed hungry, and your body needed substance. It was your own desire to continue ingesting the cookies after you had your fill."

"Why didn't you stop me?"

"My job isn't to prevent you from acting on your free will, only to observe it." Montague stands up and backs away from the table.

"You tempted me." The woman also stands up from the table.

"I only showed you what was available. I did not in any way convince you to take anything or how much of it to take. You came to that choice on your own."

"You enticed me to accept them and kept offering them freely. You are just like the last woman who beguiles and tantalizes and then criticizes my choices. You are evil." The woman laughs.

"We are neither good nor evil. We provide life with the necessary components to survive and prosper. How much you choose to indulge yourself in is out of our control."

"You poisoned my mind. You are all working against me! You would rather have me fail." The lady in orange responds in a raised sarcastic tone.

"Yes, that's right; everyone is always out to get you. All life form everywhere has nothing else better to do than to inconvenient and vex poor Montague." She lowers her voice and continues calmly. "I know your past Montague but blaming and sulking will not allow you to advance. Only once you are aware of your weaknesses will you be able to rise above them." Montague silently contemplates the woman's words. "Though you still have a long way to go you have, at least at my end, passed since you have chosen to stop consuming the cookies on your own free will."

"What would have happened if I could not stop?"

"You would continue eating until your stomach could no longer accept anymore. At that point your next swallow would cause your stomach to explode, and you would have died." Montague ponders if asking the end results of a failed trial is worth him knowing. They all seem to be grim as the lady in white had suggested. A yellow oval descends from the ceiling and pulsates near the floor. "Enter the yellow portal to meet your next challenge, but keep in mind that both success and failure lies solely in your hands."

Montague doesn't feel any resistance as he steps through the swirling energy. In a moment he is in the yellow room with the portal nowhere in view. Only a blond-haired woman wearing yellow armor is practicing swordplay with a training dummy here. What test could this be, Montague wonders. The woman takes notice of Montague's presence and smiles.

"Montague, I'm so glad you are here. I was hoping you could teach me some sword moves," she says excitedly.

"Maybe some other time. I have someone that needs my help right now."

"Oh, please. I've been watching you for a long time now and I think you are the best swordsmen. It will be an honor to be taught by you." Montague shyly smiles and shrugs his shoulders.

"Well, I've been surviving on my own for half my life. I needed to hone those skills." The lady smiles and holds her dull sword up for him to take it.

"Please let me just observe one combo move from you. That is all I will ask."

"Alright, I can show you a few things." Montague takes the sword and then lines the blade to the dummy's neck, with his legs spaced apart, before explaining his technique to his admirer.

"The first thing you need to do is make sure you have a good grip and stance. Otherwise, the sword will slip out of your hands on contact, or you could lose your balance." Montague swings the sword several times as the dummy takes what would have been fatal attacks. Montague stops to look back at the woman.

"Wow, you are so good at what you do, and you know so much. I bet you can take on anyone in a fight." Montague laughs.

"I have fought many people. But they were all bad. I killed them to save others who would have been hurt."

"You are such a brave warrior, Montague. Any woman would be lucky to have you. I know I would feel safe with you by my side." The woman offers this subtle clue, but Montague misses her hint.

"Do you know about the demon?"

"Yes, I do. It is a vile, scary creature. I get chills down my spine every time I hear stories of it."

"I have met it in battle several times, but it has never been able to kill me. I was even able to draw blood in one of my battles with it. As far as I know I'm the only one that it can't kill."

"I would never be able to face that creature. You are beyond magnificent, Montague." Montague smiles and waves his hand.

"Nah, it's really no big deal."

"And modest too. In my opinion you are the ideal hero."

"Thank you, but it's not so much about what you are able to do, but what you are willing to do."

"Everything you say and do impresses me. May I accompany you? I would love to train under Montague the great."

"You mean like an apprentice?"

"Please say yes," she says while pulling on his sleeves. "I would like it very much to stand by your side and fight all the evil of the city."

"Well, there's a lot of evil in that city and a woman needs a degree of caution."

"That's why I have you." She cozies up to Montague and lets her hand caress his face. "My strong, brave hero will protect me from the bad men." She leans in and whispers in his ear. "I would only let you touch me." Montague's boost of confidence from the woman's words allows him to ponder her request, but there's something familiar about what she's describing. He becomes lost in thought while thinking out loud.

"I already have someone who stands by my side and with no concern to her own safety. Capricorn risked her life to save mine and I would do the same for her without thinking about it." Montague lifts the tip of the sword towards her.

"What are you doing?" she asks.

"You are trying to delay me. You want me to fail. I will not fail!"

"Really, this again? I have no power over you. Only you can choose your own path."

"Then why are you making small talk instead of showing me what I need to do."

"You allowed yourself to become distracted. You know what you need to do, yet you expect me to do it for you."

"This is a waste of time. These tests are meaningless. Take me to Capricorn right now!" The woman folds her arms across her chest and glares at Montague.

"Despite your progression you still have a lot to learn; however, before your outburst, you did figure something out— What you are able to do, is not the same as what you are willing to do. But know this, willing to save Capricorn may not make you able to."

"I refuse to believe that. I already made my choice before I left. I'm willing to sacrifice my life to save hers. Nothing has changed since then." The woman holds her hand out.

"Give me my sword."

"Won't I need it?" The woman slowly shakes her head. Montague lowers the blade and hands it to her.

"I believe your words, Montague. You are willing to put someone else before yourself and that is why you pass my room." Montague hesitates to ask, but the curiosity is too much to resist.

"How would I have failed here?" The woman leaps over Montague in a single bound and lands behind him with the blade of her sword pressed against his neck.

"I lied. I'm actually quite good with a sword. If you had forgotten your true mission and walked with me through my portal. I would have betrayed you. I would have killed you in the city and everyone would ask who killed the heretic? I would be gone, and the mystery would remain unsolved." The woman lowers her sword and backs away from him. "Before you depart, I leave you with one final piece of advice. Know your mind for it is your true enemy."

The yellow room fades into green until Montague finds himself in a new room without taking a single step. This room has green vine growth on the walls and soft green grass for a floor. Montague turns around just as a man wearing a green wizard's robe welcomes him.

"Good evening, Montague. I congratulate you on making it

this far. Were the ladies good to you?"

"No, they were difficult to figure out," Montague replies. The man smiles.

"Ah, yes, most are." The man puts a hand on Montague's shoulder while extending his other hand in front of them.

"Let me show you something." The man directs him to a green bowl filled with water on top of a pedestal. "Gaze into the water and tell me what you observe." Montague looks into the water and a picture fades into view of a man and woman embraced on a park bench. They kiss each other and whisper into each other's ears before giggling.

"Seems to be some couple," Montague explains.

"Do they look happy?"

"Yes, I suppose so," Montague says while keeping a straight face. Another image fades to replace the last one. This one shows a man and woman kneeling across from each other with outstretched arms as a toddler walks in between them while laughing.

"What do you see?" the man asks.

"A baby."

"Do you know the joys of fatherhood, Montague?"

"No."

"What do you want out of life? A nice home, a big family, maybe a prestigious job?"

"The world didn't give me a chance for any of that."

"Why do you think you can no longer have that life?"

"The city is a plague. If it wasn't for the demon I would still be with Capricorn. If it wasn't for the riots and the greed of others, I could have had a peaceful life. Why do others deserve my dream, but not me!"

"Did these events allow you to meet Capricorn?" the man continues in the same calm tone, but Montague is annoyed and agitated.

"Why do my desires evade me? The selfish will scheme and scam to win their prize and thieves keep what others have to work for. Songs of victory are only sung by the villainous. Brute force overpowers the weak and the strong survive. No one good can have power because power lives when the good dies." Montague paces the floor while waving his arms wildly. "I spent my entire life fighting those who are unjust and immoral. They have no right to exist! I want to kill them all!"

"Kill? Does that ensure your success?"

"I don't know why I was cast aside. I ask for nothing grand. Why are such basic requests denied to me?" Montague falls to his knees and yells while slamming his clenched fists on the ground.

"It's all their fault! Everyone is always in my way prohibiting me from getting what I want!" Montague ends his rant while breathing heavily. The man in green advances to hover over him.

"How long are you going to blame others for your misfortunes? You are your worst enemy."

"Have I failed?" Montague asks when he has calmed down.

"You have come to terms with your true feelings. You can bury them as much as you like, but that doesn't make them go away. It is true that others can impact your life, either for the good or the bad. But ultimately, it's up to you to move past that. Your dreams don't die unless you kill them yourself." Montague feels defeated, but the man in green has not given up on him yet. "Stand. Stand on your own two feet, Montague." Montague seems hesitant to get up. "I will not help you. You must see a reason for it." Montague brings his leg up and pushes his hands off his knee and comes to a stand.

"Am I damaged?" he asks.

"We are all damaged in some way. The question is can you still function?"

"I always thought that I needed to be flawless, untouchable, the best, strongest, fastest—to have anything of value."

"Even mighty Hercules was flawed. He, like you, were also sent on several trials. Twelve to be exact. And after completing every single one his actions could not be undone. His pain was not taken away. What he received was forgiveness of all things. His grief was his final undoing, but people called him a hero and loved him. Not because he was a God, but because he was human. Because he was flawed."

"Capricorn does not deserve her fate."

"I agree, but do you think she is cursing the world for her predicament."

"No, she's above that."

"No one is above that. It is her hope in you that keeps her strong. The question is do you have hope in yourself? Or do you fear you will fail her?"

"It is unbearable for me to imagine her going through pain. I will save her. Failing is not an option."

"Do you believe you can't fail?" Montague ponders the question before answering.

"I believe our destinies are intertwined through eternity itself. If I lose her in this life. I will have her in another."

"You have kept your destiny still alive ahead of you. Go meet it." The water inside the bowl swirls upward and forms into a blueish liquid archway. Montague makes his way toward it but stops and turns back around.

"How would I have known if I had failed?"

"Hopeless sets in that you have been forsaken and will never be happy. Suicide would have been your resolution." Montague turns back towards the archway. "Go now," the man says. "The blue room awaits."

Soft chirping and the fluttering of blue birds, along with, an uplifting choir fills the air. Montague cannot discover the origin of this aria, but the atmosphere is relaxing and sure to calm any anxiety and troubled thoughts. Waterfalls gently stream down the blue walls into rectangular reservoirs at the base to recycle the water. A man in a blue robe is sitting peacefully in a yoga position with his eyes closed.

"Come and sit awhile with me," he says without opening his eyes or interrupting his meditation.

"I don't want to seem rude, but I'm too close to rest now," Montague answers.

"Do you know how devastating sleep deprivation has on the body?"

"Yes, I'm aware of the effects."

"Then sit and regain your strength." Montague sits down knowing there is no point in arguing or resisting the orders of these guardians.

"Close your eyes," the man commands. Montague obeys as the man continues. "Take in a deep breath and then slowly let it out." Montague does as the man asks hoping to rush through this as fast as possible. The birds and singing, along with the gentle sound of the waterfall, put Montague at ease. His head feels light, and his eyes become heavy; his entire body tingles with a slight numbness. Montague's ambition subsides and drowsiness sets in.

"Some wisdom is gathered by thinking; some, by dreaming,"

the man says. Montague leans back to lie on his back with his hands interlocked behind his head. The floor feels like a plush, comfortable mattress and Montague loses the gumption to get up.

"Do you know why you are here?" the man now asks. Montague keeps his eyes closed as he answers.

"No."

"What do you want to do?"

"Nothing."

"The mind and body are tired. The heart is heavy and burdened. How blissful it would be never to leave such tranquility."

Montague surrenders to the peaceful moment and drifts into a dream. A vast meadow surrounds him as he rests in the shade of an oak tree while a lazy river flows past him. "No further worries, no further pain. To live in perfect serenity without ever leaving. An illusion worth giving into." Montague turns to notice the blue-robed man sitting next to him. "It's very peaceful here, isn't it?"

"Yes, it's almost perfect," he replies.

"What's missing?"

Capricorn's image appears in the distant field and then fades.

"Capricorn. Where's Capricorn?"

"She's not here."

"Where is she?" The man opens his eyes to see Montague for the first time and then points to the river.

"She's wading." Montague glances toward the river but doesn't see her.

"I don't see her."

"You must search if you wish to find," the man responds.

Montague stands up and strolls to the bank. He looks into the water to see Capricorn sleeping on the riverbed.

"Capricorn." Montague steps into the river, but it suddenly becomes deeper than it first appeared. Capricorn opens her eyes and starts sinking deeper. She desperately tries to swim up while shouting out bubbles, but her struggles only make her sink deeper. Montague immediately dives below the surface and swims after her descending into a bottomless ocean. The light begins to dim, and she becomes harder to see in the blackness of the abyss. Bubbles rush out of his mouth when Montague yells frantically. He extends his hand downward, but Capricorn is gone. Despite his best efforts he's unable to reach her in time to save her. Montague futilely attempts to swim to the surface, but he remains stationary as he drowns. It was bad enough failing to save Capricorn, but now he can't even save himself. Perhaps he deserves death. Maybe now he longs for it.

Montague awakes and sits up in a coughing fit while taking in deep wheezing breaths as he gets on his hands and knees. He's back in the blue room with the man in the same exact place he was before. After several moments Montague glares at the man in his relaxed carefree state and finds his voice.

"You son-of-a-bitch!" The man slowly opens his eyes as Montague stands up.

"How was your nap, Monty?"

"What was that? Was that a dream? What did you do to me?"

"The mind doesn't allow the body to rest with unfinished tasks still looming overhead. Sleep is only for the accomplished."

"It felt like I was really drowning. I couldn't breathe." Montague's drowning experience felt real to him. His lungs ached, his nose could not take in air and his throat was stiff and swollen."

"What the mind thinks the body believes."

"Why couldn't I wake up?"

"Some dreams are harder to leave than others. The old hag sits on top while whispering in your ear and shaking you. Your eyelids are too heavy to open; your torment is not yet done. She finds those whose minds are troubled and snuffs them."

"How long have I been here?"

"Why are you here?"

"You are hindering me. I need to find Capricorn!"

"Then do so." The waterfall stops running and a part of the wall becomes several moving pieces that rotate and slide away to reveal a purple curtain.

"Is that my next room?"

"Yes, you've passed; if you hadn't you would've slowly aged in your sleep until eventually expiring when time decided it was so." Montague walks past the man who has never moved this entire time. The man in blue shuts his eyes and continues his meditation as Montague steps through the curtain.

This room resembles all the glory of royalty and wealth with purple rugs covering the floor and purple tapestries hanging down the walls. A kingly figure sits on his throne with a long purple cape draping over the armrests. Beside him are several closed treasure chests with one of them open. The chest is full of amethysts and other gemstones along with golden jewelry and other items such as crowns and scepters.

"You have come a long way, Montague. I think you deserve a prize to honor your progress," the king begins. "You can have anything you see in this room."

"What's the catch?"

"It's simply a reward, no catch to consider. Do you see anything you like?" Montague gazes around the room before setting his sights on the chests next to the king.

"What are inside the closed ones?"

"I do not remember," the king admits. Montague slides his hand on top of a closed chest wondering what could be inside. "You may only open one of these chests. And whatever is inside is yours."

"So, it's a gamble, or a trick. You want to make me assume what's inside these chests is similar to the one that is open."

"You can choose that chest if you like. Then there are no surprises." Montague glances at the king before turning his attention to the open chest. He picks up an amethyst and turns it over in his hands. It's a large, faceted gem too pretty to reject. While one is quite a treasure to behold, more quickly becomes desired. Why should Montague leave anything behind. He wants it all but has no way to transport the entire lot.

"Everything is very beautiful here, but how do I carry this chest with me?" Montague continues looking at the gem in his hands. This smooth, glimmering stone is desirable to him and a strong desire to possess it cannot be denied.

"Did you know in medieval Europe soldiers believed that amethysts had the power to heal," the king explains. "Many wore amulets of this stone when they went into battle as protection. Sounds like something you could benefit from." Montague rubs the gem gently in his hand.

"Yes, and plenty of battles will I have with thieves when they see this dangling from my neck. Still, this little lustrous stone contains a beauty I want to hold. A part of me desires this treasure."

"The desire to own beautiful riches is nothing new. The need for it differs from person to person. Some see only the value attached to it. Some see it as a way to raise their social status. While others still see it for what it is, a decorative piece to adorn and be admired."

"I wonder if Capricorn would like this? I would give this to her, and she would know it was from me. To see this around her neck and the expression on her face when she receives it would make me happy until the end of my days." Montague lets the gem slide through his fingers and back into the chest. "But without her, these treasures would mean nothing to me. I will continue my search for her instead."

"You are very wise," the king says with a smile. "Even as you contemplated what to take it was not for yourself." The king stands up and his throne begins to rise to reveal a secret pitch-black doorway underneath it.

"You are nearly at the end of your journey, but your most difficult test still lies ahead of you."

"What would have happened if I chose the chest?"

"You would have proved you desired riches more than finding Capricorn. And riches would have been awarded to you in great quantity. You would be given a room full of gold and gems. Gold and gems and nothing more. In a room that cannot be left, with no water to drink or food to eat. There you would slowly starve, and that room of gold and gems would become your tomb."

"I see, so I'm assuming asking for one amethyst is out of the question?" Montague inquires.

"In time an amethyst may find its way to you, but for now go further into the night, and face your final challenge."

The doorway slides closed as soon as Montague passes through. He's now standing in complete darkness with no detail to make out. He slowly stumbles forward with his hands out to feel for any obstacle that may be in his way.

"Hello? Is anyone here?" There's no response or any indication of what he needs to do. He doesn't know why he's still trying to walk as he doesn't know where he's going or what he's advancing towards. Standing still also seems to be counterproductive and the unknown begins to aggravate him. "What test is this? Answer me!" A blacklight illuminates a man completely concealed in a black cloak. He stands there motionless with nothing to say as Montague addresses him. "What is my objective?" Before this stranger responds the light disappears and the room is pitch black again.

"I do not enjoy your games. Reveal yourself!" The light comes on again to reveal Diomedes laughing.

"You son-of-a-bitch!" Montague shouts. He sprints toward him and swings his fist, but the light mysteriously disappears again. Montague's punch soars through the air but fails to connect with anything solid.

"Is this my test?! To jump at shadows?!" Montague continues to walk cautiously around in the darkened room. The light appears again, but this time it's the demon that's revealed. It roars and swings a sword at Montague. He hits the ground and rolls out of the way to avoid the attack. The demon rushes him again, but Montague attempts to kick it back. The light and the demon fade just as his foot is about to make contact. Montague lets out a frustrated growl. "Fuck! I will kill all of you!" The demon appears again, and Montague runs at it without hesitation. The demon disappears when he gets close. Diomedes takes its place on the other side of the room immediately after. Montague charges toward him now without thinking or planning, but he too disappears as soon as he dives to tackle him. He hits the ground hard and pounds his fists against the floor in frustration. "You will die by my hand!" Montague yells into the darkness. Several images of both Diomedes and the demon pop up across the room. Enraged, Montague bolts and throws himself at the illusions one by one, but Every time these images of his enemies disappear before he can make contact. Montague yells and slams his fists on the floor again. Each failed attempt to attack his foes drives him mad with anger. "Fight me!"

The man in the black cloak appears again. Montague wastes little time to punch him where he believes his face to be, but it is Montague who receives the impact. He puts his hand to his bleeding nose and feels as though he was punched instead. Montague looks back at the man in the black cloak just as he pulls the hood off his head. Montague isn't looking at the guardian of this room, but at himself.

"I am a reflection in the night," his copy begins. "A shadow, a reflection of yourself. You cannot harm me without harming yourself. If you kill your enemies, you kill yourself." Montague backs away from his doppelganger; he finally understands what his trials meant.

"I was never fighting to reach Capricorn. All this time—I've been fighting myself."

Capricorn appears suspended over a wide black pit with nothing but a rope to hold on to.

"Save me! Please, save me."

"Capricorn!" Montague hurries towards her and extends his hand over the pit as Capricorn struggles to reach it. "I can't. I can't reach." Capricorn's grip begins to slip. "I can't hold on anymore."

"You must try. Give me your hand. I will reach you." Montague leans as far over the pit as he can without falling in and reaches for her again. The tips of their fingers touch only for a moment before her grip is lost and her fingers fall in between Montague's. She leaves behind only her screams as she falls into the darkness.

"No! Capricorn!" Montague sobs as he continues staring into the black pit. "I will not lose you. I made a promise." He wipes away his tears and accepts his decision. He relinquishes his fear and forfeits his worries. "Where you go. So shall I." Not knowing what death awaits him he leans forward and allows himself to fall into the pit after Capricorn.

6

Mammon

Montague remembers falling into the dark but cannot recall hitting the ground. His eyes open and he takes in his new surroundings. The fog is still heavy in his head, as if just waking from a long lucid dream, he struggles with the concept of remembering which reality is real. Who and where he is, what happened prior to this moment and what will he do now? His life and experiences flood back into his memory all at once before he can pick himself off the cold dungeon floor.

He peers into several of the prison cells but only beaten strangers stare back. The stone walls show hanging instruments to enact deadly and painful tortures. Spiked clubs, bloody pliers, large vices, and barbed chains. Devices to restrain are also nearby such as ropes, wires, and chained cuffs. Montague continues following the wall while inspecting the gruesome decor. The next section of the wall has weapons and set of iron keys. He takes the key ring from its peg as he observes the hanging weapons. Swords, daggers, spears, and axes make up a fair collection of weaponry, but there is one weapon that does not fit among the others—a compound pistol crossbow. "Capricorn—" he whispers. He retrieves her bow and then glances down the next line of prison cells. He hurries to inspect each one while calling her name in a loud whisper. "Capricorn? Capricorn? Capricorn?" Which one of these is hers? Is she even here? What if he's too late?

Montague nears the last few cells as hope, fear, worry and anxiety blend together—he cannot tell the difference between his emotions. The next cell has a figure sitting in the corner with her face buried in her knees and wearing a torn, dirty gown. "Capricorn?" he calls out. She does not lift her head. Montague tries the keys in the lock. "Capricorn." He says again. She still does not raise her head. Montague finally finds the right key and swings the cell door open and hurries inside. "Capricorn!" Montague falls to his knees and pushes her shoulders back and then lifts her chin. She becomes startled and opens her eyes with a gasp. "It's me, Capricorn. It's alright. It's me," Montague assures her. Capricorn hugs him tightly and begins crying.

"I thought I was dreaming again." Montague cannot hide his tears as he holds her in his arms. He gently caresses her bruised cheek and pushes her hair back. They press their lips together and feel the kiss they both longed for. Montague gazes into Capricorn's eyes with vulnerability and confesses to her what he feared to say before.

"I love you. I can't remember if I ever said it before, but I love you." Capricorn smiles while relishing Montague's soothing strokes on her face. "You're hurt," he continues. "What have they done to you? I'm sorry," he sobs. "I'm so sorry." Capricorn takes his hand into hers and places her other hand on his cheek.

"It's nothing that won't heal," she says.

"I wished for the moment when I could free my caged beauty. Embraced in your loving arms until now has only been a dream."

"I never lost hope."

"I know. I know you didn't. That's where I found my strength." Capricorn rubs his arm and looks at him seriously.

"I saw darkness flow through your veins. I was afraid that you would do bad things."

"I've fought my demons." He kisses her forehead and then share another kiss. As much as the two want to remain embraced they must still find their escape. Montague helps Capricorn to her feet and then hands her bow and a single arrow to her.

"Trust your instincts," he says. Capricorn remembers that was the same message Hestia told her in a dream.

Montague and Capricorn navigate their way through the narrow corridors until they come to a circular room with three wooden doors.

"Dammit," Montague sighs. Capricorn takes his hand and pulls him towards the door in front of them.

"This way," she says.

"How do you know?"

"Instincts."

Not too long ago he would want a better explanation than that, but he doesn't contest her decision now. He trustfully follows her lead. Capricorn turns the knob and pushes the door open. They exit into a narrow alley with the brick exteriors of several buildings on both sides of them. They continue cautiously toward the street and then step out into the open after a quick peek around the corner. Almost every structure on this street has been burned down from the riots long ago. Scorched wooden beams, rubble and brick walls caked with black soot litter the length of the street as far as the eye can see.

"Where are we?" Capricorn asks.

"I don't exactly know yet," Montague admits. He's never been in this part of the city before—or maybe he just doesn't remember. He takes more time to inspect the ruined buildings from his stationary position and makes a discovery. Remains of tables, couches, chairs, and other furniture pieces occupy many of the once living spaces. "These were homes," he says in a somber tone. "People used to live here."

The demon suddenly drops down in front of Montague from the top of one of the damaged roofs.

"Did you really think you could just walk in and out of my domain without me noticing?" Montague instinctively reaches for his sword forgetting it was taken away. Capricorn hastily draws her bow and points it at the demon, but it only seems amused. "One shot, little girl. If only you had more arrows to better your odds." The demon opens its fist and lets the rest of her arrows fall to the ground at its feet. Capricorn shoots her bow without hesitation. With lightning fast reflexes, the demon catches the arrow in front of its face and then tosses it aside.

"Not this time," it growls.

"Stay behind me," Montague says while directing Capricorn

behind him.

"You had so much promise," The demon begins as it advances closer. "Your fire was something I almost envied. Little did I know a woman was the extinguisher. There was a time when you wanted nothing more than to destroy the city in its entirety. Everyone— everything—life itself. Isn't that what you still want?"

"What I want is not as important as who I am," Montague answers.

"And who are you?"

"To Capricorn I am Montague. To you and the city I am the heretic." Capricorn has never heard his real name before and looks up at him as he continues to shield her.

"Montague—" The demon lets the name linger on its tongue as it reminisces. "My past emotions no longer matter. I am pulled through life purely by instinct and need."

"What are you blathering on about?" Montague impatiently asks.

"I became what I had to in order to survive. I do not regret my sacrifice and neither did she when I came back for you. You will carry that choice with you for the rest of your life—" The demon points at Montague's face. "—In the form of that scar."

"You lie," Montague says while slowly shakes his head.

"You should remember where you are." The demon points to a ruined house that was completely consumed by fire. "That is where you lived. Flesh of my flesh. Blood of my blood. That was where we lived." Capricorn keeps a wide-eyed look glued onto Montague.

"You lie!" Montague screams. The suppressed memory of his past is unleashed back into his reconciliation like a tsunami.

Montague is fourteen when his mother takes his hand and guides him underneath the dining room table. Outside their home people are fighting and yelling amongst the sounds of shattering glass, splintering wood and explosions.

"Stay here and don't move," she tells him before pulling the tablecloth down to further cover his location. She returns into the living room just as the demon bursts through the front windows. Montague's mother hides her face from the flying glass shards and wood splinters from the framing. The demon is not hiding under a black cloak as it soon will be known for and its face and body structure still has a human quality to it, but the evil in its blood has begun to disfigure its face.

"Give him to me," it demands. Montague's mother stands firmly in place and without fear as she addresses the demon directly.

"How dare you ask me such a question after all the things you've done! You are not my husband. You are not his father. You are no longer a man!" The demon roars and waves his arm in an arch. The fire in the fireplace follows the arc of his arm and sets fire to the walls and ceiling.

"He will never be yours!" his mother yells.

"Then you condemn him to death."

"I condemn you!" The demon's claws pierce into her stomach and then swipe upwards to gut her. The demon hovers over her body before snapping his head toward the dining room table. Montague is holding the tablecloth up to observe his mother's death but has now become noticed. Montague gasps at the horrid creature staring back at him and lets the tablecloth fall back down. There will be no escape for him either.

The demon rushes forward and drags him out from underneath the table by one of his ankles. Montague kicks him with his free foot and then tries to escape. The demon proves to be faster and pulls him back. With one quick swipe it's claw rakes across Montague's face and leaves a deep bleeding gouge behind.

The demon backs away and starts howling as its facial features begin to transform. Its eyes become larger and red, its nose becomes sunken into its face and its teeth become longer and fanged. Montague hurries to his mother and shakes her several times. He looks at her wound and then her eyes, he knows she's dead, but doesn't have the time to mourn. He glances back at the demon's transformation as the fire continues to spread and the room fills up with smoke.

Montague rushes past the demon roaring in agony as its body twists and bones reconstruct. The final act of bringing harm to its family shreds the last thread of humanity it had. Montague climbs out the broken window and escapes just as the walls cave in and the roof collapses.

He runs away from everything he once knew and towards an uncertain future that will be far from kind. When exhaustion becomes unbearable to ignore, he falls to his knees and cries.

Cries that gradually morph into yells. He shouts into the night sky with his fists extended at his sides and blood still streaming down his face and neck. After his fit his body hunches over and he becomes silent. He picks himself up but refuses to look back. He refuses to accept there's anything back there at all. Ahead of him is a slain man with a black steel sword still in his grasp. He stares at the dead man for a moment before prying the sword from his stiff cold fingers. Montague holds the sword up while admiring it. He tightens his grip around the hilt and then lowers it to his side. Montague shuts his eyes for a minute. When he reopens them, he has forgotten everything that had just happened. He makes a scowl and begins walking without a destination in mind. Montague—no, not anymore. The demon is now hidden in its cloak as it watches Montague from a rooftop. It plans to cross his path many times during his life, but to Montague it will be just some demon spawned from a forsaken city that's home for the damned.

The full memory is now fresh in Montague's mind. He yells and begins to charge towards the demon, but Capricorn grabs his arm to pull him back.

"No, don't," she says. The demon draws Montague's sword from behind its cloak and walks closer until it is directly in front of him.

"You live because I've allowed you to live but deny me now and it will be deemed unforgivable. Join me." Montague reaches behind himself to hold Capricorn's hand. His words are spoken without needing any thought."

"I refuse," he replies.

"So be it." The demon thrusts the sword into Montague's stomach with tremendous force. Capricorn screams out in horror as Montague hunches over his blade. No longer able to stand, he begins to fall. Capricorn eases him to the ground and lifts his head in her lap. Her tears drop on his face as Montague tries to maintain his focus on her since shock will not allow him to speak.

The demon's cloak rips and shreds to the ground as the demon grows larger. It roars in agony as another transformation appears to be taking place. Its hands and feet grow large, curved claws and several horns sprout from its head. A long thick tail whips around behind the demon and its arms and legs become veined and muscular. Lastly, its facial features change. Its eyes become black voids, its mouth curves into a permanent snarl and its nose becomes two thin slits above its lip. The demon is now in its true and final form. No longer in hiding and standing ten feet tall, it announces its identity.

"I am Mammon."

Every evil act the demon has committed took it farther away from human and brought it closer into damnation. With this last act of hatred, the demon has finally snuffed out the only hint of humanity renaming. It now has no resemblance of a man and will never be one again. It has earned a name among the legions of Hell as Mammon.

Mammon becomes immersed in an intense flame that lights up the entire street before disappearing without a trace. Capricorn returns her gaze to Montague and rubs his cheek as she cries.

"Montague?" she says worried. Montague responds in a soft but strong voice.

"Capricorn, I'm alright." He tears his shirt around the blade a little to show the sword embedded in the bullet proof vest. "You will need to pull it out. I can't get a grip on it."

Capricorn wipes her tears away and crawls around Montague. She places both hands on the hilt and then gives him another look for his confirmation. She receives it when he nods. She pulls up the blade and notices a small dab of blood on the tip.

"It has blood on it. You are hurt," she observes.

"A scratch Capricorn. Just a scratch." Capricorn helps him to his feet and then hands him his sword. "Don't worry. I'm never leaving you," he promises. She smiles and lays her head on his chest while hugging him.

With no way of knowing how to get back to the warehouse from their current location. Montague decides to seek refuge in an abandoned house for the night. It was only several blocks away where another neighborhood had homes in a lot better shape. Overgrown yards, peeling paint, and cracked windows, but at least intact with four walls and a roof. A few furniture pieces remain, but it looks like the food had been scavenged some time ago. There's no sign of a current occupant or indication this place has been visited recently with the amount of dust and cobwebs. Far from ideal, but perfect none-the-less.

Montague finds a book of matches and a pack of twelve

candles, which he lights and then places around the master bedroom. Capricorn is excited to once again be in a bed with blankets and pillows as she jumps on her knees to test the comfort level of the mattress. "Soft and Spongy. Just how I like it," she says with glee. The lit candles around the room also reminds her of her home in the sewers, minus the tapestries, but if given the choice would rather stay here than return to Montague's warehouse closet.

Montague returns to the bed and picks up the Kevlar vest and inspects the slit where his sword went completely through.

"Do you know how much strength it takes to push a sword through this?" Capricorn shakes her head. "This is designed to stop a bullet, No one should be able to thrust a blade through this." Montague tosses the vest on the dresser and takes off his shirt. His stomach is still bleeding from the stab wound left by his sword. "I would have been dead," he softly utters after taking a long look at his cut. Capricorn crawls toward the foot of the bed with one of Montague's first aid kits in her grasp.

"You took care of me, now I take care of you." She lightly swabs the blood from his wound and then dabs the antibacterial cream on. Everything she's doing is based on memory from observing how he had cleaned and bandaged her arm prior, but it's still impressive how fast she caught on. "You're the only one in my life, Montague. I don't know what I would do without you," Capricorn continues after placing the band-aid on. Montague smiles and lightly places his full hand on her cheek.

"A Long time ago there were two people who loved each other very much. He vowed to never leave her side wherever she went. She vowed to always be with him wherever he may be. As he slept next to her in the final moments before her illness consumed her; he held her close to his heart. And both left this world together. No sickness did he suffer from; just a promise he refused to break. Neither time nor space were able to separate the bond that the two shared. That's how I feel about you, my sweet Capricorn."

Capricorn smiles and slowly unzips his pants and then pulls them down. She closes her lips around his penis and slides her mouth down to the base and then back to the tip. Montague lets her mouth and tongue explore his entire pubic area. Capricorn strokes her hand the whole length of his penis before letting it slide back into her mouth. She guides him to the bed and straddles him while pushing his penis inside of her. She rests her hands on his chest while thrusting as his fingers slither up her back. She forcible pushes her body against his and speeds up her thrusting as both let out sounds of ecstasy. She feels his release inside of her when he climaxes. They lock lips and kiss before sliding under the bedsheets.

Neither knows how long time will allow them to stay together. Living unseen is not easy and unknown is no longer possible. Montague fears he will lose Capricorn again. She has become everything to him, what an awful tragedy it would be to go on without her. Pride once ruled over him, but now love has humbled him.

His recklessness made others hesitant to cross him and hesitation allows an opportunity for a foe to act. A cautious fighter fails to strike and there are no second chances in this city. Montague must now consider Capricorn's safety, but if she's doing the same then neither is fighting alone; and that may be something no one else expects.

Capricorn lets her fingers slide through his chest hairs as she rests her head on his shoulder.

"Montague. That's your name?"

"Yes."

"Why did you tell me it was heretic?"

"Because to me, Montague died a long time ago. When innocence is lost one is never the same. I had to become someone else.

"If not Montague before, why Montague now?" He turns to look at without an answer immediately ready.

"Because of you," is all he says.

Montague remains awake as Capricorn sleeps soundly beside him. While observing her peaceful slumber he crafts a poem just for her. Maybe he will recite it to her one day.

Like the waves in the ocean my hand is a ship on your hips. I trip and allow myself to fall on your lips. Your kiss would be bliss, too nervous I miss. Your hug is like a drug that makes me feel snug.

I capsize in your eyes and get lost in your thighs. There is no surprise you saw through my disguise.

Allow me to breathe your kiss and supply me shelter in your arms. And I shall sleep to the sound of your beating heart. I kiss your eyes and dream about you until the morning, when I may see you once again.

Mammon returns to his lair where Diomedes sets eyes on him for the first time. Upon looking at him few can feel at ease, but he does his best to hide his shock. Every step Mammon takes sounds like thunder and sends a vibration up Diomedes' leg. He keeps his focus on Mammon as he stalks past him.

"You are now my proxy," Mammon growls.

"What is your wish, master?"

"The world—under my rule. Gather all black hearts and id-ridden minds. Destroy all others."

"What about the heretic?" Mammon lets out a deep rumbling laugh and turns to glance behind him at Diomedes.

"There is no more heretic."

The next morning, Montague is opening and digging through drawers of the dresser when Capricorn wakes up.

"What are you doing, Montague?"

"Looking for anything useful." Capricorn slides out of bed and strolls around the room in admiration.

"I like it here. We should stay."

"It's nice, but not at all secure."

"Can we make it secure?"

"Possibly—" Montague has been pondering a thought all night and he is now ready to voice it somberly. "There's a choice we need to make, Capricorn."

"What choice is that?"

"We can't find peace among others, but maybe in the country where no one lives we might. We build our home and farm and gather food. We have what the land provides, but that also means we let the demon win."

"Or we kill the demon and find peace right here," Capricorn says trying to be serious, but her excitement is hard to ignore. Montague tries to smile, but his concern is clear.

"I don't know if we can kill it now." Montague leans his shoulder against the wall while looking at the floor.

"I never saw you worried."

"I never used to be. Risking everything is easy when you have nothing to lose." Capricorn strolls toward Montague.

"If we leave, we may live, but many others may not. Can we live with that?" Montague lifts his head and gazes into Capricorn's eyes.

"Do we survive, or do we fight?" Capricorn smiles and places her entire hand on his cheek.

"We do what we have always done. We fight to survive."

"You do have more wisdom than me," Montague says with a small smile.

"What is wisdom?"

"It means smart."

"Oh, well, thank you." Montague chuckles and begins gathering his pants and shirt. He holds up the shirt and then makes a disgusted look.

"I was hoping to find new clothes here, but there's nothing in the dresser."

"I saw lots of clothes,"

"You did? Where?"

"In the small room."

"Small room?"

"Yes, over there," Capricorn points to a door on the other side of the bedroom. Montague approaches the door and swings it open to reveal a walk-in closet.

Montague and Capricorn shed their old clothes and dress in the new attire. Montague pulls up a pair of charcoal gray pants and then puts on the matching shirt followed by a black overcoat and then ties up a pair of black hiking boots. Capricorn fits herself with a pair of black pants and boots to match but chose a heather blue shirt and then a navy-blue overcoat with a hood. With clean clothes on and a refreshed look, Montague, and Capricorn step back out into the streets.

The city remains unsafe for any who happens to be caught in its talons. Word of the heretic's death spreads to give criminals free reign and an increase in violence takes place, even during the afternoon hours.

Five men surround an elderly man protecting his teenage daughter. Outnumbered and unwilling to give up will end in his death and his daughter to be taken and defiled. The thugs raise their daggers and close in on the helpless man armed with nothing more than a bat. His daughter his crouched low behind him while sobbing. She knows how this will play out and nothing will change their assailants' minds; nothing can prevent this inevitable outcome from taking place. Yet, hope survives even in the city of the damned; to rob evil a victory on its own turf.

A black steel sword is drawn, and a loaded crossbow is raised behind the thugs. Montague stabs one of the men in the side while Capricorn shoots another in the back of the neck. The three remaining men turn to take notice of their challengers.

"It cannot be. We were told you were dead," one of them explains.

"I've died many times. Now, take me to your leader." Montague says smugly.

"And if I refuse?" another man bravely snaps back. Capricorn waits a short moment before firing an arrow into the man's chest.

"You become obsolete," Montague replies. The last two men look at each other and then throw their weapons to the ground. Capricorn motions to the elderly man and his daughter.

"Go and do not delay." The father thanks her and then hurries away with his daughter in hand. Capricorn turns her attention back to the two would be rapists, "now, where were we?" she says as she places another arrow into her bow.

"Wait, there's a place called, The Shack. Diomedes has us meeting there now."

"I thought Neon Lights was your gathering spot," Montague asks. The second man answers his question.

"It was, but it got too crowded." Montague sheathes his sword but keeps looking at the two men.

"Now, which one of you wants to have the honor to tell your story?" The two men stare nervously ahead wondering if he means what they think he means, but Capricorn confirms it by selecting her target and then fires an arrow into his heart. Montague glances at the last man with a smirk. "I guess you win." He and Capricorn depart from the shaken man who has a message to deliver.

Word has reached Mammon of this event and he responds with a loud roar.

"Impossible!" he growls.

"My man gave their descriptions, it matches that of the heretic and Capricorn," Diomedes confirms.

"Use all your resources to kill them. When you succeed you

will gain my power."

This is exactly what Diomedes wants to hear. Having Mammon's power will put the city under his control and everyone within it will belong to him. He makes the announcement like a king to his subjects. Every villainous soul will answer his call, every one of them equipped with a weapon and every one of them with an order to kill Montague and his dear Capricorn. Two hundred men agree to slay the outmatched duo to earn a place in Diomedes' army and the celebratory drink and whore that will follow.

Montague and Capricorn have but one choice now—they must go to war.

7

By Love or By War

The Shack is accurately named for its decrepit state and small interior. It acts as a trading post for food and drinks, but neither seems to be in great supply. The walls have deep gouges in them made from a variety of blades and the tables and chairs appear to be poorly crafted from their uneven legs and tops. It's no surprise why Diomedes chose this place for him and his men to frequent. With only three tables occupied and no gambling or advertising prostitutes it does not attract the crowds that Neon Lights does. This is the end of the road for many whose untamed lifestyles has finally caught up to them. Fatigued and riddled with the long-term effects of alcoholism and untreated STD's, those that come here are waiting to die.

Montague and Capricorn take a seat at the bar as Montague slides two first aid kits to the bartender. The man opens each container before stashing them under the counter. He then fills two glasses of water and sets a single loaf of bread in between them. Montague doesn't feel like haggling and accepts the trade. Besides a man having an occasional coughing fit the entire room is silent. The door to the shack is suddenly pushed open with such a force that it slams against the wall. The disturbance gets everyone's attention except for Montague and Capricorn who does not turn around.

Diomedes strolls inside knowing he's being searched for and deciding to grant Montague an audience, but not without tilting the odds in his favor. Following close behind him are three of his men. Capricorn slowly reaches for her bow, but Montague gently lays his hand on hers and whispers, "Be vigilant first. Watch, wait, then act."

Diomedes takes his time ambling towards Montague in a cocky and taunting manner. His demeanor suggests that he's not afraid of his foe and has plenty of time to spare. His men follow him smiling and laughing intending to leave the impression that fighting them would also be foolish and that they have already won. Their tactic is meant to instill doubt in their opponents even before the fight can begin. Montague, of course, is not just any opponent.

"We meet again—heretic. Do you remember me? I'm the guy that kicked you in the face." Diomedes' lackeys chuckle loudly as Montague and Capricorn restrain from turning around. Montague is playing the same game and makes it appear that Diomedes isn't worth the time to acknowledge. "Did you know Diomedes is a famous name in some parts of the world?" he continues. "He was one of the best warriors during the Trojan War. The strength and skill to even kill Gods. No doubt a past life of mine." Diomedes gives his men a sly look as they support him in hysterical laughter. Diomedes leans his elbow on the counter beside Montague so the two can finally make eye contact.

"I didn't know this great warrior needed to drag men along to laugh at his jokes," Montague smirks.

"Watching you die will be the best moment in my life," he whispers.

"It better be. You won't have too many after," Montague responds. Diomedes glares at him before turning his attention to the rest of the room.

"Whoever helps us annihilate these two will gain amnesty from Mammon's wrath!" Chairs groan on the floor as several people stand up with their knives and daggers ready, while a few obviously have refused the offer by remaining seated.

"Some warrior. You are already looking for help," Capricorn

points out. Diomedes ignores her comment while leaning in close to Montague.

"If you survive you will make a worthy adversary." He backs away and gives the command. "Kill them!"

Montague draws his sword and stands up. He turns around just in time to jab his pummel into his attacker's face and then slices him across the gut. Montague takes the short sword from his recently slain foe and hands it to Capricorn, who had just shot her crossbow to kill her target.

"Use this instead of your bow."

"You mean twang?" Capricorn says softly to correct him.

The opposition are relentless in their onslaught, but eight feeble men are no match for Montague and Capricorn. Some are already rushing out of the shack from observing the duo's deadly blows. Tables and chairs become tipped over as men fall into them or toss them away. Capricorn proves to be just as good with a blade as she is with a crossbow, while Montague's combos are fast and accurate. He slashes another attacker down his sternum and then brings the sword back up to slice his throat. Capricorn favors the backstab technique and has agility and speed on her side. She easily avoids her attackers' offence and then twirls or sidesteps behind her opponents. Each feels the sting of her blade even before they can turn around.

Diomedes grinds his teeth as he watches the unfolding fight. He had assumed that being outnumbered would lead to their downfall, but he failed to consider the skill of The Shack's rift-raft are nowhere near Montague's or Capricorn's. His last resort is to send his own men into the fray hoping they can finish them off. Forgetting about Capricorn, he pushes each one toward Montague.

He relies solely on parrying those surrounding him while letting Capricorn strike behind them. His enemies' one-track minds give him the victory and the last man's intestines spill to the floor from Montague's sword. Blood soaked wood and broken tables and chairs are now added to The Shack's appearance.

Diomedes stands alone with a focused glare on Montague. He ignores the fact that after just fighting eleven men both Montague and Capricorn remain unscathed. He expects Montague should be slow from exhaustion by now and that this will give him the upper hand.

"This is just between you and me, heretic," Diomedes announces. Montague gently guides Capricorn behind him.

"Montague?" She says concerned.

"It's alright Capricorn; this man only thinks he's a warrior," Montague taunts. Diomedes pulls back the flaps of his overcoat to reveal two swords on either side of him.

"When I kill you. Capricorn will make a decent trophy, and when I'm done with her, I'll give her to the street." Diomedes says as he draws each sword.

"Capricorn won't be able to feel your touch," Montague replies calmly.

Diomedes flails his swords around him before charging toward Montague. The wild swirling blades pose a new threat to Montague, who only has one blade to deflect. He's forced into defense against the double blades whizzing around him by parrying and dodging or ducking. Capricorn rolls over the top of the bar to get out of the way as the two carry their duel across the entire floor.

She squats down below the counter and unexpectedly discovers a young boy hiding nearby.

"It's okay, you'll be safe here, we won't hurt you," she says while gently taking his hand into hers.

Diomedes' swords slice through a chair as he advances toward Montague, who has little choice but to keep backing up. Diomedes fumbles with kicking the broken chair out of the way giving Montague his long-awaited moment to strike. His aim comes in at an upward angle forcing Diomedes to lean back. The sword catches the flap of his overcoat and shreds through its side. Diomedes becomes aggravated and hastily swings both swords down, but Montague quickly rolls an overturned table in between them. The swords slice deep into the wooden side of the tabletop and become stuck. Montague takes this opportunity for another attack. His outstretched reach, across the table, manages to allow the tip of his blade to graze Diomedes' cheek. Unable to free his swords, Diomedes backs away unarmed and then lightly touches his wound to take note of the blood on his fingertips.

"I could make a comment on your claim about killing Gods, but I do not believe in such petty insults," Montague jokes.

"Mammon has marked you for death. I'm surprised you've survived this long, but you fight a war you cannot win. You're just standing in line for the guillotine, and I will be there when it falls."

Diomedes leaves his swords in the table and brashly walks out of the shack with one side of his coat hanging considerably lower than the other.

"Are you going to let him go? Capricorn asks after standing up from behind the bar.

"I don't know why. I just have a feeling that I should," he answers while sheathing his sword.

Capricorn holds the hand of the boy as the three walk outside. A worried father hurries toward them and scoops the boy up into his arms.

"Thank you for keeping him safe," the relieved father says to Capricorn. She smiles and nods for her reply. "For so long no one dared challenge what this city had become. Most of us found it easier to accept it or join it," a bystander admits.

"Don't fight the city. Fight only for yourself and the ones you hold dear. If everyone does that the city will eventually heal," Montague responds.

"Hide with us, you'll live longer, the boy's father suggests."

"I was hiding my entire life—and I never once considered it living," Capricorn points out.

"You will be in our prayers," the man says as he departs with his son and the few others in his group.

Capricorn takes Montague's hand and looks at him as they begin their walk.

"A baby. A little boy or a little girl. I would like one of our own." Montague smiles.

"Someday. When life will be fairer, need will be rarer, and greed will not pay." They continue heading toward the setting sun with not much else to say. Both are pondering the similar thoughts centered on a future they may or may not have and about their ill-spent pasts.

Montague's shelter proves to still be out of reach when dusk blankets the city. He and Capricorn have reached the commercial district and seek refuge inside a five-story office building. The dark, cold lobby is littered with trash and broken chairs and benches that offer no place to rest. A short climb to the next floor takes them into a large cafeteria where a smashed in vending machine provides a few chocolate candy bars. The third floor are all cubicles and the fourth consists of conference rooms and a security office that has long been out of commission. The fifth floor are executive offices and present the most comfort with their couches, chairs, private bathrooms, and large windows to keep watch on the streets below.

Montague keeps a keen eye on the outside as the last of the light slowly fades. The streets appear to be deserted when he turns his attention to Capricorn. It didn't take long for her to fall asleep on the loveseat behind him. While he admires her several men hurry across the street toward the office building. Montague redirects his sights back outside but has missed the chance to spot the small force coming his way.

The sound of hurried footsteps in the nearby stairwell alerts Montague that a peaceful night is out of the question. He quickly retrieves his sword resting on the ornate desk and then hurries to wake Capricorn.

"Capricorn," he whispers while shaking her shoulder. "We are not alone."

Despite making such a ruckus, running up the stairs, these hired assassins now gather silently outside the closed office door while holding their daggers or clubs. They exchange looks and nods before one of them kicks in the door. The mob rushes in and immediately spreads out through the darkened room. It looks like no one is here, but they are not ready to give up until they've made a thorough search.

The moonlight casts a dim glow that illuminates some of the office, but a potted Ficus stands in a corner that's still encased in shadow. Montague stands motionless behind the foliage with his sword raised up and pressed against his chest. He takes careful note where everyone is and where they may be heading as his presence is not yet known.

The men continue conducting their search in the adjoining restroom and behind file cabinets. One of them strolls around to the back of the executive desk with front and side walls that meet the floor. Capricorn is hiding in the leg space with her bow pointing at the pair of legs that has just crossed her sights. The man lets his fingers tap on top of the desk and then plays with rolling the chair back and forth. There's only one place left to look. He glances up at his party members before averting his eyes downward. He lightly pushes the chair away and then slowly lowers his body until his investigation concludes with Capricorn's arrow speeding towards him. He falls back with an arrow in his forehead before any thought had time to form.

The men become alerted closer to the desk just as Montague jumps out of his hiding place. With a war cry he advances behind the men and begins slicing through them with short, fast strokes. Capricorn crawls out and fires another arrow at one of the thugs before climbing on top of the desk. She lands a direct kick into the face of another who attempts to grab her legs.

Montague's ambush was able to cull most of the threat down from an overwhelming force into something a bit more manageable; however, now surrounded by three men is proving to be challenging. Capricorn jumps off the desk and grabs two clubs from a fallen foe and begins clobbering her assailants. She finally reaches those around Montague, but not before one of them gets a lucky swing across his chest. The attack interrupts his flow and results in a moment of hesitation. He is swiftly tripped and kicked down to his knees. Capricorn rushes into the middle and stands over Montague with each leg on either side of him while flailing the clubs around her. Anyone who dares get close receives a bone-cracking impact.

One of the last few men flicks his dagger at Capricorn from a safe distance only to find it embedded deep into one of her clubs. Unsure if it was a lucky block or a skillful interception, the last four men retreat with broken bones and gushing wounds—the remaining six have succumbed to their injuries.

Capricorn tosses the clubs away and then squats down over Montague.

"Montague, my love," she says worried. He grunts as he lifts himself up to lean his back against the wall.

"I'm alright. It looks worse than it feels," he says with a sigh.

Capricorn begins digging through his pockets to retrieve the first aid kit he always keeps. She helps him take off his coat and shirt and then lightly dabs the blood away with a cotton swab. She disinfects the wound and finally, wraps a cloth around Montague's back and across the gash.

"This wasn't a coincidence. They knew exactly where we were, and they were well reinforced," Montague says as she mends him.

"Shh, don't worry. No one will get to you while I'm here,"

she says softly while drawing him close to her body and holding him against her. Capricorn has a way of bringing down his defenses, even now he can't help but feel as vulnerable as an infant while resting in her arms.

"I love you, Capricorn. Do you know what that means?" Capricorn stares into his eyes and places her hand on his cheek.

"It means a deep care for someone. An extension of your own soul. When it hurts to be away from them or not be able to hold them. Is that how you feel about me?"

"Yes."

"That's how I feel about you too."

Montague gazes out the window to notice the city's limits in the distance and the rolling hills of the countryside beyond it.

"Look outside Capricorn. See those hills? That's the outskirts of the city. We are being hunted by demons that can smell our very blood, but we can leave all of this behind us."

"I have a feeling those hills are too far away, my love. Besides, we promised to bring an end to Mammon's rule."

"Somewhere in the middle of nowhere we spin at a thousand miles per hour. Heavy now is the world, yet it floats effortlessly in space. Tired now are the weavers of this quilt. Pictured here are all who have walked the many paths of this labyrinth through time; however, our story is yet to be sewn."

"Our story will reach those who will never know us; told from those who only saw us as some image in the fog. I promise—I will always be with you."

"And I promise never to leave your side—either by love or by war."

Later that night, a single flame-lit lantern casts its flickering amber glow on a bottle of whiskey and the shot glass nearby. Diomedes takes the gulp and then refills the glass as he sits alone at a table. Only two assassins from the assault on Montague and Capricorn approach the table and wait silently.

"Tell me," Diomedes commands somberly after another swig and already pouring his next shot.

"We found them, but they got away," One of them replies.

"Did they get away, or did you?" Diomedes asks refusing to pause his drinking. His men exchange looks but fail to respond, leading Diomedes to conclude his assumptions are correct. "I cannot fathom how so many can fail to kill only two rebels," he continues after a sigh.

"They fight with passion," the other man confesses. Diomedes slams his fist on the table.

"Don't preach passion to me!" he yells and then downs another shot. "My wife was pregnant with our first when the riots reached us. Our house was invaded forcing us to abandon it. There was a mad rush of people carrying torches—her hand slipped out of mine. Lost in the crowd—I never saw her again.

Diomedes remembers searching frantically for his wife and unborn child in the midst of the angry mob. The stampeding crowd rushes by while forcing him in their direction of travel with no amount of pushing helping his outcome. He becomes pinned against a congested cluster just before a man carrying a torch is forced into him. Unable to pull away, the fire scorches the left side of his face, but his screams are not heard above the roar of the mob. Shortly thereafter he covers his deformity with half of a black mask. Since that day, it has never been removed.

Diomedes snaps out of his recollection and then stands up. He stumbles and falls into one of the men. He puts his arm around his shoulder and lightly taps his cheek.

"Do you know what a heretic is?"

"Um, someone who is stupid," the man answers with a laugh. Diomedes smiles and laughs sarcastically.

"It's someone who goes against the common majority. Do you know how one remedies that?"

"No," he replies while shaking his head. He may have hoped that Diomedes' drunken state may make him less of a threat, but unpredictability can never be properly defined.

"Ah, and that is why I know I chose the wrong man for the job." Diomedes pushes a dagger in his gut and twists it before stabbing him several more times. He pushes the dying man away and watches him bleed from his mouth until his body stops twitching. Diomedes turns to the second man who is trying hard not to show how frightened he is. "Gather everyone to block every exit out of this city and cover every rabbit hole," he orders him.

"Yes sir, absolutely," he answers and then swiftly departs before Diomedes changes his mind. Diomedes returns to his chair and stares into the flickering flame as it reflects dancing shadows on his face.

"They have proved they can resist a few. Let's see how well they fair against an army."

Dawn. The beginning of a day that will go down in infamy. A formidable army of two hundred eager myrmidons follow Diomedes through the city streets. The meek watch from windows of forgotten homes and workplaces with horror and disgust, while others cheer from the sidewalk as if watching a parade. The boisterous wants to be seen showing their support for Mammon and Diomedes, while the silent few, consumed by fear, struggle with their guilt. How can there be so many willing to kill for scrapes and empty promises? How can there be so much hatred toward two who are only guilty of protecting others and surviving? A man with a megaphone advances among the legion while repeating his recruiting prompt.

"Mammon reigns supreme. Aid in the destruction of the heretic and his slut and be rewarded. Mammon reigns supreme—"

"My God—what has become of us?" an observer asks in disbelief while peeking out of slightly opened blinds.

"There's nothing we can do," an older gentleman says. "He who lives unseen lives well," he continues before fully shutting the blinds.

Montague and Capricorn are not oblivious to the plot against them as they watch the mob from a crouched position on a rooftop.

"It's a modern-day witch hunt and just as primitive," Montague observes.

"Why are there so many when we are only two?"

"Because we fight cowards, Capricorn, and cowards will always find a way to win." Montague remains fixated on the staggering numbers while lost in thought. He recalls a reoccurring nightmare from his childhood. A dim light is all he has to repeal the encroaching darkness around him. Something unseen shuffles in the dark, it is always heard, but never seen. Montague knew it was coming for him and that one day it was going to find him. It was an illness that was not a disease. It was a monster that lacked a form. In his dream it was death. Death hides in the fading light; the shade of a shadow. Something you think you see out the corner of your eye, but when you turn to glance there's nothing there. That's where it lives. So close, yet always invisible.

Montague rubs Capricorn's cheek. "I think you were right,

hon. Those hills aren't meant for us." Capricorn brings his cheek to hers and hugs him.

"Thank you for saving me," she says.

"It was I who was saved by you, Capricorn. You gave me a world to believe in," he replies softly and then hands her a sword. "Keep this with you."

Montague and Capricorn maintain a cautious pace as they proceed through secluded alleys on their route to the city's limits. What choice do they have now? There'll never be a hiding place secure enough for them to seek refuge in and they can't risk staying another night. This city was never on anyone's side but its own. Even now it watches and listens to every step they take. Every whisper, every shuffle, lets the city know where they are. They press their backs against a brick wall and follow it to its end. A quick peek around the corner reveals an eerily deserted sector. Several shops, cafes and an apartment complex meet the sidewalk that surrounds a grand plaza. It was once an attractive place to shop, eat and gather, but it's hard to visualize it past the litter and rubble. From the collapsed stage to the shattered windows and the overgrown weeds sprouting up from the cracks in the pavement. Countless rainstorms and looters finished what the fires had started. The vast area now rests in a dilapidated state until time plays its final hand. It's a long sprint to reach cover again, but the desolate appearance doesn't convince Montague it's safe. The ruined and darkened building interiors are perfect for concealment and avoiding detection won't be easy.

A breeze stirs loose papers up into a mini tornado and gently rocks overturned trashcans to and fro. Montague and Capricorn slowly advance while glancing up into the windows of the high-rise apartment in case someone may be spying below. They also take turns observing around them to be sure no one is following behind. They reach the center plaza to put half of their trek behind them, but this also puts them the farthest from cover.

A dreaded voice is heard that halts their march.

"You weren't the first to try to leave the city—" Diomedes strolls out from behind a heavily damaged large-screen television and sound system. He's resting both hands on each handle of his swords that are strapped to his sides. Montague had left them behind after their previous squabble and never thought to try to deprive him from regaining them. "—The misses had the same idea," Diomedes continues as he faces the two with only a few yards in between them. "Let's go to the cliffs and live on the beach. Beyond the hills and far away from this city, she said." Neither Montague nor Capricorn respond, and Diomedes continues. "I didn't want to live in a hut or leave my things behind. So, I contested. Of course, none of that ended up mattering," Diomedes pauses for a slight moment and shows a hint of remorse, but it fades almost as soon as it had appeared. "What were you planning anyway? Building a log cabin? Start up your own little homestead? No, you aren't a shelter building expert. Face it, heretic, you are just like all of us. Your survival relies on others failing."

"For once you've said something I agree with. Our survival does rely on someone failing." Montague's reply gets a smirk out of Diomedes, but he's not at all amused.

"I'm happy to disappoint." Diomedes lets his hands slide off his sword and his arms fall to his side. He then lifts one arm and points toward them. "Here lies Montague!" he yells.

Doorways and front windows become flooded with charging mobs of thugs as they rush out of the surrounding buildings with weapons drawn and hollering. The rampaging army is quick to cut off any hope of escape as they close around Montague and Capricorn. The two remain standing back-to-back as they skillfully slash, stab and slice their opponents. Despite being severely outnumbered the duo are holding their own with impressive tenacity while trading off defensive and offensive tactics. Montague slashes a man across his belly and then strikes another under his chin with the pummel of his sword. Capricorn kicks another man in the crotch before stabbing him through the chest.

Today an excess of two-hundred men has been sent to kill two. And two may have killed two hundred if it were not for one. Diomedes watches his men falling at the blades of these two warriors with shock and frustration and finally decides to get involved. He reaches behind the downed television screen and picks up a tactical crossbow. "You aren't the only one with a crossbow," he says under his breath. He holds the bow steady and takes careful aim at his target before squeezing the trigger. The bolt rips through the air and hits its target with such force that only the fletching is seen protruding from Capricorn's abdomen.

Her body goes numb, her sword falls from her grasp, her mouth becomes frozen in a scream that cannot be heard. Colors blend together, sounds are fading out, her breathing slows, and she begins to fall. Montague sacrifices his sword to catch her in his arms. She tries to speak, but nothing comes out.

Montague gently eases her down until his knees come to rest on the ground. She wraps her arms around him and forces a small smile through her quivering lips. The onslaught ceases to allow Montague and Capricorn to exchange their last words. It's not because these men have honor or respect, but more so to remember the moment and prolong the experience.

"Capricorn—" Montague begins, but he cannot finish his sentence. Blood trickles from her lips and nose as she feels the blood pooling in her throat; somehow, she manages to speak. "I can see myself in your eyes. That is where I will always be." Montague kisses her lips and holds her close to his heart.

"You exist within me. I cannot be without you," Montague sobs.

"I can see the daylight peeking over the rolling hills. It is here that I wait for you," Capricorn whispers. "I—love—you," she forces her last message to him just before her head falls back. Her arms fall from Montague's shoulders and her eyelids shut. At this moment her breath becomes no more. She leaves this world and one like her will never again grace our presence. Montague kisses her again and with his arms refusing to set her down he forfeits his fight.

This concludes the truce, and the men decide to finish what was started. Sword and dagger, knife and stiletto stab and slash into Montague's ribs, back, chest, and stomach. Yells filled with pain and sorrow echo throughout the city as a hush falls over all who hears him. His blood pours into a pool around him and all warmth departs from him. His numerous wounds have become too great, and his body falls over Capricorn's. In their final embrace his heart beats its last and his soul follows his love.

The mob retires from the plaza after their conquest and two lovers are left alone in a desolate plot; even the breeze has become still. In this city the dead were never given much notice. No one ever mourned them or thought to move them from their concrete coffins. They were left where they fell until hungry dogs made them into meals. But today is not like the days before. These two will not be ignored. The plaza gradually becomes occupied by people who respectively advance with lit candles toward where Montague and Capricorn lie. Several volunteers lift the slain couple and carry them while the humming procession follows.

They are cleaned and cared for with the utmost respect and then wrapped in white linen. They are gently placed side by side inside a grave as an assembly gathers around. A young man steps forward and bows his head.

"Our hearts are heavy and ache as tears dry on our cheeks. We shiver from lack of heat and cry to deaf ears. We reach up to arms that never hold us. We live in invisible cages holding onto dreams that never come true. We are the forgotten few—and we never met." A woman advances to his side while holding a rose.

"You may have hated this city, but you saved it. Both of you—" The woman releases her rose and watches it fall onto Montague's chest. Everyone follows her lead and drop their flowers on Montague and Capricorn. This is how they are buried. They are remembered by those they had helped and by those who found hope in just their stories.

"You never got to hear it—but thank you." That was spoken by the people, not the city. Not by those who believe they owned it or should rule it, but by those few men and women who hid and prayed for change. They now stand in great numbers and in the open. Neither afraid to morn, nor afraid to be seen or to be heard. Home always seemed so far away—until now when it's realized it was here all along.

While the city remains somber, Mammon and Diomedes celebrate with laughter back inside Mammon's grand hall.

"You did very well," Mammon praises.

"Thank you, it was my finest conquest." Diomedes answers.

"It is time. Relinquish your soul and receive my power."

"I'm ready and humbly accept," Diomedes responds and bows his head.

"First is knowledge. A fragment of information. Something your human mind is oblivious to, but to be like me requires more than you know."

"I'm ready to know everything you are willing to share," Diomedes eagerly responds.

"Your beloved was not murdered as you had thought."

"She lives?" Diomedes says with a glimmer of hope.

"She escaped the mob and survived long enough to give birth—to a girl. A girl born in seclusion. A girl she named after her zodiac sign. A girl named, Capricorn." Diomedes eyes become wide. This information cannot be true.

"What do you speak of?" he asks dumbfounded. Mammon lets out a long rumbling laugh. "Are you implying Capricorn was my daughter? Did you make me kill my daughter?!" he shouts. Diomedes' distress fills Mammon with a drunken blissfulness that one has after drinking too much wine as he continues his hysterical laughter.

"You hate because I told you to hate. You've killed your family just as I have killed mine. Now, you are like me." Diomedes yells an agonizing yell while Mammon continues laughing. Diomedes' sorrow quickly becomes anger.

"Why did you not tell me?"

"You never wanted to know. You cared more about being king and ruling than the truth about your past. Did you not want power? Did you not ask for the city to bow to you? Did you not desire a harem of harlots? You chose your destiny, now embrace it."

"You lied to me!"

"I never lied. I just never told the truth."

Diomedes picks up a spear from the nearby weapon rack and points it at Mammon.

"Tell me this claim is false!"

"Don't be a fool. You have reached your goal. Do not folly now."

"There is nothing left for me." His greatest triumph has lost its luster. His victory feels more like a failure. While Mammon found acceptance in his sacrifice, Diomedes is unable to. He's driven mad and charges forward to trust the spear through Mammon's chest. Mammon roars while trying to back away from his attack, but Diomedes follows through with great force until the spear tip explodes out his back. Mammon is brought down to his hands and knees and glares at Diomedes.

"You will never be able to hide from me. I will find another, and he will hunt you down. My power is enduring, many will fight for it."

Diomedes doesn't respond with a comeback. He draws one of his blades and slashes a deep cut on the left side of Mammon's neck. Mammon swipes his claws in retaliation, but Diomedes pushes the embedded spear further to force Mammon away. He brings his sword around again to the right side of Mammon's neck to hack another deep gash. With one more final blow Diomedes swings his sword through his previous slices to lob off Mammon's head once and for all. His roars and growls end with his head rolling away from his lifeless body. The hall falls silent following Mammon's corpse plopping to the floor. Only Diomedes is here to witness Mammon's demise. Who would question the demon's death? Diomedes finally achieved everything he had strived for. With Mammon dead the city is now his, the people are his, but he no longer wants any of it.

The fact stands that after the slaying of Montague and Capricorn both Mammon and Diomedes disappeared; however, no love was shown to them. No one searched for them and soon all conversation concerning the matter became short or no longer discussed. Those that were promised glory and prestige for their aid and association with Diomedes fell into obscurity. To the inhabitants of a broken city Mammon and Diomedes are operating in the shadows, but who is to say that Montague and Capricorn are not doing the same?

Beyond the rolling hills are the oceanside cliffs towering over the crashing waves. The beach below is a mile away; only piles of jagged rocks occupy the ground here. The howling wind harshly bombards Diomedes relentlessly as he maintains his footing near the edge.

"What have I done? My abhorrent hands. My passionless heart. What have I done? Will compassion be showed to this doppelganger? Will forgiveness be given to this forlorn soul?" Diomedes questions to himself. He pries his black mask from his face and hurls it over the side of the cliff. The concealed side of his face is riddled with burn scars and a blind eye, white with puss, is revealed. He lets out a long painful cry and stretches his arms out. "I leap against the resisting winds and find freedom. A few seconds of peace." Diomedes leans forward and his feet slide off the solid surface.

"Time is slow. I find my redemption—
on the rocks below."

Diomedes plunges down the cliffside towards the rocky ground where he meets his end.

It took seven months for the tales of Montague and Capricorn to spread and flourish. Hiding civilians leave their refuges to band together and overrun those who used to prey on them. Another bout of chaotic upheavals and disorder ensues that gradually eliminates the loyal forces still obedient to Mammon and Diomedes. The aftermath from this civil unrest; however, is peace.

A lush park of flowing bushes and paved walkways offers an inviting respite for the citizens of a rebuilding and modern city. A young scholar is reciting his poetic tale to an engrossed crowd engaged in his words. They sit on the grass before him as his voice carries his story to all who celebrates this much-loved event year after year.

"Listen to my tale of the fair and beautiful Capricorn and her beloved—the brave and troubled Montague. I was there when he breathed his last few breaths in her loving embrace. I was there when both left this world together. I saw them my entire life, but only noticed them in their final hour. Formally known as the heretic, remembered now as Montague. Hear me, and I will tell you their story."

Not far behind the storyteller is a limestone statue of Montague with his sword held above him and pointing up while kissing Capricorn's lips, while she has her bow grasped at her side. Engraved at the base are the words,

By Love or By War.

The sidewalks once again welcome parents pushing strollers and businessmen and women holding their briefcases and cups of coffee.

If one visits the art district, they will find an exhibit called,

The Hexagon of Light.

It is here that a glass case holds a compound pistol crossbow and a black steel sword. Never again to be needed, but always seen, and never forgotten.

Nestled among the infinite rolling hills is a small stone cottage with a fenced in vegetable garden behind it and a line of mixed flowers along each side of the house. Capricorn delicately inspects her growing crops until she hears her name being called in the wind. She looks up and around her, but no one appears to be close enough to call for her.

"*Capricorn—*"

She lifts her head a second time to look around and this time spots a figure advancing toward her. She exits her garden and waits for the man to come closer. She remembers him now and runs to meet Montague, who no longer bares a facial scar. She jumps into his arms and presses her lips against his as he twirls her around him.

"My love. My love, you have returned," she says after her feet become planted back on the ground.

"I will follow you wherever you may go. Never will I leave your side," he replies. She smiles and lays her head on his warm chest.

"Here we are free. Here we are home. This is home," she says with her eyes closed.

"I have something for you," he says.

"You do?" She lifts her head to see what he had brought her.

Montague reaches into his pocket and takes out an amethyst amulet and then carefully places it around her neck. She lifts the amulet up and gazes admirably at the perfect stone "Thank you, it's beautiful," she says with a broad smile. They kiss again before Capricorn takes his hand and leads him towards their countryside cottage.

Montague and Capricorn are finally where they belong—

Together.

There comes a time when a man must forgo familiarity, and venture into uncertainty. Risking obscurity, but also quite possibly—finding meaning.

"If writing isn't fun, you're doing it wrong."

UTOPIA

*Sometimes **perfect** comes with fine print.*

Contents

1
CPQ

The greatest challenge to an individual is how they perceive reality, and how they are connected to it. It's based on the point-of-view of the one who's exposed to it, and their acceptance or rejection of it. Such as in the cases of lucid dreaming, one may be confused for the first few moments of waking up as they struggle with their recent experience while becoming self-aware in the current time and place.

In a child's mind, reality may only be a present moment, but tomorrow could be very different. This allows the child to develop their imagination while pretending that any given reality could be true. In adults, knowledge, and experience, dictate what can and cannot be real. For those who have mental disorders, the line between reality and illusion become blurred and their actions become unpredictable. What most of us call civilized and sociably acceptable may differ greatly from another.

For Brian Troth, a young defense attorney in his mid-thirties, reality is centered around his job. He lives solely for his career. A career which he considers a game; a game of who can talk the best. Whether it's half-truths or pointing out the loopholes; it's all about how you present the facts. He doesn't care too much if his clients are actually guilty or innocent, he just finds a way to instill doubt into the jury or focus on the lack of facts, or some irregularity in morality. He only cares about winning the case given to him and the truth is just a matter of opinion. His methods must be effective since to date, he's never lost a case. Many would not consider him a moral man, he seldom does anything for others and if he does, it's usually attached to some financial gain. He lives only for himself and shares his time and space with no one else.

For Brian this reality is permanent and everlasting. He has planned out his whole life at the age of thirty-three and any possible change was never taken into consideration; however, an extreme shift in reality is about to occur for Brian. A change so severe that it will be impossible for him to accept or understand it. In fact, he will disregard it completely and demand an end to the charade. His reality is about to be questioned.

Brian's current hearing involves Mr. Allen, who's convicted of murdering fourteen women and then engaging in necrophilia with them. Brian is not here today to try to prove Mr. Allen's innocence, he is most diffidently guilty in the eyes of the law. Brian is forced to change tactics and try to prove if Mr. Allen was aware of his actions at the time of committing them.

The courtroom is silent as the observers and jury members sit patiently waiting to hear Brian's rebuttal. Mr. Allen is sitting with his hands clasped together on the table while Brian skims through the report in front of him. After a short moment he slowly closes the manila folder and stands up. He removes his reading glasses and sets them on top of the folder before advancing towards the jury and begins calmly pacing back and forth.

"Good afternoon, ladies, and gentlemen of the jury. My name is, Brian Troth. You have been told that my client, Mr. Allen, is a ruthless murderer. Some have even been so bold to call him evil, but please consider the following facts. At the age of thirteen his mother committed suicide leaving him alone with his alcoholic father, who beat him mercilessly. Mr. Allen also suffers from schizophrenia and prone to experiencing vivid hallucinations."

Brian picks up several black and white photos on a small table and holds them over his head. The gruesome crime-scene photographs show the women victims in pools of blood, dismembered and nude.

"Do not be coaxed by these crime-scene photographs into the belief that Mr. Allen is a monster. In his unstable mentality he has no recollection of his actions and should not be held responsible for deeds he does not recall committing." Brian rests his voice before starting again.

"In the Old Testament Cain is labeled the first murderer after killing his brother Able. Do you know how he committed this act?" Brian pauses as he glances at every member of the jury. "He threw a rock at his head. There wasn't any biological research on the brain at that time, or medical knowledge of the results of brain injuries. As this also was the first time a life was taken by a human hand, there wasn't a concept that this act could even be committed. Mr. Allen, like Cain, is accused of taking life, but neither of them, in their minds, understood what the end result of their actions would have been. Mr. Allen did not plan to kill; he did not stalk his victims; it was a trigger that set him off. A trigger that he was unable to control or predict.

In closing, I only ask that you see my client, Mr. Allen, for who he really is. Not a predator, but a victim himself. Thank you."

Brian heads back to his chair next to Mr. Allen. The groans coming from the audience proves many did not care for Brian's explanation. He doesn't look at his defendant or try to whisper reassuring phrases to him. He doesn't even acknowledge the grieving family members sitting in the audience or the prosecutor who's watching him intensely. Instead, he opens another folder and begins reading the facts for his next case while jotting down notes.

The judge asks the opposition if they have anything to add. The prosecutor shakes his head, and the judge dismisses the jury so they can discuss the case and come to their decision about Mr. Allen's fate.

It only takes twenty minutes for the jury members to reenter the room and take their seats.

"Have you come to a verdict?" the judge asks.

"We have, your honor," one of the juror answers.

"You may proceed." Brian lifts his head only to hear the final result from the jury.

"We, the jury find, Mr. Allen guilty on all fourteen accounts of murder."

The judge slams his gavel several times to quiet down the observers of friends and family members who either have become relieved or upset. Brian just sighs with a shake of his head and then returns to his papers. When the chatter and shuffling of feet subside the judge continues.

"Mr. Allen, you have been found guilty of murders in the first degree by a jury of your peers. By the laws of the state of Maryland you are hereby sentenced to death by lethal injection. This courtroom is dismissed." One final slam of the judge's gavel ends Brian's winning streak.

The bailiff directs Mr. Allen out of the courtroom in handcuffs while Brian carefully packs his papers and folders away in his briefcase as the prosecutor approaches him.

"How does it feel to lose?" he asks. Brian continues packing his papers and answers apathetically without making eye contact.

"Same as winning; I got paid and now I wash my hands of it."

"I'm told you can always spot a lawyer who has no case when they start quoting the bible as part of their argument," the prosecutor continues.

"I wasn't quoting the bible. I just told a story." Brian snaps his briefcase closed and heads out of the room still busy with straggling observers.

The parking garage is nearly empty at this late hour as Brian strolls past the few parked cars. The only sound he can hear is the echo of his dress shoes against the pavement. A squeaking of a large metal car door opening and then slamming shut resonates from someplace in the garage. Another pair of feet seem to match Brian's pace as they follow him from a distance.

Brian digs into his brown trench coat pocket for his keys as he nears his new BMW M3. The person who was following him slides his feet to a halt nearby. Brian turns around to notice a man with both hands in his pockets staring at him.

"Can I help you?" Brian asks.

He was one of the men sitting in the audience, but Brian would not have known that.

"Did you look at those pictures you held up today?"

"I don't know. Why?"

"Did you take the time to see who those girls were? Their names, their dreams, did you?"

"None of that has anything to do with me. Now please excuse

me." Brian turns his back to the man to unlock and open his car door.

"One of them was my daughter," the man continues. Brian sighs and turns back to face the man.

"Look, he was found guilty. Justice has been served."

"Yeah, he's being sent to some psych ward with padded walls, a plush carpet, and a comfy mattress. He will be fed three full meals and play board games with his caretakers. The worst he will endure is occasional sedation. You gave him a better life than most of us have out here."

"Look, when your case lands on my desk. I'll be sure to advise you on an insanity plea too. I'll even get you a vase of flowers as a housewarming gift."

"You really are an asshole, aren't you?" The man pulls a handgun out of his pocket and points it at Brian. "I doubt anyone will morn your passing."

For once Brian does not have a response as he stares speechlessly into the barrel. The man cocks the gun and then pulls the trigger. The bullet enters the far side of Brian's forehead. He's knocked back into his car and then collapses to the ground.

An hour had passed before someone finally discovered Brian unconsciousness beside his car. There's no sign of anyone else nearby or any possible cause that led to this man being shot.

Paramedics rush through the hospital doors pushing a gurney with Brian on top. A nurse jogs alongside them as a doctor hurries to meet them.

"Male, early thirties, gunshot to the left side of his head," one of the paramedics calls out.

"We have a pulse, but he never regained conscious while in our care," another responds. The doctor inspects the head wound and then opens each of Brian's eyes to shine a flashlight in them.

"No pupil dilation. How long ago was he shot?" the doctor asks the first responders.

"We don't know. He was found by a janitor at the end of his shift."

"Has his family been contacted?" the doctor continues.

"We only found a number for his secretary on him," the nurse answers.

"Call her." The doctor directs the paramedics to follow him to the operating room while the nurse hurries to the counter and picks up the phone.

In an unpredictable moment everything in Brian's life is about to change, and everything about him will never be the same.

Lena never suspected she would be starting her day in the waiting room with her boss in surgery. A doctor refers to his clipboard while walking into the room.

"I'm sorry for making you wait so long, Ms. Lena," the doctor says as he sits in a chair that's facing Lena. "You are Mr. Troth's secretary, is that correct?"

"Yes, is he going to be alright?" she asks.

"Mr. Troth is out of surgery, but I'm afraid to report that he's in a deep coma."

Lena puts her hand to her mouth while shaking her head in disbelief. She's holding herself together quite well, but it's obvious she's upset from the news.

"According to the Glasgow coma scale his collective score is a 4, with 3 being the most severe. This indicates a deep state of unconsciousness. There's no eye opening, no verbal response and no motor response to pain or speech."

"How long will he be in this coma?"

"That's difficult to say. It can be anywhere from six hours to several years. There's just no way of knowing." The doctor pauses. "The longest coma ever recorded lasted 37 years." Lena's tears begin to show now. "All we can do is wait." The doctor continues. "Is there anyone else associated with Brian to contact? Children, wife?" Lena shakes her head as she dabs a tissue in her tear ducts.

"No—no, there is no one else."

Hours turns into days, and then weeks into months. The world left Brian behind as it slowly continued without him. After six months, his career abandons him, and his office is cleared out. The vinyl letters that spelled his name are peeled off his door and any sign he was ever there is thrown into a dumpster. Lena packs up the last of her things and looks back sorrowfully at the empty office that once belonged to Brian Troth. She's no longer needed there and must leave it as well.

After a year, his possessions are auctioned away, and his condo and car are sold. Every sign of Brian's existence is erased. Years become more years and finally into decades. The world advances into a new era as it evolves and society adapts.

Brian lies in the hospital bed with wires connected to machines to read his vitals and tubes to feed and give him oxygen. The soft beeping fills the room as his pulse reading slowly ascends; his fingers start to move and his eyelids twitch. The bullet wound on his head is now a faint scar. Brian flinches to pinches on his arm and moans to jabs underneath his fingernails. Day by day his score improves until the moment when he opens his eyes. To Brian it was only a moment from feeling the sharp pain in his head to waking up. In actuality, it's been thirty years.

Brian lies awake in a daze as nurses and doctors swarm around him while taking notes and performing tests. Brian isn't fully aware where he's yet; similar to the confusion, and uncertainty of awaking in bed other than yours for the first time. His eyes expected to see the familiar sights of his bedroom. When they don't, his mind must explain why. For most people it only takes a moment to remember something such as traveling. For Brian it takes a lot longer.

Later that day, the room is finally free of visitors as Brian lies in bed staring at the ceiling. No one who was there when Brian was admitted is there now. Brian Troth is only a name on a piece of paper with a history that cannot be confirmed by anyone else.

"Mr. Troth?" Brian turns his head to see a nurse standing in the doorway with a clipboard under her arm. She smiles and enters before taking a seat beside his bed. "Do you remember anything?" Brian waits for an extended moment without saying a word. The nurse continues to wait for his response while he keeps a focused stare above him. When she feels he may not answer her question she clicks her pen tip down and places it to the paper in front of her.

"I remember my name," Brian finally says. The nurse looks up without writing anything. "I'm a defense attorney," Brian continues. "But I don't know why I'm here."

"That's good that you remember who you are. Most people in your condition have amnesia for quite some time after waking up." Brian turns to look at the nurse.

"What happened to me?"

"You were shot in the head, Mr. Troth. It's a miracle you survived." Brian remains silent while searching for the memory, but he's more concerned with getting back to work as soon as possible.

"When will I be released?" he asks. The nurse jots down a few notes on the clipboard before lifting her head.

"I don't have that answer, but I know the doctors will want to keep monitoring you and run some more tests. When we begin your physical therapy, we will have a better understanding if you will make a full recovery or not."

"Why do I need physical therapy?" he asks. The nurse seems confused at his question.

"You haven't used your legs in a very long time, Mr. Troth."

"Fine, can you at least call my secretary, Lena and have her bring my papers? I have several cases to go over." The nurse looks bewildered and unsure of his question.

"There's no need for that anymore. Everyone now fills out a CPQ."

"What's a CPQ?"

"Citizen Placement Questionnaire. It determines where you live, where you work and the perfect romantic match for you. It truly is a testament to the advancement of our society."

"What are you talking about? I already have a home and a job."

"The world is quite different now than it was as you remembered it, Mr. Troth."

"I don't know what you mean. The world can't change overnight."

"Hasn't anyone told you?"

"Tell me what?" Brian asks while shaking his head.

"Oh dear, I'm sorry. I thought you were informed—You've been in a coma, Mr. Troth—for thirty years."

He doesn't reply; his first reaction is to disbelieve the nurse's claim. He built his entire career on fact checking or finding ways to work around them, but this time he doesn't know where to begin.

In an undisclosed section of the hospital is a darkened conference room where two government officials in black suits sit at the long table facing a doctor with his fists closed on top of a folder.

"What can you tell us about Mr. Troth?" one of the officials asks. The doctor opens the folder before him and shares what he knows.

"Mr. Troth was a defense attorney. He was shot by a grieving father who had lost his daughter to a murderer who Troth defended." The doctor flips to the next page. "No surviving family or friends. The only person associated with him was his secretary, Lena." The doctor pauses as he skims the text. "Who apparently got married and moved back to her home country of Albania."

An official writes certain key points on his pad of paper as the other continues with his questions.

"Roughly, how old would you place Mr. Troth?"

"When a person is in a coma, or any form of deep hibernation, the heart rate, metabolism, and body temperature drop significantly. Mr. Troth's average body temperature was between 36 to 39 degrees Fahrenheit instead of the normal 98.6 degrees. His oxygen consumption was 2 percent of normal rates and his heart rate decreased by a factor of one hundred. When the body cools it needs less oxygen, therefore slowing the aging process. While Mr. Troth's actual age is 62, we have calculated his biological age at only 47."

After making his final notes the official holds his hand out to accept the folder from the doctor.

"Thank you. We will file this with our agency."

"Thank you, doctor for your time," adds the other official. The doctor nods and then stands to let himself out.

Brian resumes his therapy as doctors and nurses either help him or stand on the sidelines monitoring him while taking notes. He uses a variety of physical therapy and exercise machines to strengthen his legs including walking between two metal bars as he holds onto them for support. He's clumsy and seems to struggle at first, but he gradually gets stronger and faster. He also lifts weights to work his arms and then jogs on a treadmill while hooked up to suctions and wires that read his heart rate and breathing. After several months of constant workouts and monitoring he finally meets the hospital's requirements to be discharged.

Brian finds himself sitting alone in a conference room that's solely lit by the two desk lamps in the middle of the table. He's dressed in jeans and a button-down polo that had been sitting in a cubby since he had arrived thirty years prior. Other than the clothes on his back he has no other personal possessions within, or out of his three-decade prison sentence. He ignores the glass of water that had been placed in front of him as he waits for someone to arrive. The dim lit room has nothing to look at or pick up to read. Boredom and frustration are starting to show as he squirms in his chair.

Finally, a beam of light cuts through the room when the door behind him opens. He turns around as two men wearing black suits enter the room with one of them carrying a briefcase. These men resemble the government officials who had interviewed Brian's doctor several months before. The door is gently shut, and the men walk around the table without uttering a word to Brian. The men sit down across from him, and the briefcase is placed flat in front of them. There's no greeting or handshakes exchanged between one another or an explanation or apology for the long wait. Brian hides his annoyance but refuses to be the first to speak or smile. The popping of the locks opening on the briefcase is the first sound to break the silence. Brian watches the man take out a pencil and a piece of paper before sliding both across the table towards him.

"This is your CPQ. It contains ten of the most perfectly worded psychological questions ever to be compiled. Your perfect residence, the perfect job, where you will feel a state of accomplishment, and of course your perfect mate, will all be determined by how you answer these questions," the official says.

"After you have completed this questionnaire you will become a permanent citizen of this utopia," the second official adds.

Brian glances at the sheet in front of him while wiggling the pencil through his fingers and tapping its eraser on the table. "Utopia, huh? I have a question," Brian begins. The two men exchange looks before turning back to Brian. "How are these ten questions supposed to tell you everything about me?"

"Because that's what they were designed and researched to do," the first official answers.

"No one is ever dissatisfied with the results. You are about to set foot into a perfect world; where no pain reigns and no crime is present," the second continues.

"Everyone has everything they want and need. Shelter, self-worth, companionship, and no worry of financial burdens."

"We provide you with everything and as long as our rules are followed, nothing can be taken away."

"You will be happy—I assure you." The officials' monotone

responses feel as if they have been poorly rehearsed without any emotion behind their phrases. To Brian it seems almost like they don't really believe their own explanations. They share a quality of bad actors trying to remember their lines while also attempting to make them believable. Brian lets a moment pass before asking his next question.

"Why can't I just remain a lawyer?"

"There's no further need for those."

"Crimes are no longer committed, Mr. Troth."

"I'll believe that when I see it," Brian says underneath his breath. He starts reading the questionnaire and making his marks or writing out his answers.

Some questions refer to subjects about the ideal evening after work and social events that do not trigger anxiety. Other questions ask how much living space is needed in order to feel comfortable, and lastly, sexuality questions and preferred mates. Older women who act motherly, dominate women who are more in control, or docile women who desire to please others before themselves.

After Brian has answered all the questions, he hands the sheet back to the men. The form is immediately taken and put into the briefcase without being looked at. The latches lock into place and the key to the case is handed to the other official, who quickly places it into a small flat box that resembles a holder for business cards. The man then places the box into his inside chest pocket of his suit. The two men stand up and then hold their hands out to shake Brian's hand. It seems to be a forced gesture without sincerity, but Brian decides to shake their hands none-the-less.

"Thank you. You will have your results in a few days. Statistically the romantic match is always last, but we can get you settled into your new apartment and employed by this time next week."

"Welcome to your new life, Mr. Troth." The officials exit the room without waiting for a response. The bright lights from the hallway creep into the darkened room once more and then dissipate when the door shuts. Brian is alone with his thoughts again in the dimly lit room.

"My new life? I wasn't yet done with my last one."

Three days have passed since Brian's meeting with the government officials when he's notified that a favorable placement has been decided. Brian has his doubts, but he suppresses his natural desire to resist and fight back. He has no choice but try to conform to this new way of living.

Brian follows the government official through a posh apartment hallway decorated with paintings and golden room numbers. The official finally stops at room, 505.

"This is you," the man says. Brian observes that the door handle has no keyhole.

"No key?"

"No locks."

"No locks?"

"No need for them."

The official swings the door open and enters with Brian following him. The spacious open concept living quarters consist of a kitchen with its breakfast bar counter and two chairs acting as the only partition from the living room, which is furnished with a couch, coffee table and a big screen TV. A large glass patio door opens to the balcony which overlooks the Community Gardens across from the apartment building. Lastly, the bedroom and bathroom are to the left of the kitchen and behind the living room. So far Brian is impressed with the room. It looks like no expense was spared to make this desirable for him.

"This isn't too shabby, actually, and it comes already furnished?"

"Yes, everything is provided." The official then reaches into his inside coat pocket and withdraws a sealed envelope. "This is your job assignment. Inside are all the proper payment forms and job information."

Brian takes the envelope entitled:

Employment Title & Duties
–Brian Troth–

Just then, a slight continuous squeaking draws Brian's attention to the still open apartment door. A medical worker, wearing a respirator, soon passes Brian's door as he wheels a body fully concealed under a white sheet on top of a stretcher. Brian remains focused on the incident until the worker disappears from his view as he continues down the hallway. Brian looks back to the official who has picked up on Brian's curiosity.

"I thought you said this is a perfect world," he says sarcastically.

"Illness is unavoidable, Mr. Troth. It's a disease called Loquacitis, it can fatally consume individuals in less than three days."

"What does it do to the infected?"

"We believe it's similar to a brain eating virus. Those infected flail wildly and rant nonsensical words and are prone to delusions and making false claims or realities based on fiction. Unfortunately, there is no known cure for it; fortunately, it kills fast. Otherwise, it's feared it could be highly contagious."

"I guess even perfect comes with fine print."

"You don't need to worry about any of that, Mr. Troth. We have a good system in place to keep the virus contained." The official points to the envelope. "You start Monday at The Daily Curator, our local newspaper. It's in walking distance from here and quite important since everyone receives it. I look forward to reading your name under future headings."

Brian smirks as he shakes the official's hand before he escorts himself out of the room. Brian gently closes the door and then looks at the sealed envelope in his hand. After a moment he lowers it to his side and then redirects his gaze out the patio door. The sun is setting behind the apartment complex on the opposite end of the gardens as several people make their rounds along the floral paths.

"Is this even real?" he mutters to himself.

Brian lies awake almost the entire night thinking that perhaps he's still in a coma and that this is nothing more than a lucid dream. There's a clear disconnection between what he sees and how he feels about it. Brian is at war with his thoughts and soon they will betray him.

2

The Glass Rose

Brian wakes up to a sunny day with a cool breeze that dances through the leaves of the trees lining the sidewalk. Casually dressed in a short-sleeved button-down shirt and khakis, he strolls the ten-minute walk to his new job. An observation that he makes almost right away is the fact that the roads do not have any cars parked or driving on them, in fact they seem to almost serve no purpose. Everyone is walking alone, or in small groups as they head to their jobs. It's a strange sight to not see vehicles during a morning commute, and Brian must wonder what happened to them. If vehicles are no longer needed, then why have the roads been left behind? Perhaps, it's cost related.

Brian arrives at the double doors with full view green-tint glass inserts and the building number, *314*, located on the right side of the entrance. *The Daily Curator* also appears in large, block, golden letters above the doors. Brian enters the lobby and advances toward the receptionist's desk. She looks up from typing on a computer when he arrives and gives him a big smile. Brian hands her the letter from the government official.

"Hello, my name is Brian. Today is my first day." The woman

unfolds the letter and then folds it back up and hands it back to him.

"Welcome Brian. You may take the elevator, or the stairs to the third floor. Have an excellent day," she says still smiling. Brian thinks it a bit odd but returns the grin with a nod and then thanks her before heading to the elevator doors.

Brian steps out of the elevator into a white hallway that feels void of the company's culture. There are no posters or pictures hanging on the walls, or any sort of phrases, words and mottoes, nothing resembling its values, history, or achievements. It feels like a rented space, or temporary location, not even the floor holds any pattern to give the area any depth. There's only one open door on this floor so finding his destination is quite easy. He stands in the doorway to The Daily Curator's newsroom. It's almost a completely open concept office where all the desks are in rows of two that face one another except for an office in the center that extends inwards from the outside wall. The base of the office is drywalled that comes up about two feet, and then meets glass windows that extend up to about a yard from the ceiling with raised blinds on the inside. Everyone has a cup of coffee next to them and is typing feverishly or making copies. A half empty box of doughnuts sits on a table as people take turns making their selections and then going back to their desks.

The setting looks normal enough, but Brian is a little apprehensive to step inside. Finally, a middle-aged man named Lenny, approaches him.

"Hello, you must be Brian." Lenny greets him warmly, and then extends his hand as the two men shake.

"Yes, how did you know?"

"I'm Lenny; we were told you would be joining our staff today." Lenny picks up a freshly printed newspaper off a nearby desk and then hands it to Brian. "There's been some talk about you lately."

The cover headline reads:

Man wakes up from 30-year coma; will work for newspaper.

Brian turns the page and then another page before coming to the back page.

"Where's the story? I just see the headline."

"We find most people don't read past the headlines, so we have no reason to include anything more," Lenny says.

"So, this is a newspaper of headlines?"

"And crosswords," Lenny places a hand on Brian's shoulder blade as he waves him forward. "Come on, I'll show you to your desk."

Brian follows Lenny past the box of doughnuts.

"Help yourself to some doughnuts," he says with a hand gesture.

"Oh, no thank you. I had breakfast before coming in," Brian respectfully declines.

"You sure? Chocolate Glaze, Bavarian Cream, bluuueberrrry? Brian smiles and shakes his head.

"Some other time maybe. But thank you."

"Well, if you change your mind, you know where they are." Lenny continues leading him towards two desks that's facing each other. "This is your home away from home," he begins while pulls out the gliding chair. "Right across from me. If you have any questions don't hesitate to ask."

"Thank you."

Lenny strolls to his desk and then sits down while Brian wheels himself closer to his computer. He rotates the cup of pens on his desk until he feels the contents are leaning in the best direction, he then picks up a pile of writing pads and stacks them as even as he can next to the pens. Lastly, he lifts his keyboard and places it back down gently only a few inches from where it originally was, but this makes Brian feel like his area is now better customized to him. He peeks around his computer monitor at Lenny reading from a manila folder. He moves back to his side and tilts his monitor to where he likes it before pushing the power button in, a short moment later the screen fades into view. He taps his fingers on the desk a few times and then looks around the room. Everyone appears to know what to do except for him.

Brian glances around his monitor again to see Lenny typing away. He turns back to his screen and grabs a pen from the cup holder and clicks the point out. He clicks the point back in and sets it next to his mouse. He stares at his computer screen for a moment before looking around it yet again. Lenny doesn't seem to notice Brian observing him.

"Excuse me?" Brian says. Lenny looks up and smiles. "What am I supposed to be doing?" Brian asks.

"Write an article," Lenny answers.

"What kind of article?"

"Anything."

"I just spent two months learning how to be human again."

"Write about something you know."

Brian returns to his screen and rolls the mouse pointer around the screen a few times. Finally, Brian slides the mouse away from him and leans back in his chair. He sighs and softly announces his problem.

"Everything I know—no longer applies."

Brian spends his first day testing every pen on his desk to ensure they are all in good working order. He collects several papers, torn from the pad, that have scribbles and circles on them, and tosses them in his garbage pail. Despite not having an assignment or any expectations, Brian still feels unaccomplished and contemplates why he should return tomorrow. Does he have a reason to be there? Does he have a purpose anywhere? The world buried him thirty-years-ago, and now was forced to find a place for him. Everything feels strange to him, even the people feel imaginary. It's as if he's suffering from culture shock and jet lag at the same time.

Brian begins his walk back to his apartment while forcing himself to smile or wave to those who pass him. He doesn't feel like talking or interacting with anyone, but also doesn't want to reveal his melancholy to others.

Brian passes a tiki atmosphere restaurant called, The Hut. He stares through the large window with both hands in his pockets and expressionless. A party of people are laughing and standing up with glasses raised while listening to someone making a toast. They cling their glasses and clap or hug one another. Brian slowly turns away and continues walking with his head down. He feels like a ghost in a world where everyone belongs except for him. He always lived a solitary life, but the difference was before he had a job that he was good at and status, now, his existence is meaningless.

Brian reaches his apartment complex and stops before walking inside. He glances up to where he believes his room might be and then looks across the street at the Community Gardens. After an uneventful day at work, he hopes a walk in the park will make him feel somewhat better. There's nothing waiting for him there any way, his things are not there. Not his chair, not his bed, nothing resembling his personality, or hobbies and talents. That living space is nothing more than a glorified hotel room. He can never feel home again. A few minutes into his stroll he sits on a park bench just off the main path. He's surrounded by a variety of flowers with pleasant aromas and the ambient sound of a nearby water fountain; however, the calming atmosphere has failed to lift his mood.

A continuous stream of happy couples walk past him while holding hands. He remembers being told romantic matches are chosen, but are all these relationships arranged? Unnoticed, Brian continues to observe the content people around him until deciding to head home. His dinner consists of microwavable popcorn and his evening is spent watching nature shows. So far, Brian has failed to see the perfection he was promised.

The next day, it's business as usual for those who work in the newsroom of The Daily Curator. Everyone lines up to fill their cups with coffee and then heads over to the box of doughnuts before going back to their desks. Lenny places his doughnut in his napkin and then turns into Brian's path just as he enters the room.

"Good morning, Brian," he says with more energy than one should have first thing in the morning.

"Morning," Brian responds with little emphasis.

"Doughnut?" Lenny insinuates by rising his doughnut resting on the napkin.

"No thank you."

"Coffee?"

"Maybe later," Brian says with a smirk as he struggles with staying friendly. He's not ready to join the crowd in their daily routines.

Lenny accompanies Brian to his desk and then points to a manila folder beside Brian's keyboard.

"Today is your lucky day; you get to write the forecast." Brian picks up the folder and looks inside as Lenny explains his task.

"Everything that needs to be written is in there, and the referenced images are all stored on the server. All you need to do is input the data into the forecast template and then upload a PDF to the folder with tomorrow's date."

"I have a law degree and they want me to copy and paste all day," Brian says underneath his breath when Lenny walks away. He figures this is a pity move because he was unable to write anything the day before. He sits down and removes the single page to read the text. "Sunny with a chance of rain." Brian sighs. "Well, that covers all the bases." Underneath the copy block are two dotted boxes with Image #4 written in one and Image #8 in the other. He turns on his monitor and waits for the computer to boot up before glancing toward the center office, which is separated from the rest of the room by large windows with raised navy-blue blinds. Inside is a man who's sitting behind an elegant desk as he occasionally glimpses at a piece of paper beside him and then returns to typing.

"Who's that?" Brian asks softly. Lenny follows Brian's gaze to the office.

"Oh yeah, you were never introduced. That's Victor Heart, he's our editor in chief."

"So, he's the boss?"

"Yeah, I suppose so, but I never had to talk to him."

"How do your work in a place and never interact with your boss?"

"We do our work and then hand it in. Sometimes it's approved, sometimes someone modifies it. That's all we have to do." Lenny returns to his work leaving Brian shaking his head.

"This world doesn't make any sense," he says to himself.

He follows the paths to his needed files to write his supplied forecast report and then drags the image of a sun and raincloud into their appropriate boxes. Lastly, he exports the file and drops it into the last folder on the server. Within fifteen minutes, he's done with his shift. The remainder of the day remains awkward as he appears busy by rearranging his pens.

Another day ends for Brian, but he still feels trapped in a never-ending dream. He doesn't think he will ever get used to this new life. He exits the lobby of The Daily Curator along with several other co-workers.

"Great job on the forecast page, Brian," a woman says when they reach outside.

"Thanks," he replies while trying to hide his opinion that the work was undeserving of praise. Any eight-year-old could have done the same task. He considers this newspaper obsolete, but he won't admit his thoughts to anyone just yet. The woman begins to walk home in the opposite direction just as Lenny joins Brian's side.

"Looks like we're going the same way," he says, but Brian only smirks for his reply. "Do you still have writer's block?" Lenny continues.

"I remember writing case reports and legal documents, but my talent wasn't writing, it was talking."

"Well, writing is talking without sound. Maybe you are thinking too much. You have to allow a chance for your subconscious to talk to you. Try to analyze a dream you've had or how you saw the world when you were seven," Lenny advises.

"The world is one giant, never-ending mind game, and I know those well," Brian begins. "I can give you facts hidden behind obscurities, half-truths and lies, then let you determine what it means." Lenny thinks for a moment before responding.

"Maybe you can create the crossword puzzles if you like brain games." Lenny, of course failed to understand his point, or the subject matter, but Brian doesn't want to take the time to explain it. He decides to change the subject back to his companion instead.

"What do you write about?"

"Sometimes I write about food and the best wine that goes with certain dishes. But most of the time I write poems and short stories; putting words together to express a similar feeling but told in a different way."

"You write stories for the paper?"

"All the time, nothing too crazy, less than 500 words. I can't draw so I have to make people laugh with words."

"You write comedies then?"

"Yeah, that's all there is."

"There's a lot more genres than comedy."

"I mean, I know that, but we can't write anything that might give people bad feelings. Everyone is happy."

"*I'm not happy.*" He doesn't say it and thinking it may even be considered a crime. Everything seems to be carefully controlled right down to everyone's individual feelings. Anything that could instill fear, sorrow or anger has been outlawed; what side of the law is Brian on now?

The eastern and western apartment complexes frame the Community Gardens that lies between them. Brian lives in, East Garden Apartments while Lenny resides in, West Garden Apartments.

"I've been thinking about something ever since I came out of my coma," Brian begins as they venture into the garden.

"Oh, yeah? What's that?"

"How did this happen? The world—how did it change?"

Lenny and Brian sit down on the next bench they find as Lenny silently tries to recall past events before beginning his explanation.

"There was a time when housing and food were going up and wages were going down. No one wanted to work for what everyone was paying, and no one could afford what they needed. Something was bound to snap, and it finally did. People took to the streets and rioted and looted. Government buildings were stormed, and everything was burning. The police enforced curfews, but that had no effect. People didn't respect or obeyed authority and they weren't afraid to rise against it. Soldiers were ordered to turn their guns on citizens and a second civil war was born. After months of fighting a new idea arose from the ashes of a collapsing government; give the people what they want. The concept was based on three fundamentals, rent free housing, jobs that bring self-accomplishment, and lastly, companionship. That's when the questionnaire was distributed; a way to find a place for everyone. No trial, no error, perfect and accurate results. We earn enough for food and gifts, but everything else is provided. No one is better off than someone else. They said happy people don't commit crimes." Lenny and Brian sit in silence for a short moment.

"I defended many happy people who committed crimes," Brian begins. "This one guy, he had everything. A beautiful, loving wife, three kids, high up in his company too, made good money, well respected, then one day he set fire to his house after killing his wife and kids. No reason, just felt like it, I suppose."

"What was his sentence?" Lenny asks. Brian doesn't immediately answer. He remains looking ahead in a daze until finally answering in a mono-toned voice with little expression.

"I convinced the jury he wasn't aware of his actions due to a multiple personality disorder. I got him some cushy minimal security sentence at a penitentiary with three square meals and daily foot rubs." Brian lightly rubs his forehead. "It was too good for him, but my own success was more important than seeking justice. I was better than the prosecutor, and that's all there is to it."

"I can't imagine anything like that happening anymore," Lenny says.

"Are you familiar with Maslow's Hierarchy of needs?"

"Never heard of it," Lenny admits.

"It's something we had to memorize when I was a law student. Visually it's a pyramid made up of five different layers. On the bottom are basic needs, everything you need to survive such as food, water, and shelter. Then comes security, knowing you are safe from harm. The third layer is being loved and having an intimate relationship. The fourth layer is esteem and self-accomplishment. The government believes they have provided you with all of this, except for the fifth layer. Self-actualization, creativity, spontaneity, acceptance of facts, and hobbies. They give you almost everything but make it very hard to achieve this last layer. Once we have everything, we start to look for something else. You can't change humanity."

"Everyone is given everything they need and desire. No one is left behind or made to go without. How can anyone be unhappy about that?"

"It almost looks like a path has been chosen for us. What happens if we stray from it? Has anyone ever asked that?"

"No one ever asks questions."

"In a world where no one asks questions, no one needs to come up with any answers. Ignorance is bliss, especially when gifts come attached to it."

"The government is like a battery. You don't need to dissect it to know how it works; you just need to know that it's working."

"If the government is the battery, then we must be the robots." Brian pauses and then continues. "We have something called curiosity. And someday that curiosity will find even the best hidden secrets." Brian stands up, but Lenny only glances up. "The biggest threat to those in power is a man who can think for himself. I think somewhere down the road everyone gave that ability up." Lenny stands up to meet Brian's eyes.

"I understand the effects of your coma haven't completely worn off yet. As a friend, I'm asking you to keep all these ideas to yourself. Resistance is natural, but soon everything will make sense." Lenny lightly places his hand on Brian's shoulder and smiles before slowly walking toward his apartment complex.

Brian shakes his head wondering if he made a mistake trusting Lenny with his feelings. Lenny has fully adapted to this lifestyle or is too afraid to dive into the inner workings of this engine that runs society. Brian likes him as an acquaintance but considers him naive. He can't trust him as much as he had hoped and will now have to watch what he says out loud. He must pretend to fit in because standing out may have consequences that even Brian cannot fathom. The two men walk in opposite directions toward their homes.

Later that night, Brian pours himself a full glass of a red wine at the breakfast bar, and then steps out onto his balcony. He leaves the sliding door open as he looks across the gardens, silhouetted by the lanterns and lampposts that glimmer through the nightly fauna. He sips his wine while being immersed in a cool breeze that makes the trees sing a mysterious lullaby and the streetlamps cast a soft amber glow on the sidewalk below. Brian tries to let go of all the questions and worries plaguing his mind. He attempts to find comfort in the silence of night and the robustness of his wine. He closes his eyes and takes in the sounds of the crickets and the wind tugging at his shirt. Only after everything has stopped does it appear peaceful and pure.

His restful surrender is soon interrupted by several consecutive knocks at his front door. Brian opens his eyes and looks behind him. Who would be at his door at this nightly hour, he wonders? Perhaps, someone heard his conversation with Lenny earlier? He hesitates before walking back into the room. He closes the balcony door behind him and then sets his wine glass on the counter. The knocking continues once more, and he cautiously approaches the door. A door without locks doesn't necessarily need to be knocked on to gain entry. Brian's curiosity gets the better of him and he slowly opens it. A beautiful woman, in her late thirties, excitedly waves while grinning wide.

"Hello future husband." The woman picks up her single suitcase and walks into the apartment and past Brian who looks flabbergasted. "I know it's late," the lady continues. "Were you sleeping?" She sets her suitcase on the floor and looks around the room seemly impressed with her surroundings. "I like it," she says nodding. Brian rubs his forehead and turns around to look at her.

"Um, I'm sorry, but I think you have me mixed up with someone else." The woman reaches into her pocket and takes out a folded piece of paper.

"No, I don't think I do." She unfolds the paper and reads it. "East Garden Apartments, suite 505, Brian Troth, that's you, right?"

"Well, yes but who are you?"

"Oh, I'm so sorry, I was so excited, I forgot to introduce myself." She grabs Brian's hand and shakes it with both of hers.

"My name is Chloe; I'm your spouse to be." Brian runs his hand through his hair as Chloe heads into the kitchen.

"Oh, yeah. The questionnaire results—" Chloe opens and closes the cupboard doors as if she's already comfortable making herself feel at home.

"That's right; I was on the waiting list for so long. You can't imagine my excitement when I got notice that they found a match for me." Chloe takes out a pan and places it on the stove. "I hope you don't mind. I haven't had anything to eat all day."

"Um, no, please, help yourself."

"You're so kind," she says happily.

Brian sits at the breakfast bar while Chloe opens the refrigerator and then returns to the pan with two eggs. She looks up at Brian and smiles again.

"Do you want some eggs?"

"No, thank you, I already had dinner."

Chloe cracks the eggs into the pan and watches them carefully as not to miss the perfect time to turn them. Brian can't help but focus his stare on her suitcase before turning his eyes back towards Chloe.

"So—you have a suitcase?"

Chloe flips her eggs while seemly satisfied with her timing. "Yes, perfect! Oh yeah, I just brought some of my clothes and perfumes and a few other little things I wanted to keep."

"Are you moving in?"

"Of course, we are about to begin our lives together."

"And you are comfortable with this? I mean—you never met me before."

"Yeah, but you're my soulmate. We would have met and fell in love and have gotten married at some point anyway.

"Well, if that's true then we would have gone through the necessary stages to finally reach that mentality and mutual agreement."

Chloe puts her eggs on a plate and then grabs a fork. "But if it's meant to be then it's still meant to be."

"How do you know it's meant to be? Because the magic sheet of ten questions says it is? What if they read it wrong or got names mixed up? It's probably one guy's opinion. I doubt this is backed by scientific facts, or proven psychology evidence.

"Oh honey, stop analyzing everything." Chloe gently touches Brian's cheek before sitting down with her eggs.

Brian maintains a bewildered look before reaching for his bottle of wine and pouring the rest of it into his glass. He can't understand how quickly she has embraced such a sudden change. He's a bit more apprehensive as he gulps the wine down.

"What are your thoughts on children? I think we should start tonight."

Brian chokes on the wine and coughs it back into the glass.

"Start what?!"

"Why having a baby of course," she says sincerely.

"Okay, look—" he begins with a sigh. "I don't know how this process is supposed to work."

Chloe looks at him surprised. "Oh, well—I guess I can initiate it."

"What—no, not that," Brian says while waving his hand in front of him.

"It's okay, you don't have to be embarrassed. I've had all the proper education."

Brian huffs and then picks up the bottle of wine and tips it over his glass forgetting it was empty. "There's not enough wine in the world," he says softly before setting it back down disappointingly. He then continues with clarifying his point. "What I meant was, I don't know how you can be so trusting."

"Why shouldn't I trust you?"

"Well, for one, you don't really know me, but I was talking about the system."

"The system has never been wrong."

"So, your faith in a system that no one questions tells you to marry me and you pack your bags?"

"For love, yes."

"Love? You can't feel love because someone tells you to feel love."

"I know you're still adjusting from a medical procedure."

"I was in a coma!"

"It's okay, I was informed. I'm here for you; whatever you need."

Brian lets out a deep sigh and finishes the last of his wine.

Brian's wine buzz does little to put his mind at ease about this new situation. Maybe some men wouldn't mind a pretty woman walking into their apartment ready to spend the night and share their bed, but Brian is used to being alone in his own space and sticking to his rigid schedules. A woman just adds complication to an otherwise simple lifestyle.

Chloe does not think it odd to take her place in Brian's bed. She tuns down the covers and builds up the pillows on her chosen side of the bed. She looks around the room with her finger on her lip as she familiarizes herself with her new surroundings. She picks up a small stack of books, Brian had on his nightstand, and returns them to the bookshelf, she then decides his reading lamp is better on the headboard surface rather than on the nightstand. Brian observes her actions from the couch in silence. She's been here an hour and is already moving his things. Chloe picks up Brian's shirt, he had draped over a chair, and places it on a hanger and then hangs it up in the closet. Brian has seen enough. He lays down on the couch and pulls a blanket over him.

Chloe questions Brian one last time about joining her in bed. "Are you sure you want to sleep on the couch? It is our first night together."

"I think that's exactly why I'm making the right choice," he replies. He can't get used to the concept of opening his whole life to someone else instantly. He never did before, and he especially can't now. There are too many changes happening all at once, and his feelings can't catch up to his reality. Everything feels like a dream, a vivid dream, that once awaken from manages to confuse the dreamer about their location and identity. Brian woke up into a world that was not his and must now adapt to it while also trying to understand it.

Chloe accepts Brian's decision and turns off the lights before crawling into bed. Within moments she's fast asleep, but Brian remains staring wide-eyed at the ceiling. His mind is too busy to allow sleep to set in. What else can possibly happen to him?

The next morning, Brian arrives at work earlier than usual. The office is still mostly empty except for Victor, who's in his office, and some girl on the far side of the room who Brian never met. She taps loudly on her keyboard and seems oblivious to anything else around her.

Brian decides today is good day to try the coffee. He pours himself a cup from the machine while gazing through the windows into Victor's office. Victor is expressionless and focused on his computer screen as if in a deep trance. Brian looks away soon after fearing he will be spotted. Brian returns to his desk while sipping his coffee. He glares at the flashing black cursor on the blank document page for several moments wondering what Lenny would advise him to write. Perhaps, it was the wine last night or maybe the coffee this morning, but a thought finally enters his mind, and he begins typing.

> *Some might wonder if people dream while in a coma. As someone who just woke up from one, I can tell you that you never stop. I can recall places I've never visited and conversations with people I've never met, and each event is part of a riddle to be solved. If not in this life, maybe in the next.*
>
> *I traveled the world in a paper sailboat. Alongside rocky coastlines, around forgotten islands, and past mysterious floating cities. Orange clouds would rain Chardonnay and purple ones rained a fine Cabernet. For thirty years it was just me and the sea.*
>
> *I remember distinctively the night sky consisting of red, blue, and green nebulas. It is the only color in otherwise complete blackness. Although it sounds beautiful the feeling was unnerving. Almost like I was going to sail into space and never be able to return home.*
>
> *Right before awaking the butterfly people came to me. What lesson can a dream teach? For all they said was, there is courage in surrender when knowledge is given.*

Lenny lowers Brian's paper after just reading it.

"I like it. What does it mean?"

"I don't know what any of that means. It was just a dream," Brian admits.

"Now you're writing as good as me," Lenny says with a chuckle. "I think we can include this in our poetry section."

"I was never really creative, I never had an imagination, and wasn't one for fictional stories," Brian says.

"Maybe you are now." Lenny turns toward Victor's office with Brian's paper still in hand but stops when he observes his blinds have been closed. "Looks like Victor is busy. I'll give this to him tomorrow." Lenny places the paper on Brian's desk and then motions him to follow him. "Come on, let's go. Every Friday we get out an hour early."

Brian laughs. "*What a perfect world,*" he jokes to himself.

Brian and Lenny walk home together as Brian confides in him once more.

"Are you married?"

"Yes, it's been—about five years now."

"Did you adapt to it right away or did it take time?" Lenny chuckles.

"I suppose I just went with the flow. Why do you ask?"

"My match showed up last night."

"Well then congratulations are in order. What's her name?"

"Chloe."

"Beautiful name. You need to get her a gift now."

"A gift?"

"Yes, it's customary to give your wife a present upon meeting."

"I don't really know what she likes yet."

"Lucky for you, I know a gift shop up ahead. I can help you pick something out."

"Thanks. It's just the way things are here differs so much from what I'm used to."

"Understandable. We've been living this way for over a decade now, and our children will grow up knowing only this way. You literally woke up into it. We all know adjustments will take time."

"It's not that I dislike her, but it's another sudden change for me, and she seems perfectly at ease with it. I can't help but feel apprehensive about it."

"I remember when Clerissa first arrived at my apartment. We cooked spaghetti and meatballs and shared a bottle of wine. What did you and Chloe do?"

"She arrived late last night. She made herself eggs and I drank the full bottle of wine." Lenny lets out a hardy laugh as Brian continues. "I'm not used to a woman being around. Much less having everything rearranged." Lenny laughs again.

"There's an old saying that goes, men are the head of the household, but women are the neck; wherever the neck turns the head will look."

"Have there even been couples who end up not being compatible?"

"Well, no, the system can't falter. The officials make sure mistakes do not happen."

"How can anything maintain one-hundred percent accuracy?"

"Science and research."

That's not very reassuring," he says followed by Lenny chuckling.

"You just have some new relationship jitters. It'll pass. She's perfect for you, that's all you need to know." He advises while directing Brian towards the door of the shop. "Here we are. You'll find something in here."

Bells & Whistles specializes in gifts for events and occasions, and stocks quilts, glassware, candles, figurines, and other knickknacks. Brian inspects the shelves and displays but nothing seems to stand out. Lenny points out little statues of puppies, or hands him decorative ceramic jars of potpourri, neither of which appeases Brian's idea of elegance. Brian doesn't like to spend a lot of time in stores, and he almost wants to leave this errand for another day, but Lenny insists and the two continue perusing around the store.

In the far corner of the store is an area dedicated to steppingstones, garden gnomes and floral décor. He picks up a long, slender box and opens it carefully. Inside is the perfect gift for Chloe.

The elevator chimes as it stops on his floor and the doors open. Brian strolls down the hallway with the gift bag in his hand before entering his lit apartment room. On the breakfast bar counter are two plates, silverware, and two wine glasses neatly set near a bottle of wine yet to be opened. On the stove is a pot with steam rising from underneath the lid and the smell of a home-cooked meal almost brings him to tears. He never had anyone to come home to, much less find dinner waiting for him. He takes a long whiff of the air, and picks up scents of basil, Cabernet, and hints of Kalamata olives. He hears the toilet flushing and quickly hides the bag underneath one of the pillows on the couch before Chloe advances out of the bathroom.

"Oh, you're home. How was your day, love?"

"Not too bad actually. I wrote my first article today," Brian answers proudly.

"That's great, I'm so proud of you. Dinner will be ready shortly. I hope you like spaghetti with veal patties." Brian can't help but laugh.

"I was talking about spaghetti with Lenny on our way home."

"See, it must be a sign." Brian heads into the kitchen to get a closer look at the dinner he can't wait to receive.

"How did you make all this? I didn't have any of these ingredients," Brian asks.

"I'm a big girl, darling, I know how to go shopping."

Brian smiles and lifts the lid to smell the simmering sauce. He closes his eyes and lets the aroma surround his senses. Yes, this is where the smells originated. Tomato pasta sauce with herbs, olives, and red wine to tie everything together. Chloe can cook.

"Can you open the wine for me, dear?"

"Sure," Brian replies. He lowers the lid back in place and then picks up the corkscrew and begins uncorking the wine. "I have to admit, this is a new experience for me."

"Marriage?"

"Well, yes that too, but I was referring to coming home to something other than darkness and emptiness. I never had someone home waiting for me."

"The only thing I ever wanted was to find someone who couldn't wait to come home to me," Chloe admits. They shyly grin at each other as Brian pours the wine. In no time at all, the awkwardness is gone. The two giggle and chat throughout dinner with all the euphoria of first dates pulsating through their brainwaves. At this moment Brian as a thought that he keeps to himself, *"perhaps, I can be happy here."*

After dinner the two sit beside each other as they watch TV. Chloe lowers her head on his shoulder and lightly brushes her fingers against Brian's hand. He smiles and turns his hand over to open it. Chloe willingly places her hand into his. Several moments pass before Brian remembers what he had hidden under the nearby pillow. He stretches behind the pillow to take out the small bag and then hands it to Chloe.

"What's this?" she asks.

"Something I hope you will like?" She takes out the slender, rectangular box from the bag and admires the silver trim around the cover. She continues to smile as she lifts the top off to discover a glass rose carefully placed on white padding. She carefully picks it up and admires it as it glistens in the light from the lamps.

"It's beautiful, I love it."

"Its beauty and perfection will always endure; it can never wilt or wither. It cannot become dull or fade. It will last forever," Brian says softly.

Chloe brings her lips close to his and lightly kisses him. He returns the small kiss, but she can tell he was hesitating.

"I want to be with you," she whispers.

Brian gently caresses her arm before she moves in to kiss him again. He allows their lips to lock and her tongue to find his as they continue kissing. She straddles him and then lifts his shirt and tosses it behind the couch. She leans against him and continues kissing him as her hand slowly unzips his pants. She guides her hand through the open zipper and rubs his penis with her full hand. She draws away from him only to pull his pants down and to take off her shirt and bra. She then takes Brian's hand and positions it over her breast, he cups it and begins to massage her nipple with his thumb.

"Come to bed," she orders softly. She picks up the remote to turn off the TV and then takes his hand and leads him into the bedroom. She presses her body against his to gently lower him into bed. Chloe proceeds to remove her skirt and panties before climbing on top of him. Brian caresses her breasts and ribs as she thrusts above him. Brian gives in to the moment and the passion intensifies as each let out moans of ecstasy. Chloe's repetitive gyrations finally causes Brian to ejaculate. She slows her movements but continues steady thrusts until his erection subsides. Chloe sinks into the sheets beside him as they embrace.

"Are you happy with me?" Chloe asks. Brian looks at her and smiles.

"I was never happy, until now." She returns the smile, but she can also tell something is bothering him.

"What is it? What are you thinking?" she asks while stroking his cheek. Brian remains silent for a short moment before responding.

"I was a good lawyer. I defended both the scum of the earth and good people caught in a bad situation, but I always looked at them the same. They were the hand I was dealt. My challenge was trying to find a way to bluff the jury in my favor. I was a good lawyer—I was not a good person."

"That is not your fault. The world was a cruel place, survival demanded just thoughts and fair actions to be sacrificed. Life is now how it was always meant to be, a perfect Eden."

"Perfect is a fallacy born from ignorance," Brian says.

"You don't think people can be happy?"

"I think to legitimately feel happy, one must feel unhappy. I remember those dark, cold nights and felt the bitter chill of loneliness. I know what feeling empty feels like and that's why I can cherish this moment right now. If people are given everything, they appreciate nothing."

Chloe kisses him and snuggles under the covers with him. "Don't dwell on what is no longer relevant." Brian brings her hand to his lips and softly kisses it.

"I hope this isn't a dream. It would be a very good dream, until awaking, then it becomes a cruel joke."

"When you wake up. I'm going to wake up right next to you," Chloe replies before turning off the lights. Within moments the two fall soundly asleep.

Brian begins accepting his new life. There's always a part of him that wants to resist it, but there's also a large part of him that's happy with it. He has adapted to his new job and receives some sort of satisfaction from it. He now finds himself with a cup of coffee and a doughnut on his desk, just like the rest of the office. He has become less critical of others and sometimes agrees with their viewpoints.

His apartment is comfortable and provides him with the posh lifestyle he desires with a great view of the Community Gardens. He also can't deny that Chloe is the best thing that has ever happened to him. They frequent the gardens while walking hand in hand and everyone greets them warmly.

Could this system really work? Everything people search for throughout their entire lives are automatically provided to them without challenge. It appears his results are indeed true to his persona, values, and mentality. He doubted it at first. His nature is to test authority and prove lies, but he has everything he needs and desires nothing more. Despite his happiness, Brian cannot shake the nagging feeling that this is somehow a form of brainwashing, or control—a temporary calm before the coming storm. What lengths will those in power go to maintain order? It's this feeling that's playing havoc with his emotions. He can't ignore the single demanding question that bore itself in the back of his mind. If deception brings you satisfaction, is it acceptable? Would you sacrifice your dreams to fight against it, or allow it to continue for fear of retribution?

Another ordinary day begins, and nothing unexpected is considered. Brian eats his breakfast, kisses Chloe goodbye, and then walks to work. He arrives at The Daily Curator a few minutes later than usual and takes the elevator up to his floor. Brian enters the newsroom to discover a disturbance. His co-workers are huddled in several small groups while talking amongst themselves as two government officials rummage around in Victor's office. They open and close desk drawers and file cabinets, then shuffle through stacks of papers and folders. Lenny notices Brian entering and waves him over.

"Brian, over here." Brian joins Lenny while keeping his focus on the two men in the office.

"What's going on?" he asks.

"I'm sure it's nothing," Lenny replies.

"Nothing? It looks like something."

A female co-worker overhears their conversation and walks toward them. "Victor didn't show up for work today."

"So, the question is—why are they here instead?"

"It's frowned upon to question someone else's job, Brian," Lenny warns.

"Then I'm about to break the law." Lenny quickly grabs Brian's arm just as he takes a step forward, but the men walk out of Victor's office at this moment.

"Victor Heart has recently moved to a new area to seek a better opportunity," one of them announces.

"A new editor in chief will be assigned within a few days," the other explains.

The room is filled with the "ahs" of the newsroom staff content with this explanation. For everyone this is enough to move on without further thought, but for Brian this reason does nothing to convince or relieve his prying nature.

"Where did he move to?" he asks.

The chattering and laughing stops as the room becomes deathly quiet. The two men jolt their attention towards Brian with a menacing glare.

"Does that concern you?" one of them asks.

"What concerns me is the amount of apathy that surrounds this case."

"This isn't a case, Mr. Troth," the other government official adds.

"It's in your best interest to ignore Victor's fate," warns the first.

"For my safety—or yours?"

Brian's response manages to even stump the officials with an immediate reply. The room remains silent as all eyes are fixated on Brian. Few have talked back to the officials, and fewer still have actually witnessed it. The officials are used to dealing with an occasional outburst or one disobedient individual, but their shock of Brian's demeanor indicates he may have gone too far. With the striking of one little match, a flame takes shape, what happens next is either its spread, or its extinguish. Lenny decides to intervene before the situation becomes any more out of hand. He pats Brian's shoulder and then steps in front of him while laughing and looking at the officials.

"You have to excuse my friend, gentlemen. Last night we were celebrating quite late and went through a lot of champagne. I think he may be acting out a scene from a movie."

"Everyone, have a pleasant day," one of the men responds with a hint of sarcasm. They begin to leave the newsroom, but their intense glare on Brian is a silent warning for him to watch his words in the future.

"Let it go," Lenny whispers close to Brian's face after their departure.

There's no reason for Brian to defend Victor. He hardly knew him and never talked to him, but he's still curious about the truth. This entire situation doesn't sit right with him, and he can't help but wonder if an injustice has been carried out. It's hard for him to think about anything else for the rest of the day, yet he manages to finish his day without further incidents.

Brian meets Chloe in the Community Gardens after work to tour the exotic plants and flowers on either side of the cobblestone path. Brian buys two chocolate cones at an ice cream truck and hands one of them to Chloe. They continue their walk across a bridge extending over a gently stream while savoring their cones. After their walk they enjoy hamburgers and margaritas in the popular tiki themed restaurant, The Hut. The relaxing evening helps Brian to calm his restless mind at ease his troubling conundrums. By the end of the evening, the morning event has been pushed out of his head.

Brian and Chloe return home to continue their date night by slow dancing to smooth saxophone music playing from the wireless speaker sitting on the wall shelf directly behind the apartment door, and beside it is the glass rose inside a vase. Brian glances at the rose and then back at Chloe. *"For 30 years and 212 days I've been dead; and before that I was killing myself. Life is short; I don't care what keeps the world turning. I just want to enjoy the time I have with you,"* he thinks to himself. Chloe looks up and smiles as if she had read his mind. He holds her against his chest while admiring the glass rose again. It could last forever, but it's also fragile.

The next morning, Lenny waits for Brian at their usual meeting spot in the Community Gardens. He leans against the lamppost with a pen hanging from his lip as he concentrates intensely on the week's crossword puzzle. Brian arrives right on time at 8:10. Lenny smiles and folds his paper under his arm and then puts the pen in his shirt pocket as the two begin their walk.

"You made this crossword too hard, Brian. I only have six filled in," Lenny admits as Brian chuckles.

"Okay, I'll give you one free answer," Brian agrees. Lenny unfolds the paper and thinks for a moment.

"Fifteen across," he says while handing the paper to Brian.

"Solid AU—AU is the periodic symbol for a metal." Lenny remains looking at him with a blank stare. "Gold," Brian gives the answer realizing Lenny did not know it. Lenny takes the paper back and folds it under his arm again.

"Why don't you just do flowers and animals like everyone else?"

"I thought this was supposed to be challenging," Brian laughs.

They cross the street and continue their commute, but this also reminds Brian of a question he's had since noticing the vacant roads. Maybe, his trusted colleague can answer it.

"I must inquire, why are there roads? I have not seen one car, or any vehicle for that matter."

"That's because cars and driving have been banned. The roads remain because they make the city look complete."

"Why was driving banned?"

"It was decided that people cannot be trusted with the privilege of driving. The allowance of cars gives an opportunity for their improper use by disobeying rules, ignoring ethics, and will, almost always, instill rage in other motorists."

"They thought of everything, haven't they?" Brian says while rolling his eyes. "So, there's no more cars?"

"I'm sure there's a place where a few of them are stored. They are restricted for government use and for citizen transportation or placement after authorization."

"So, there are other cities?"

"Of course, and more of this one as well. This is just where we feel the most secure, but someone else may desire a different setting. I can't see myself living anywhere else, but then again, I never saw anywhere else."

"Why's that?"

"No one travels outside of their assigned location. If people are too different, they may not get along." Brian decides not to press the issue. Freedoms allow many to consider their own advancement and success without awareness of the costs to themselves or others nearby. Ambition is always blind.

Brian and Lenny arrive at work and enter the lobby. Brian recalls his exchange with the government officials the week before. He's aware that his questioning is sometimes unavoidable, it's his nature to wonder, but his rejection of that addiction is starting to wane. He's growing accustomed to his work/life balance and ensuring Chloe stays by his side every step of the way. Now he understands the risk Lenny took to defend him and can't put him in that position ever again. He also understands his warnings; he can't jeopardize his life, or Chloe's over an unanswered question, or mysteries surrounding suspicious secrets, and unsolved events. The elevator doors open, and the two men enter.

"I don't know what I was thinking last week with those guys in Victor's office. I have a good life now; I don't need to worry about everything anymore. Thanks for stepping in."

"Everything is fine, Brian," Lenny answers while smiling.

They step out of the elevator and make their way to the newsroom door to discover that it has been closed.

"That's odd. Why is this door closed?" Brian asks.

"I don't know. It never was before," Lenny replies before gently pushing the door handle down. It's not locked as Lenny swings the door open. They are greeted with an ensemble of cheering and clapping from the rest of the office as balloons float to the ceiling. One of them steps forward and shakes Lenny's hand.

"Congratulations," he says.

"Is all of this for me?" he says bewildered.

"Yes, we were informed yesterday that you are now our new editor in chief," a second colleague responds before turning to Brian. "We tried contacting you to tell you about the surprise party but could not reach you."

"Oh, I was out most of the day with Chloe," Brian says.

"That explains it then."

A spread of cakes and pastries take up an entire folding table, while coffee, juice and iced tea fill up another.

Brian helps Lenny move his computer into Victor's office as Lenny brings in a box of his folders. Besides the desk, computer chair, and a rug, all of Victor's personal belongings have been stripped away. Even the walls are bare except for several forgotten tacks that once served a purpose. Brian sets the monitor down on the desk as Lenny sets down his box.

"How does it feel being the boss?" Brian asks.

"I don't know yet." They share a laugh before Lenny waves Brian towards the door.

"Alright now, get back to work you," he jokes. Brian brings his hand to his forehead in a salute while snapping his heels together.

"Yes sir."

The mystery surrounding Victor's sudden disappearance is all but forgotten, or completely disregarded. Even Brian tries to dismiss the questions he has concerning the topic. He eats, drinks, and celebrates his friend's promotion with the rest of the office without a worry crossing his mind.

Little does he know that this celebratory moment is a ruse. The wool has been pulled over Lenny's eyes, his success will soon ask him to betray Brian. They want to call it a perfect world, but perfection can only be reached when nothing has the ability to surpass it or be allowed to try.

3

The Eden Project

Misfortune seems to follow soon after euphoria. Maybe it's the natural order of things, nature's way to limit perfection. There's an unsettling calm before the storm, then the sun fades, and the winds pickup. Without time to prepare, the clouds unleash its barrage of pounding rain and thunder growls like hungry wolves. As the storm rolls on time becomes difficult to gage, and in its wake is nothing but memories.

For Brian, the passing weeks give him a false sense of security. It almost never fails, as soon as one feels they have accomplished their goals, another problem arises.

One evening, Chloe welcomes Brian home while holding an envelope before handing it to him ecstatically. He pulls out the heavy stock paper and reads it out loud—

This certificate hereby recognizes
Brian and Chloe Troth
as husband and wife.

"It's official, I'm yours forever," Chloe says while softly clapping her hands.

"I won't have it any other way," he replies with a smile as the two embrace and kiss.

Brian, Chloe, Lenny, and Clerissa frequently double date at popular eateries, such as *The Hut* for dinner and drinks. Brian shoots a glance out the windows and can almost see his former self looking in and feeling like a complete outcast. Now, he's laughing and joking with the people who mean most to him. He never noticed the official spying on him from a corner table, he's having too much fun to care what is going on around him. Delicious appetizers of stuffed mushrooms, jalapeno poppers, and mozzarella sticks keep his focus, and the two pitchers of margaritas drops his guard. This time it may have worked in his favor, as his carefree demeanor and jolly disposition keeps the official on low alert.

"Assimilation appears to be taking hold. No further action needed, but will continue to monitor," he reports into his collar mic.

For a month Brian manages to stay under the radar and follow the rules of this new world. He and Lenny become close friends, and the couples are often together on Friday nights, dining out, drinking, or playing games at one or the other's apartments. Brian's mind appears to have been calmed and his questioning nature stifled; for once he's happy, and he plans on keeping everything the way it is.

It's neither strength nor wisdom that ensures victory over time, but the ability to adept and the will to do so. One's path is ruled by how they perceive it, but sometimes there's an unexpected bump that knocks everything off balance. Just as soon as Brian adapted to this lifestyle, one choice will change everything forever.

The day at The Daily Curator feels like another typical day. Some work on articles that they think others may find interesting. They're closely related to printed forms of blogs that have more opinion than fact, but no one seems to care about the sources. Lenny's phone rings and he answers it with a smile that gradually fades. The conversation is short with this unknown caller, but as soon as he hangs up, he exits his office and waits by the main entrance into the room. Brian observes Lenny and wonders why he appears nervous while waiting for some guest to arrive. The reason soon becomes clear when two government officials meet him. They talk in hush tones for a minute before Lenny turns around to address the room.

"May I have everyone's attention please?" Everyone stops what they are working on and listens. "I have been informed that due to a potential cyber threat we will be wiping the server. Please copy all your current work to your thumb drive. After the server resets you can move your folder and files back. Anything that is not copied will be lost." The office scrambles to save their work and important assets.

Brian's cursor scrolls over a row of folders until he stops at the one entitled, *B. Troth*. He clicks and drags several folders to the attached thumb drive and then waits for their completion. On the next row down is the folder, *V. Heart*. This was Victor's personal folder that must have been overlooked. Brian wonders if this is the real reason behind the server's wipe. Could there be a clue in there to explain his disappearance? What was he working on? Brian hesitates for a moment before moving his cursor to open Victor's folder. Inside is only one file entitled, *The Eden Project*. Brian has never heard of this project and cannot guess to what it could be. Is it even worth knowing? If he decides not to investigate it, will he always wonder what it was?

The two officials scan the office continuously from the doorway. Brian has the option to ignore it, he doesn't need to be involved in the affairs of others. He can leave it alone and never look back, but that's not who Brian is. Something tells him that this is important, and someone is going to great lengths to acquire it before it can be discovered again.

His folders successfully finish copying, and he now finds his cursor hovering over the icon of, *The Eden Project*. He clicks on it and holds it while thinking about his intention one last time before dragging it over to his thumb drive. All that's left is for him to lift his finger. He does, and a tab appears on the screen.

Copying...

Brian taps his fingers nonchalantly on the desk before glancing up at the men standing in the doorway. One of them makes eye contact with him and he quickly looks away. He realizes his mistake and looks back nervously, hoping they didn't pick up on his avoidance. The man whispers into his partner's ear before starting to walk towards Brian. Brian softly voices his concern under his breath.

"*Shit.*"

Brian moves the cursor to close the folder, but the copying tab flashes indicating he's unable to change screens despite his desperate clicking.

Copying... 86% Complete...

He tries to cancel the action, but the **x** button is grayed out prohibiting him from abandoning his mission. He curses under this breath before glancing up to see the official getting closer.

"*Damn, damn, fuck.*"

Copying... 92% Complete...

This must be a large file and it's taking a lot longer to copy over than the rest of the department's work. He's the only one still seemingly working and it catches the attention of the second official who keeps his focus on him. A fellow co-worker unknowingly wheels back into the first official's path to stand up. The official puts his hand on the man's shoulder and lightly pushes him to the side as he advances closer to Brian with a serious expression.

Copying... 98% Complete...

Their eyes lock. There's no place for Brian to go. The official turns his glare onto Brian's screen that shows an image of kittens playing with balls of yarn.

"Hello, sir," Brian says with a smile while pretending everything was fine all along. The official doesn't return the greeting, instead he frowns and heads back to his partner with nothing more than a shake of the head for his report. Brian lets out a sigh of relief and takes a sip of his coffee. This file better be worth it—

Later that night, all the windows of Brian's apartment complex are black except for one which illuminates a dim amber glow. The hour is late, but Brian is wide awake with little chance of him going to bed. He sinks into his couch and sets his laptop on his lap before booting it up. He inserts the thumb drive and then moves, *The Eden Project* file to his desktop. This was the last thing Victor was looking at before he mysteriously vanished. The fact that two government officials were going through his papers soon after has not escaped his attention; they were looking for something. Could this be it? Brian double clicks the file and begins reading.

Rules, Regulations, & Codes to be obeyed by all Citizens

- Every citizen, of age, will be assigned to a career, and must remain employed until retirement is allowed.
- Every citizen, of age, will be placed into an apartment complex or townhouse, which they will inhabit for life.
- Every citizen, of age, will have arranged for them a spouse whom they will remain betrothed to until death.
- No citizen will own or maintain property.
- No citizen will own or operate vehicles.
- No citizen will question any government official.
- No citizen will ask or want more than what is provided.
- All citizens will be paid a fair market allowance.
- All citizens will have major expanses covered, such as medical, utilities, and rent.
- No citizen can collect inheritance—monetary or physical items.
- No citizen, for any reason, can fight, steal, argue, disagree, or curse.
- All deceased citizens will be cremated, and their ashes will be stored in our facility—visitations will not be allowed.

Dire consequences will ensue to any offender of these rules with extreme prejudice and little forgiveness.

This file marks the beginnings of utopia, this is how it all started. Under the guise of perfection lies a darker agenda and this file reveals it—a new world order.

Twenty years ago.
A meeting is being held in an unknown high-rise conference room. The attendees consist of six men on each side of the room-length table, and another occupies the head chair. The room is silent as they study, and flip through the report packet in front of

them. The men give the head guy their attention when he stands up and takes an assertive pose.

"This civil unrest is showing little signs of dying down. The people want a world without government, without order, without supervision, and somehow, they think they will be better off if they get it." He points to the packet in front of everyone before continuing. "What lies in front of you is the solution. In order to end a war, we must remember what started it; 55% unemployment, raising rent and food prices and falling wages. We give the people a choice—door number one is the world outside that window—" He shoots his arm out to point toward the large windows without taking his gaze off his audience. "—A city consumed by fear and worry, or door number two; a perfect world where everything will be provided. An end to poverty, and wages that don't match the cost of living. We demolish single family housing to save land while limiting society's responsibilities. We cure road rage by taking away their cars, we convince them that we know each and every person better than they know themselves. We provide the job best suited for each individual, a place to live, and lastly, their ideal romantic connection. Like a pet, we put food in their bowls, and a roof over their heads, and they will stay loyal."

He then strolls to the windows and looks outside for a moment with his hands held behind him.

"We give them everything, and by doing so, we also give them everything to lose. We will own this entire monopoly board." He turns back around to face the group. "After that happens no one will dare cast their dice, they will just stay where they are—safe." A member raises his hand to speak, and the department head lifts his chin to grant it.

"How do we predict everyone's actions?"

"To reduce probability of the public's actions, we limit what they are allowed to do. Predicting their actions then becomes easy."

The man paces back and forth at the front of the room. "We stand unopposed with our future plans, gentlemen. We win the people over with kindness and gift giving and they will thank us. They may even love us for it. Welcome to, The Eden Project, men. We stand on the cusp of a new world."

"How do we deal with those who will not conform?" another

man asks.

"We cannot be allowed to be proven wrong; our word can never be tested or questioned. Anyone who exhibits signs of discontent, melancholy, paranoia, greed or any other negative thought or action must be eliminated. How do we do this without arising suspicion, you might ask?" the department head smiles. "We say they are sick." The men chuckle in agreement. "It's an incurable cerebral illness that explains all abnormal behavior. Throughout history, from the bubonic plague to coronavirus, everyone has shared one common fear, the fear of disease. This fear will give us control of where people go and who they talk to. Everyone will fear this disease so much that anyone we say is infected will be shunned. How else do we control masses of people? We convince them they are in danger and that we alone know how to keep them safe. Controlled Oppression Via Infectious Diseases." The men stand up while clapping in unison. The department head sits back down and puts his fingers together as his lips form a grin.

Presently.

Brian finishes reading though the files as the morning sun rises. He has obtained forbidden knowledge, he can't pretend not to know, and he can't assume the government won't find out. In some way, he had always known something was operating the cogs of society from some undisclosed location and away from prying eyes. There's no going back from this now. Happy is he who lives unknown, and Brian cannot live unseen any longer.

Chloe shuffles out of the bedroom while stretching and giving Brian a smile. "Good morning, love. You're up early," she says as she begins to prepare the coffee maker. The consequences of his actions will also affect her.

"Chloe, come here and sit down," he says somberly. Chloe abandons her brewing preparation and approaches the couch concerned.

"What is it?" Brian takes her hand into his.

"If I inquired about moving to a different place, would you join me?"

"Move? Why would we move?"

"Would you," Brian repeats with anxiety clearly in his voice. Chloe becomes increasingly nervous about the nature of his question.

"Of course, but what is this about?"

In another part of town is a heavy-duty barricade and fenced in area that's manned by a guard kiosk. Inside are the only signs of vehicles; these charcoal gray SUVs with smoked headlights, grill, rims, and tinted windows remain parked and ready for departure. Every SUV is identical and outfitted with an engine upgrade that produces 1000 horsepower—they're called Trackhawks.

Behind the row of cars is a plain brick, four-story office building with dark blue tinted windows. Inside this building are endless rows of supercomputers, hard drives, and operating servers. These large server rooms are connecting by clean hallways throughout all four floors. This is a data center, and it controls and sees everything going on around this city and other nearby settled cities. This is where the government makes sure everyone is following the rules.

Three officials are listening to phone conversations at a station that resembles a high-tech switchboard.

"How about a drink after work guys?" someone suggests somewhere in the city. The officials continue to listen but make no action.

"Everyone is so nice where I work. I'm glad I'm there." a woman explains during a phone call. The officials continue to listen.

"I wish there were more entertainment here. It's kinda boring." The officials exchange looks and then writes something on a pad of paper—*Observe closer. Code 4.*

The codes increase in severity based on public disturbance or risks to order. A code 2 may represent someone in a temporary bad mood. A code 4 indicates someone may be involved or exposed to a thought or idea that may be considered unfavorable. Anything above a code 7 demands immediate attention and could be anything from being tailed to being removed from society, or even elimination.

On the floor above are security camera feeds of every public place or business. They are small and never noticed on the streetlights, inside apartment hallways, over doorways, and on exterior walls. Monitors show people going about their daily routines without knowledge they are being watched.

In another room, officials read lines of text that are constantly being updated on their screens. This is real time information of everything everyone is doing on a digital device. From what they are reading to what they are typing and what websites they are visiting. They know what you are saying, what you are doing, and what you are thinking all the time.

The top floor is the true command center of the government, and where orders are given out. A government official has an external hard drive plugged into his computer as he types on the keyboard while clicking through files. He finally raises his hand to signal a high-ranking official to come over.

"I found it," he announces when the general approaches his desk with a stern expression.

"Where was it?"

"Victor hid it on the Curator's server—It looks to be fully intact—Wait—That's odd."

"What's the matter?" the general says gruffly.

"The code looks different—This file has been copied."

"Where, and by whom?" The man continues typing and scrolling through the lines of computer coding.

"It was accessed from another computer at The Daily Curator." The man continues typing with sort fast strokes. "It may have been moved directly to an external hard-drive as there's no evidence of it being stored on any of their local drives."

"I'm losing my patience," The general announces. The official turns to his second monitor and pulls up a login screen.

"I think I can track the file itself. We know Victor hacked the password, but the PDF also connects to the server every time it's opened, that means we will get an IP address from whoever has viewed it." The official enters his command, and a single IP address shows up on the screen.

"Who is that registered to?" The general asks. The man types the address in another tab and a name and address reveals where the file was last opened—

Brian Troth
Community Garden Apartments, Suite 505
Last Opened: 11:52 PM
Device: Macbook Pro

The general picks up a remote and points it to one of the large monitors on the wall. Brian's photo appears on the screen along with information on where he lives, works, and Chloe's name and image as his partner. Below the main data is also his CPQ answers, personality report, and medical files, as well as information on his former life before the coma. Next to his name is also an icon of a small red flag.

"He's already been flagged as a potential threat," the general says. "I'll get someone on it."

Meanwhile, Brian and Chloe are continuing their conversation on their couch.

"Things are not as they appear to be," Brian begins.

"What do you mean?"

"Victor Heart, I don't think he moved. I think—I think he was killed." Chloe pulls her hand away from Brian and gives him a worrisome expression.

"What has kept you up all night, Brian?"

He places his hand on his brow before combing his hair back with his open palm. "The government officials are part of some secret organization. They give gifts with one hand and steal them back with the other."

"I don't understand, Brian," Chloe says while shaking her head.

Brian notices a deck of playing cards on the coffee table and grabs them. "Think of it like this. I'm going to quickly show you three cards. I want you to remember the numbers you saw."

Brian shows the top card to Chloe before laying it face down on the table. He then shows her the second, and lastly, the third. "What were the suits?" he asks.

"You told me to look at the numbers," Chloe says with a confused glare.

"Yes, but now I'm asking for the suits."

"I don't know. I only paid attention to the numbers."

"When you focus on one thing you become blinded to everything else in plain sight. In this case you saw what I asked you to see." Brian flips the three cards face-up. "The suits are right there, yet you did not see them." Brian pauses. "Victor saw something he wasn't supposed to see, and they got rid of him because of it."

Chloe puts a hand on Brian's cheek. "I feel bad for Victor, but I beg you not to pursue this any further."

Brian takes her hand in his and squeezes it tightly. "Chloe—I already saw it. It was right there, how could I not? If they know I have it, they will be here soon."

"Then we must leave now," Chloe says jumping to her feet. Brian rises to meet her eyes while grasping her quivering hands.

"We cannot veer away from our daily tasks. Everything must look normal. If I don't show up to work, they will start tracking us right away. We will leave tonight when it's unexpected."

"I can't sit here all day worried out of my mind."

"I'll be back in seven hours."

"They will arrive before you." Chloe turns away and puts the tips of her fingers in her mouth.

"I shouldn't have done it. I put both our lives in danger. I'm so sorry." Chloe rushes into his chest as both begin to show their tears.

"Nothing is going to change my love for you," she says. They share several kisses before Brian pulls away and takes a step towards the door.

"Stay here, Chloe. Don't trust any of the government officials. If they come, deny everything, you know nothing. You—know—nothing. Make them believe it, and perhaps you will be ignored. I love you—I will always love you."

Chloe stands still while watching Brian leave, but the lump in her throat stops her from expressing her love for him. The door shuts, and she fears she will never again see him.

Brian's senses are heightened to a level he has never felt before. The world looks different to him now. The smiling people, that once looked friendly, now appear to show sinister grins, and the gardens look like an overgrown cemetery with forgotten tombstones. His walk to work feels like a long drug trip with his heartbeat lodged in his ears.

Brian enters the newsroom with a straight face while walking to his desk without greeting anyone or making eye contact. He sits down and notices a manila folder beside the keyboard. He flips it open and reads the forecast report.

A stationary front is moving in. Expect several days of cloudy skies and torrential rains.

Chloe tries to force herself to think about something else as she sits on the couch with both hands wrapped around a warm cup of coffee. This option becomes challenged when knocking explodes like thunder on the other side of the door. She looks at the door for a long moment afraid who might be standing on the other side waiting. Her hesitation is surely noticed as the knocking continues. She sets her coffee cup down and then slowly stands up. She takes a deep breath and advances towards the door before opening it cautiously. Her heart skips a beat, and her mouth becomes dry when she discovers two government officials looking back at her.

"Sorry to disturb you ma'am. May we come in?" one of them asks. Chloe can feel the hairs on her arms stand on end, and her heart pounding inside her chest. She should have smiled and said "absolutely," and then offer them coffee. She should have done that, but she didn't. Instead, she slightly closes the door while hiding her body behind it. The two men exchange looks when their request is denied. One only fears authority when one is aware of their wrong doing. To them, her action is that of a deviant, and those are usually punished.

"We believe your husband may have come down with Loquacitis. For your safety we ask that you come with us," the other official explains.

"I—can't believe that."

"We have a vehicle waiting. You will not be harmed," they continue to explain.

"I have to refuse—whatever illness he is believed to have, I shall have it also."

"Is it worth your life?" the official asks.

"I only know one life," she replies. The men exchange looks again before returning their gaze to Chloe.

"Have a good day ma'am," They conclude before walking away peacefully, and without an incident, or showing any hostility, but that was the most terrifying thing they could have done. Their departure signals that Chloe wasn't compliant, and disobedience cannot be tolerated.

She closes the door and puts her hand over her mouth before starting to cry uncontrollably. In less than an hour she does the one thing Brian told her not to do; she leaves the apartment. Overcome with fear she quickly scans around down both ends of the hallway before jogging towards the elevator. Chloe didn't notice the government official peeking around the corner of the far wall; he lifts his collar and gives his report into the clipped-on microphone.

"She left."

Brian takes note of the black clouds rolling in fast outside the window. The day is now more closely related to dusk as rolling thunder crackles in the distance. He turns back to his computer and tries to focus, but his thoughts are elsewhere.

"Do you have the next crossword puzzle ready yet?" Brian glances up at one of his co-workers.

"Crosswords and word searches. This isn't a newspaper, it's a God-damn activity book," he says frustrated. Lenny lifts his head and looks out of his office window as the startled man walks away in disbelief. Lenny needs to defuse this situation fast. He steps out of his office and approaches Brian as fast as he can get there.

"Are you okay, Brian?"

"You should stop calling this a newspaper. Because a, news...paper contains news. What happened to reporters and uncovering the truth? This is all headlines, but no stories. Well, I got a headline for you—When did activism die? This utopia is an acceptable grave and everyone goes along with it. Sometimes we should question the origin of even our most valued gifts. But no one ever asks why! Is that word still used today?"

Two government officials run up the staircase as an unknown voice sounds out from their earpiece.

"We have a code 9! Code 9!"

Lenny lightly touches Brian's arm attempting to calm him, but he pulls away from him.

"You don't understand, no one understands. We are given food, water, shelter, and companionship, but trade freedom for the dangling carrot. We are all animals locked in beautiful cages, but always underneath the zookeeper's control."

The government officials burst into the room to draw everyone's attention.

"I'm sorry everyone, but this man is infected with Loquacitis," they exclaim. Most of the room utter signs of worry and swiftly back far away from Brian, except for Lenny who remains by his side.

"Yes, let's talk about Loquacitis," Brian begins. "It isn't an illness, it's your cure; sounds like it was taken from the word, loquacious, or someone who talks a lot. I don't think that's a coincidence."

The thunder rolls in the distance as Chloe enters the lobby of The Daily Curator. She strolls past the empty chair behind the recipient's desk and then pushes the up button on the elevator. She waits impatiently for the doors to open unaware that she's been followed this whole time. The doors open, but her relief suddenly turns to despair when an official darts out at her. She avoids his tackle and continues to back away in horror.

"Hold it right there, miss," he says sternly while approaching with a dominate stride.

The officials have been dispatched across the city in a force rarely seen and none has ever escaped. More officials rush into the lobby from outside to cut off her escape route. She was so close to being united with Brian, but now she must retreat. Brian, unfortunately, will never know she was there. The officials close in, but Chloe fakes out two of them with a step in the direction she never takes. This gives her a lead around the mob that almost had her surrounded. Her sprint allows her to make it out of the building as the officials scramble after her.

"Don't let her get away," one of them demands. The pursuit will now continue through the streets.

Meanwhile, the officials advance toward Brian.

"You are not well, sir."

"Who are you? Illuminati? Majestic 13? What do you call yourselves?!" Brian responds. "I'm the only one with their eyes open. This utopia is a fallacy!"

"What we have here is a perfect world," the official snaps back.

"No, what you have here is intellectual suicide!" A loud clap of thunder explodes overhead, and large raindrops fall like millions of tiny missiles that rival hailstorms.

"Take him down," the voice from their mics order.

The officials rush toward Brian, but he backs up into the coffee machine. He quickly grabs the hot pot and smashes it over one of the official's head. The scalding liquid burns his flesh while the glass shards pierce into every part of his face sending him to the floor in agonizing pain.

Lenny can't help Brian any longer. He's forced to stand by as a helpless observer. He can hope for the best, but expecting the worst is usually the safer bet.

The last standing official and Brian throw fists at each other until Brian lands a jab to the man's jaw and then slams his head against the corner of the table with enough force to snap his neck.

Brian's co-workers scream out, or gasp as they witness the violent act of murder. Brian can never go back from this—his only option is to run out of the office.

Lenny bows his head and shuts his eyes. "Goodbye, Brian," he whispers to himself. He knows he will never see his friend again.

Brian hears the elevator chime and catches a glimpse of two officials exiting. He quickly darts through the door leading to the staircase and dashes down the steps.

One flight down, he intersects an official scurrying up the steps toward him. Brian punches him in the chest and then kicks his legs to send the man tumbling down the steps.

Brian bursts through the door into the lobby where he's welcomed by more men. They must have called everyone they had. He dodges around the group and makes it out into the street as the men pursue him. He still doesn't know Chloe was just there a few moments ago and is being chased at his very moment as well.

The pouring rain is accompanied with thunder and lightning as Chloe sloshes through the puddles of the vacant street towards her apartment. She crashes into the community hallway only to find an official waiting for her.

"I have her at the apartment," he says before sprinting towards her. He grabs her and then throws her against the wall as she screams while he attempts to pin her arms behind her. She never needed to fight, but a primal instinct takes over that forces her to kick her heel up into his crotch. He stumbles backwards before receiving Chloe's fist in his eye and another kick into his gut. Another official is rushing down the stairs from his stake out of her room. With Chloe's passage blocked, she must retreat back outside.

"Target on the move. Send more men," he reports while stepping over the incapacitated man and taking off after her.

Trackhawks roar towards Brian's reported position as several officials chase him on foot. Brian ignores the relentless rain and the deep puddles his feet fall into. Strangely, there are no signs of citizens anywhere. Naturally, they wouldn't be out in this storm, but all the buildings are dark and appear to be unoccupied.

Mysteriously, the city resembles one that's been completely evacuated and now only him and government officials remain.

Brian reacts quickly when an official jumps out in front of him from behind the corner of a store. Brian punches him and then grabs him behind the neck to slam his face into the nearby streetlamp pole. A Trackhawk screeches to a halt so close that it almost fails to stop before colliding with Brian. He detours from his intended route and darts down an alleyway with the driver running after him. He swings a garbage can into the path of his pursuer to successfully make him fall over it. This gives Brian enough time to regain his lead.

Chloe thinks maybe she can run through the Community Gardens towards Lenny's apartment. She doesn't know but hopes that Clerissa will offer her refuge. She glances behind her and almost seems relieved to see no one there. The moment is short-lived; however, when a Trackhawk scales over the grassy incline on the outer edge and growls through the field ahead of her. Chloe abandons her current destination as her adrenaline reserves kick in and she seeks another path for her escape. Another SUV crashes through the bushes nearby to make her yell from being startled. Four officials are now in pursuit and her tiring legs feel as though they may buckle any time. Chloe pushes herself and veers off the main path and into a cluster of trees while passing a sign that the lightning lit up too late for her to read—

Garden ends here.

Brian's escape is also proving to be troublesome when two more vehicles speed through the street and stop right behind him. Three officials dash out of each car and quickly gain ground over him. He puts the last of his energy in the final push into his apartment entrance. He then slams the door before dead-bolting it, and then slides the solid oak bench, hiding in the ingress, in front of the door as an extra precautionary step. His decision proves to be valid just as the six officials reach it and begin slamming their shoulders into the door or try to kick it in. He hurries up the stairs to his floor unaware Chloe is no longer there.

Meanwhile, Chloe continues through the dense trees until she comes to a gravel circular clearing. Her feet slide across the uneven surface as stops abruptly. She has run out of ground to traverse, and her next few steps leads her to the edge of a steep cliff. She whirls around hoping to backtrack, but this too is futile as the four officials slowly advance toward her. They don't need to hurry, there's no place for her to go. She takes a step back towards the edge of the cliff and glances down. She's trapped.

Brian barges into his room and sends the apartment door slamming into the shelf on the wall. The vase and glass rose tip over and shatter across the floor. A gift that was supposed to last forever had one fatal flaw—it's fragile. Only when undisturbed can it last.

The apartment is dark and lifeless as the flashes of lightning occasionally lights up the area for a brief moment.

"CHLOE! CHLOE!" Brian yells out frantically as he runs into the bedroom and then peeks into the bathroom. He walks back into the living room and looks around, but there's no sign of her. He swings the patio door open and steps onto the balcony. He yells into the rain and wind at the top of his lungs.

"CHLOE!"

Panicked, and fear laden, Brian returns inside overcome with grief. Soaking wet and dripping water in his wake, he sobs. He lifts his head and notices a folded piece of paper on top of his closed laptop. He advances toward the breakfast bar and begins unfolding it.

Behind him, a pair of feet has just stepped out from a darkened corner of the room. A recessed section in the wall where a potted plant occupied was one place Brian never thought to look.

Brian tilts the note towards the window so the streetlight can illuminate the tiny piece of paper.

The man behind Brian takes another soft step forward and becomes half illuminated from another flash of lightning. His face shows a scowl and dead eyes as if he doesn't contain an ounce of humanity.

Brian makes out the handwritten note containing Chloe's last words for him.

I love you. Your soulmate, Chloe.

The man slowly reaches inside his overcoat and draws a pistol. Brian is unaware he has a barrel of a gun pointing at the back of his neck.

Meanwhile, the relentless rain refuses to ease up as the four officials stand directly in front of Chloe. Tears swell into her eyes before she shuts them and relinquishes herself to her fate. The officials' hands connect with her shoulders and her body is forcefully pushed backwards. Her feet leave the ground as she plunges downward in a silent reverie. Several bolts of lightning shoot down from the clouds over her descending body and the following crack of thunder explodes over Brian sobbing with her note in his grasp.

"Chloe—" he whispers.

The assassin cocks his gun. Brian hears it but does not have time to spin around. The trigger is pulled, and a dart is sent into the back of Brian's neck. He clenches his fist around the note and gasps as he attempts to reach for the dart, but the poison acts fast as he begins to lose basic mobility functions and is eyesight blurs. He falls over the counter to knock his laptop to the floor, resulting in the thumb drive popping out of the USB slot and sliding partially under the fridge.

Brian slowly slides off the counter while toppling over the chairs and coming to rest on his side. In less than ten seconds his heart stops. In death his eyes remain open, as if trying to learn the identity of his killer as the storm rolls on.

The assassin stands over Brian and pries Chloe's note from his hand and then retrieves his dart. He then reaches into his shirt pocket to pull out an old flip phone. He flips it open and dials one and then a three. After one ring, the receiver is answered without a greeting.

"I got Adam," he reports.

"Eve has been dealt with—report back."

The next morning, Lenny leans against the streetlight pole in the Community Gardens waiting for Brian to meet him. As the minutes tick by he becomes more and more worried. Brian is never late. He lifts his watch to observe the time, 8:13. He looks in the direction he will be approaching from, but there's no sign of him. His worse fears begin to take shape. He checks the time later, 8:23. He bows his head with a sigh and begins walking out of the garden and across the street. He glances in the direction of, The Daily Curator, and then turns to face Brian's apartment. Instead of continuing to work, he makes an unplanned change in his schedule and heads to his friend's home.

Three government officials interact with one another in Brian's apartment when Lenny walks in. The fact that the door is wide open, and the presence of these officials prepare Lenny for what he will soon discover.

He takes a moment to scan the room. The laptop is sitting on the breakfast bar as if it never fell the night before. The chairs are all neatly pushed in, and the spot where the glass rose fell and broke had been cleaned up.

Brian is lying in bed with his shoes neatly placed at the foot of the bed. Lenny sighs and shuts his eyes. The struggle from the night before seems to play out in his mind, piece-by-piece, as if Brian is showing him the truth through a way he cannot explain. He observes the dark room, and the assassin's dart firing out of the gun before seeing Brian falling to the floor. Lenny opens his eyes and lets the light filter through his eyes. This experience is new to him, but he can't deny it. Lenny begins to walk towards the bedroom where Brian lies, but he's interrupted immediately by one of the officials.

"Excuse me sir. You can't go in there."

"He was my friend."

"That may be, but he's a victim of Loquacitis and I don't want you to get infected. You shouldn't be here."

"Is that where you found him?" Lenny asks. The official looks at him for a moment and nods.

"Yes, he died peacefully in his sleep." Lenny now has reason to believe he's being lied too, and that Brian may have been right to question what others easily accepted.

"Are you sure?" Lenny asks. The government official appears stunned with his question.

"Are you serious? I think you should go back to your crosswords, my wife loves those," he responds hoping to unnerve him enough to make him leave.

Lenny begins to understand what Brian was fighting against ever since he woke up—the notion that there's no such thing as perfect.

Lenny played by the rules his whole life, but he never had to feel a loss as deep as this. It wasn't that long ago that he would never have thought to question an official, or deliberately being late to work, much less walking into a government occupied location. He plays it cool, but a thought creeps into his mind that was never allowed to fully form before. Maybe this world is not what it appears to be after all, and maybe Brian knew it from the start. The safety of his well-being is now questioned if he lingers here any longer.

Lenny sighs and bows his head in defeat but catches a glimmer of the thumb drive hidden under the fridge. He gets an image of Brian's laptop crashing to the floor and his thumb drive sliding to its current location. He doesn't know what it is, but he cannot deny that it must be important in some way. He looks up at the official, but he's looking away. Lenny puts his foot on top of the thumb drive and then takes a pen out of his shirt pocket before dropping it near his foot.

The official darts a glance at Lenny briefly, but then looks away when only a dropped pen seems to be the disturbance. Lenny bends over to grab his pen and the thumb drive at the same time. He then quickly shoves both into his pocket.

Lenny makes his way to the door, but glances back one last time.

"Hey," he says. The government officials stop talking and all glare at him. He lifts his head in an upward motion towards Brian's body. "He was the one who did the crosswords." Lenny calmly departs the apartment without hearing a response.

Lenny enters the newsroom to see everyone working as if nothing had happened the day before. He respectively strolls past Brian's empty chair and continues into his office. He gently shuts his door for the first time and then proceeds to his desk. He wants to look up and see Brian at his computer, but his absence creates an eerie void that's home to only ghosts. Just another day at the office—almost.

Later that night, curiosity leads Lenny to plug the retrieved thumb drive into his computer at home. The images and words reflect in his pupils as he flips through the pages of the document. The sun rises as it becomes dawn and Lenny now knows everything that Brian had found out. Brian's action of saving over the original file localized the PDF making it a different version and free from detection. He didn't plan it that way, it was nothing more than an instinct to continuously save his work throughout the day.

"I understand, Brian," Lenny softly says to himself.

The government officials tried as hard as they could to tamper with Brian's apartment to make it look completely normal, but when picking up a fallen laptop a missing thumb drive was overlooked. Perhaps, a more thorough investigation would have located what was not that far away.

Call it fate, call it happenstance, call it whatever you like, but sometimes things can occur outside the control of even the most prepared powers. It may be incomprehension, or arrogance, but some leading forces disregard the meek and humble, yet they tend to be the ones who find the best kept secrets.

Lenny drags himself into his office and closes the door behind him again. When he gets to his desk, he observes a manila folder beside his keyboard. He looks at it for a long moment until finally flipping it open.

Report on Brian and Chloe's death.

HEADLINE: **Troth Couple Found Dead.**

Brian died suddenly due to Loquacitis. Chloe, who was running to the aid of a doctor living nearby, became disoriented in the storm and headed towards the cliff by mistake. Due to the wet earth and pour visibility she slipped and fell off the edge to her death. Her delusion may have been due to the beginning stages of Loquacitis as well.

Lenny falls into his chair with a blank stare. Lies, all lies. He knows he's expected to write the story exactly how it appears in the report; despite it being completely false. In the past he would have without question because it was his job, but now it would be because of fear. Knowing what Brian knew has given birth to a disturbing question in his mind. *"How long can I hide what I know before I'm dispatched like those before me—and the secret dies yet again?"*

He puts the report in front of him and begins typing the first few words as it appears in the report before stopping. He's torn between playing it safe or risking everything and telling the truth. Lenny pounds his fist on his desk and puts his forehead in the palm of his hands. He looks up to notice some of his co-workers looking at him through the window. He smiles and waves pretending it was nothing. He turns back and glances down at the pile of papers on his desk. He narrows his eyes and lifts the first sheet on top of the stack—it's Brian's poem that was never shown to Victor, his dream that may have been more of a message. Lenny reads Brian's words one last time, but this time one passage stands out. *There is courage in surrender when knowledge is given. Some of us are solely here to pass the torch, while others are meant to light it. Heroes are born from sacrifice. The brave should honor those who came before and teach those who come after.*

Lenny stands up and shuts his blinds, an action that is unusual and may be looked at as someone who's trying to hide their actions. Lenny treads in the footsteps of Victor and Brian, soon one will need to follow his. He sits back down and gazes at the few words he had already typed. He holds down the backspace button until everything has been erased. Lenny reaches into his pocket and sets Brian's thumb drive in front of him.

"I have a headline that needs a story," he says without lifting his gaze from it. He pushes the, *Do Not Disturb,* button on his work phone and then drops the manila folder into the garbage before resuming his revised report.

What is the price for happiness? Is resigning basic freedoms in exchange for a peaceful surrender acceptable? It was perfect—but even, **perfect** *comes with fine print.*

They called it Loquacitis, but they were wrong to call it a disease. It's not; it's a way to limit intelligence, control information and prevent unfavorable opinions from spreading onto others. But they were right about one thing—it is contagious.

Tomorrow everyone will have an article to read.

An article that will give birth to a resistance.

A resistance that will change the world.

"Sometimes writing is the only way you can discover yourself, and when you learn more about yourself, you also learn more about others. There's nothing antisocial about it."

Days
Gone By

Hope.

Contents

1

The Anniversary

In the wake of great sorrow, the mind can sometimes build a wall that shuts everything negative out; however, this can also modify the memory and create lasting emotional disorders. Following the event, a person will become distant, angry, or numbed to feelings that once brought joy or triggered a common reaction. The individual becomes trapped in a private safe place, such as the boundaries of their home, a condition known as, agoraphobia, or the fear of open spaces. Treading too far from this familiar space or being around too many people at once will fill the person with anxiety and dread. Over time it becomes more taxing to break free from these mental chains, and many cannot do so without outside assistance.

Unable, and unwilling to accept a life-altering tragedy made one Wisconsin man, named Caleb, succumb to an extreme case of this condition. If it were not for a series of bizarre and magnificent events, Caleb would be consumed by his depression and remain alone until the end of his days.

This is his story—

I always thought God had a personal vendetta against me. I don't know what I did to deserve it, but four years ago is when I lost my faith.

It's Sunday morning and church is nearing an end as the pastor speaks his closing sermon to a full congregation.

"Several years ago, I met a man who did indeed have his ailments, but after some time had passed, we finally become good friends. One day he opened up to me and said,

When I was young, I believed in God and angels, and said my prayers every night. When I got a little older, I only spoke to him when I needed something, all the other times he was just a nice idea. By the time I became an adult, life demanded all my time.

And after he said that I began to mull it over in my head, over and over. And I realized, that's how many of us probably treat God. When we are sad or in trouble or lacking in a want or need such as a better job with better pay, or to find that special someone, or maybe just to get a really good deal on a brand-new car—" The congregation shares in common laughter at his comment as the pastor continues with his sermon. "—We raise our hands up and say help me, God, I need your help. But when we are doing well in life, we justify our lack of prayers on being too busy for God at that moment."

Members of his congregation nod their heads in agreement. In the front row are Carl and Melissa, who are currently engaged with a wedding planned for this coming spring. Sitting next to Carl is his sister, Carrie, but their younger brother, Caleb is missing. He's been estranged for the last four years and even the other churchgoers stopped asking about him, he has become a distant memory in a place where he was once frequently seen.

"But now think about this," the pastor continues. "Does God need to wait for us to fall on hard times to hear from us, or is the fact that we are not deprived of necessities a result of God's everlasting love and care for us? Is it so hard to say thank you? Thank you, God, for all you have given me and all that you will give. How long did that take? Say it with me now." The congregation repeats along with him. "Thank you, God, for all you have given me and all that you will give. Amen."

After the closing prayer the pastor concludes his sermon, and the room begins to empty. Some head outside toward their cars, while others descend the stairs to enjoy rolls and coffee. Since Carl can't pass up a snack of any kind and Melissa and Carrie love any chance to socialize, they make up the latter group.

Flurries gently fall over the wintry city of New Berlin, which shows evidence of a previous snowstorm. Snowbanks line the street curbs and encase the bare branches of the park trees. The snow-capped houses hide behind mounds of freshly shoveled snow and cars slowly drive through the slush. On a quiet side street, overlooking the residential park are a cluster of four mailboxes. Directly behind them is a quaint home with an ornate glass design on the front door and a Christmas wreath. This is Caleb's home, and he's about to receive a visitor for the first time in a very long time. Little does he know how this interaction will trigger a significant series of unexplainable events that will change his life forever.

It's been four years since the tragic car accident that left him partially disabled. Caleb slowly limps toward the front door, while leaning heavily on his cane. His handicap has become his excuse why he can no longer be part of society and over time he's convinced himself that's the only reason.

Caleb is speechless when he opens the door and finds his brother, Carl standing on his doorstep.

"Hello, Caleb," he says while smiling.

"Carl?" After a pause Caleb finally steps aside. "You wanna come in?"

"Thank you." Carl walks in and stomps the snow from his feet and then shakes the flurries from his coat. He pulls his coat off and then drapes it over a chair next to the foyer table with a top drawer. The staircase to the second floor is behind it and the open concept living room is directly across. The hallway continues into the kitchen and the door to the backyard. "We're supposed to get more snow tonight," Carl continues. Talking about the weather seems to be a good way to start the conversation, but Caleb has little interest in the subject as he shuts his door again.

"Would you like some tea?"

"Sure." Caleb leads his brother into the kitchen while Carl looks around somewhat surprised at the lack of holiday decorations.

"No tree this year?" Carl asks.

"I put a wreath up."

"Ah, yes, I saw." Caleb begins pouring two cups of tea from the pot sitting on the counter.

"I was at church this morning," Carl begins.

"I remember the place," Caleb replies without looking up from his pouring. "Have they stopped asking about me yet?" he continues. Carl hesitates with his response, but then nods.

"They have."

"Good," Caleb says. Carl accepts the tea from Caleb and holds it up to his nose. "This smells good. What kind is it?"

"Earl Grey," Caleb responds before pulling out a chair and sitting down.

"I should have guessed. You always did like Earl Grey." Carl sets his tea on the table and then pulls his chair out to join Caleb. He lets a moment of silence pass before talking again. "I was in the area. I suppose I could've called."

"No, it's okay."

"Tomorrow's the anniversary."

"I know."

"Three days after Christmas."

"I know!" Caleb raises his voice; he doesn't want to be reminded about the day of the accident. He lived it once already and any talk of it now just agitates him.

"We missed you at the funeral," Carl continues.

"I couldn't do it. I couldn't look into that coffin and see his face. I couldn't see that tiny lifeless body."

"He was our nephew, Caleb."

"He was just shy of five, Carl. He would be nine now. How could I watch him be buried?"

"Everyone asked about you."

"I figured they would."

"Carrie still hasn't forgiven you for not showing up."

"Is that why her Facebook page only lists one brother?"

"She lost her only son, and with you locked up in here she lost a brother also, but *you* can come back."

"She blames me."

"No, she doesn't. Why would you think that?" Caleb takes a sip of his tea.

"Because I was the only one there."

"I know she misses you. We all do."

"That's fine; I'll be the black sheep of the family. Every family needs one so everyone else can look better."

"That's not what we want. You look pale, when was the last time you went outside?

"I sit on the patio when it's nice."

"But you never venture far from it, do you? You don't leave the house." Carl stands up and paces around the kitchen. "We're worried about you, Caleb."

"I'm not suicidal; at least not yet."

"That's not what I'm talking about. Prolonged solitude isn't good for the mind. You need to be out with people."

"Why? So, I can get mugged or shot, or maybe hit by a drunk driver?" Carl lets a moment of silence pass.

"We've been praying for you."

"To who?" Caleb sarcastically chuckles. "No one was listening four years ago. No one is listening now."

"You had a bad experience, we all felt that blow, but you didn't move on, you ran home and hid behind closed blinds."

"Would it have been better if I never came home at all?"

"Dammit, Caleb. You know that's not what I meant."

"I know everyone wishes it was me in that coffin instead of him."

"That's not true."

"I wish it was." Carl ignores his latest comment and opens the blinds to the kitchen window to let the sunshine in.

"It's the middle of the afternoon, but you would never know it standing in here."

"There's nothing to see anyway."

"Where are the pictures of Tommy you used to have out?"

"I put them away."

"Why? So, you can forget him?" Caleb pounds his fist on the table.

"I don't need to hear this. Is this why you came over? To lecture me about Tommy's death? Look, it's nice to see you, but I don't need you."

"I don't know what got into you." Carl says with a sigh. Caleb stands up while using the surface of the table for support.

"What do you mean, what got into me? My legs are useless. I need this Godforsaken cane for the rest of my life. I may have closed the blinds, but you closed that door. Four years, four fuckin' years. Why show up now?!"

"I wanted to see you. This rift in our family needs to end."

"Everyone has been getting along fine without me."

Carl shakes his head and walks back to his coat with quickened steps.

"I don't know how you can live like this. I know you aren't happy." Caleb grabs his cane and follows him.

"I don't need anyone to tell me how I feel."

Carl throws his coat on and opens the front door but turns around on the doorstep.

"I'm sorry; I didn't mean to talk about Tommy. The real reason I came over was to tell you that I'm getting married. I want you to be at my wedding." Caleb hesitates but cannot fathom the thought of being in a crowd much less a church.

"I'll send you a card," he says. The shutting door separates the two brothers again with them no closer to a resolution than four years ago. But something is about to happen that never happened before. Carl's appearance weakened Caleb's defenses just enough to allow others to visit him. Now, I don't know if it would be considered a miracle, but it does transcend what the mind believes to be possible and rational. Caleb will soon be visited by another relative, but this one had left this Earthly plane when Caleb was still a child.

Later that evening, Carl finds himself sitting at the dining room table delicately sipping his glass of brandy. Melissa strolls into the room and immediately takes note of the closely guarded bottle. She scoops it up and studies the label before setting it back down.

"Okay, what's wrong?" she says lovingly. Carl gives her a smirk and sets his glass down.

"I went to see Caleb today," he replies calmly. Melissa pulls out a chair and sits down eager to hear more.

"You mean your brother, who no one likes to talk about?"

"Uh-huh."

"I still haven't met him."

"I'm afraid you never will. He has agoraphobia."

"That's a big word."

"I looked it up. It's a fear of leaving one's home. He's afraid of the world."

"What happened? Every time I bring it up someone changes

the subject."

"No one likes talking about it. I'll tell you, but not right now."

"That's okay. How is he doing?"

"I felt like I was talking to a complete stranger. He never ever refused to put up a Christmas tree. He used to put it up the day after Thanksgiving and kept it up all the way into February. He also tried to be the best house on the block with Christmas lights. I thought he had moved when I arrived; a single wreath and nothing more. The person I remembered him to be is gone."

"Everyone deals with sorrow in their own way."

"That's just it though. He never actually dealt with it. He just shut down."

"Maybe we can call someone to help him."

"He would only refuse it, Melissa." Carl takes another sip of his brandy.

"It's partially my fault. When he didn't show up for the funeral, we all alienated him. I wanted to invite him back to the family so he could be there at our wedding, but maybe I waited too long." Melissa gently caresses his arm.

"I'll put his name on the guest list. Maybe he will show."

"I don't think so, Mel. I'll send a card, that's what he said to me." Carl takes another sip and then lightly tops off his glass with a generous pour. "He walks with a permanent limp, and he thinks it's the same as dying. I don't know how he can be so close-minded."

"I don't know him, but I think he kept a lot of pain trapped inside and doesn't know how to release it."

"When we were kids, he was like a little explorer. He always came home with cuts and bruises, but he always went back outside; trying to learn how something grew or how some insect survived. Now he's afraid to walk past his mailbox. He lives in that tomb he calls a home."

"What do you want to do?"

"What can I do?"

"Well, you went to see him. That's a start."

"I went to see someone who used to be my brother."

"He's still your brother."

"I should have made it right with him a long time ago, but I kept telling myself that he should be making the first move. That single thought stopped everything.

"Meet him in the middle. It's never too late."

"Four years is a long time to expect forgiveness." Melissa leans over and kisses his forehead.

"I'll pray for him." Carl smiles.

"How did I get so lucky to have your love?" Carl says as he takes her hand in his.

"If you need me, I can stay here tonight," Melissa smiles.

"That's a very tempting offer," Carl jokes. "But I'll be okay."

"Kay, then I should get going. I'm going to Carrie's in the morning, but I can stop over after." Carl stands up and helps her into her coat before escorting her to the front door.

"Sounds good, have a good night." They share a soft kiss before Melissa heads to her car. They wave to each other one final time as she drives away.

The next morning, Carrie is admiring a picture of Tommy, Caleb and Carl smiling with presents piled under the Christmas tree in the background. She lowers the picture with tears in her eyes and takes a moment to dab them with a tissue. Melissa meets her on the couch with two cups of coffee in hand. She sets them down on the coffee table before joining her side.

"This was the last time everything was perfect," Carrie says. Melissa picks up the picture and points to Caleb.

"Is this Caleb?"

"Yes."

"He has a nice smile."

"I don't think he has smiled since that day. In fact, I haven't seen Carl smile until you came along." Carrie wipes her eyes and then sips her coffee.

"I'm very happy. After years of searching, I'm finally marrying the best man out there this coming spring."

"We need this celebration," Carrie agrees.

"Thanks, Carrie. This was my first Christmas with you and Carl. I've always loved the season, but I don't know how to express it without coming off as inconsiderate."

"It's hard not to think about it, but you don't need to hide your feelings from us," Carrie tells her.

"I know Tommy is looking down right now with that same smile he has in that picture." Carrie grins through her tears and embraces Melissa.

"I'm so glad you are going to be part of our family."

"Me too." Melissa hesitates for a moment before continuing. "Carl visited Caleb yesterday. He wants him at our wedding, but I don't think he was very receptive." Carrie appears shocked at first after hearing Carl went to visit Caleb, but she soon relaxes.

"I have so many different feelings toward Caleb ranging from anger to indifferent to worried, but I do miss him."

"Has he always lived alone?"

"He was seeing some girl from Jackson, but it didn't work out." Carrie shakes her head and continues. "I don't think he knows how to live any other way than alone."

"Caleb will find his way back, I'm sure of it," Melissa assures her.

"We all have wished things were different, but when one dwells on it, they tend to fade away from reality. That's what happened to Caleb."

"Did you talk to him at all this Christmas?"

"No, he buys one thing for me and Carl on Amazon and has it shipped to us, but he never calls."

"Maybe you could call him." Carrie thinks about Melissa's suggestion for a moment.

"I don't know what I would say," she finally admits.

Later that night, the temperature drops to minus six and the frigid wind rattles Caleb's windows. He has changed into his robe and pajamas and enjoys a warm cup of Jasmine tea before turning in for the night. During the day he prefers black teas, but at night he changes to green teas. Honey ginseng, Jasmine, or Chamomile is brewed after 7:00PM while Earl Grey, with an occasional Irish Breakfast, is enjoined from the morning through the afternoon. He places the teacup in the sink and runs water in it with a little soap. He shuts off the water and leaves the cup soaking.

He grabs his cane and turns off each light switch before slowly making his way up the staircase. He enters his bedroom where the soft amber glow, from his salt lamp, illuminates the space. Everything he does is very meticulous and routine. He pulls off his robe and then hangs it up on the hook behind the door. He then limps to his bedside and slides his slippers off, but ensures they are neatly side by side in front of his nightstand. Lastly, he carefully leans his cane against the wall in between his headboard and nightstand before sitting on the side of the bed. After he pulls the covers up, he reaches over to click the salt lamp off.

The hours continue to creep pass until the whistling of a teapot awakes Caleb from a sound sleep. He glances at the clock, 3:14 in the morning. He lifts his head to gaze into the hallway and notices the faint glow of a light on downstairs. He knew he made sure everything was put away and turned off before retiring. He immediately becomes baffled with the unexplainable state of his downstairs and the circumstance that led to it.

"What's going on?" he mutters to himself. He reaches for his cane and then slides his slippers on. He makes his way to the door and ties his robe around his waist and then ventures downstairs to investigate the mystery further.

When Caleb reaches the bottom landing, he can hear the clinging of a spoon stirring inside a cup followed by the cup being set gently on a saucer. He peeks around the corner to see the kitchen light is on.

An intruder has broken into my home to drink my tea, Caleb thinks to himself. He considers calling the authorities to report the possible home invasion, but the mere thought of his explanation convinces him out of it. Instead, he decides to deal with the matter himself and advances slowly into the kitchen to find an elderly man enjoying a cup of tea while sitting at the table. Caleb is now more confused than he was before as he shuffles his feet across the floor. He knows this man to be his grandfather, but this must be an impostor. The old man looks up and smiles at Caleb.

"Hello, Caleb. It's been a while."

"This cannot be. This is impossible."

"What's impossible?"

"You being here. This goes against the laws of physics."

"Yes, I suppose physics can't explain how your grandfather, who's been dead for 22 years, can be sitting in this chair and talking to you right now. But then again here I am, and here we are." His grandfather takes another sip of tea.

"And you're drinking my tea too? Am I dreaming?"

"No, I'm really drinking your tea," his grandfather jokes.

"This can't be explained. I don't know what this means," Caleb sighs.

"It means you need to find another explanation," the elderly man says. Caleb sits down across from his deceased grandfather lost for words. His grandfather continues sipping his tea before

Caleb finds his voice again.

"How did you get here?"

"Well, we migrated to this country from Portugal in 1959—"

"No, I mean here, right now."

"Well, I didn't mysteriously come back to life if that's what you're implying. No, sometimes individuals are recycled back into the world for a reason, and sometimes it remains a mystery."

"Are you here for a reason then?"

"Yes, I'm here for you, Caleb"

"You mean I'm dead!" He says flabbergasted.

"No, no, no, you're neither dead nor dying. You never used to be wound so tight. You need to calm down."

"Calm down? My dead grandpa is talking to me in my kitchen in the middle of the night while drinking my tea. How can I calm down?" His grandfather stares at him for a moment without uttering a word. "Okay, you know what?" Caleb begins while waving his hand in the air. "I'm going back to bed, and when I wake up in the morning this will just be a fascinating dream with no logic to debate." Caleb lifts himself from the chair, but his grandfather's story forces him to sit back down.

"Before I moved to this country, I used to go for late night walks near the cliff overlooking the ocean. One night, about midnight, I came across a woman who was blocking my normal route. She told me to go no further and to return home. I, of course, told her I was not yet done with my walk and questioned why I should go back home. She insisted and was very adamant about making sure my next step was in the opposite direction. She eventually talked me into it, although I don't really remember how she finally convinced me. The next morning, I saw that the cliff-side path had slid into the ocean. At night I would not have noticed the disturbed foundation and would have fallen to my death."

"Why are you telling me this?"

"Because I never saw that woman again and living in a small town you don't usually come across an unfamiliar face. Especially not on some secluded rural path at night. I believed she was an angel sent to save me. So, if I can accept that as a rational possibility, you can accept that I'm here talking to you right now."

"Why are you here?"

"Because you did fall from your path and I'm here to guide

you back."

"I don't have a path." Caleb's grandfather stands up.

"Let's go for a walk."

"Are you kidding me? I'm in my pajamas and it's in the middle of the night. Not to mention six below."

"Are you sure?"

"Yes," Caleb forcefully argues.

"Open that door," his grandfather says while pointing to the door that leads into the backyard."

Caleb sighs and gets up. "This is crazy," he says as he turns the deadlock and opens the door.

An unexpected blinding light forces him to raise his hand to shield his eyes. When the light dims Caleb lowers his hand and then blinks. He and his grandfather are standing in a large, well kept, backyard garden full of flowers, fruits, and vegetables on a warm summer afternoon.

"Now, you are just in your pajamas," his grandfather jokes.

"How did you make this happen?"

"You're the one who opened the door, Caleb." Caleb's grandfather inspects his tomato plants and then the peppers growing nearby. "Everything in this garden I grew from seed. Can you believe that?"

"I suppose."

"You used to help me. Of course, you were only three so you wouldn't remember; digging with your little plastic shovel—" His grandfather recalls the memory with delight, but Caleb appears only to be frustrated and interrupts him.

"Why did you bring me here?"

"You ask a lot of questions. Why don't you try to look for some of the answers?"

A child laughing is suddenly heard as a three-year-old Caleb plays hide 'n seek while his grandfather looks for him.

"Is that me? You brought me back to the past?"

"Yes, I did. You were such a happy child, always full of energy."

"Children usually are."

"No one has to stop feeling like that. It's a choice, Caleb."

"I didn't choose to be dependent on a cane."

"We can't always choose what happens to us, but we can choose how we deal with it."

Young Caleb is picked up by his grandfather and is held over his head as the two laugh. Caleb appears distraught as he tries to recall moments with his grandfather.

"I only have bits and pieces of you in my head, but never a clear picture."

"Perhaps it's because you are afraid of how that memory will make you feel." Caleb lacks a response and remains silent. "When was the last time you were fishing?" his grandfather asks.

"I never went fishing," Caleb answers while thinking with narrowed eyebrows.

"That's not true." His grandfather places his hand on Caleb's shoulder and in a single moment Caleb and his grandfather are now sitting in a rowboat on a calm lake. Caleb looks around amazed at the sudden change of the environment. His grandfather gets his attention back by handing him a fishing pole.

"I don't know how to fish," Caleb says as he accepts the pole.

"Then you must have forgotten. You used to be quite the angler. Just wait until a fish takes the bait and then reel it in." Caleb watches his grandfather cast his line out first and then tries to cast his own line. His reel spins and the line unravels before the bobber drops into the water.

"Ah, nice cast," his proud grandfather says. They wait in silence as the boat gently rocks against the waves slapping its sides. "The last time we were out here you were ten," his grandfather begins. "I didn't know that would be my last summer with you. I didn't know I was going to get sick. I didn't know I would be buried before Thanksgiving."

"We are just pawns on a chessboard," Caleb somberly replies.

"Pawns? No, we are the products of a much larger picture. When humanity needs us; sometimes we become heroes without even knowing it."

"I don't know what that means," Caleb admits, but his grandfather only smiles.

"That's my message for you, Caleb."

"You went through all of this just to give me a riddle?"

"More like a clue; a clue about your life."

"There's nothing special about my life."

"We all get older, but a child's laughter can bring youth back into your heart. That's what you did for me. All life is special."

"It wasn't enough. There's so much I wanted to learn from

you."

"Well, here I am. Ask me a question." Caleb thinks for a moment before speaking again.

"How do you grow an apple tree?"

"Plant an apple seed."

"I did that."

"Water it."

"I did that too, nothing happened."

"Try more than once." Caleb's line suddenly goes out.

"Whoa!"

"Reel it in," his grandfather says with excitement. Caleb begins reeling the wrong way.

"No, the other way," his grandfather instructs. Caleb begins reeling in the line while listening to his grandfather's advice.

"Lift up the pole as you reel." His grandfather stands up and leans over the side of the boat to lift the perch Caleb had caught. "You did it. This will make a good fish fry." His grandfather sits back down with a proud smile. Caleb almost had a smile himself, but it didn't quite take hold.

"I wish we had more time."

"I may not have had time to teach you all of my fishing secrets or all my gardening tips, but that doesn't mean I haven't been watching." Caleb directs his gaze across the lake and then admires his surroundings.

"It's peaceful here."

"This was my favorite place. I'm here all the time now. That's why you should never be sad when you lose someone, because they always go to their favorite place."

"I never had a favorite place."

"You will someday. It's getting close to that time when we must part once again."

"You're leaving?"

"We only have a limited time to give you our message and to show you what you need to see."

"Who's we?"

"I am but one visitor out of several that you will encounter. In the coming days there will be others. All of whom will come with a message. Some of them you will know, some of them you won't, but all of them will know you. Remember their words and what they show you. In the end you will understand why you were chosen. Chosen for a task, not because you are forgotten, but because you are loved. Goodbye, Caleb."

Caleb wakes up in his bed with the early morning sun shining through his blinds. It was just a dream, he thinks. He dresses and then heads into the kitchen where he stops abruptly. On the kitchen table sits an empty teacup in the same spot his grandfather had placed it. Caleb looks at it with a puzzling expression before walking up to it. He finally lifts the saucer and cup up and finds a folded piece of paper underneath it. He places the cup back down to unfold the paper. It's a hand-written note that reads:

Sometimes we are heroes without even knowing it.

How could this evidence be here if Caleb's experience was indeed just an elaborate and lucid dream? Caleb searches for an explanation and may assume he started sleep walking, but the handwriting isn't his. If the event that took place last night was a dream, then the cup and note would not be on the table. His grandfather's spoken message would also not be written before his very eyes. He must consider the strange possibility that his experience was not a dream after all, but if it wasn't a dream— then that means Caleb's journey has just begun.

2

A Friend from the Past

Carl and Melissa are spending their Saturday morning looking at a display of fabric samples at the Wedding Supplies & Gifts Boutique. Most of their weekends are occupied in and out of stores or on the phone talking to venues. More often than not, Melissa is usually the one picking up the phone and pushing Carl out the door. While Carl's priorities consist of making a list of his favorite songs for the DJ and planning a menu, Melissa's is quite a bit more involved.

"I think this light blue looks nice," Carl points out as he slides the cloth sample through his fingers. Melissa flips up the cloth sample and reads the tag.

"They call this cornflower."

"What's a cornflower?"

"Must be a type of blue flower." Melissa continues in a playful, elegant, and aristocratic tone while checking the tags on the two adjacent fabrics. "I like this Celadon or maybe this Magnolia."

"You mean green and white?" Carl says trying to simplify it. Melissa giggles just as a male clerk approaches them with an ecstatic grin.

"Can I help you look for anything special?" He says flamboyantly.

"Well, we are getting married this coming spring," Melissa begins.

"Oh, congratulations," the clerk replies eccentrically while clapping his hands

"Thank you." Melissa continues. "We are still trying to decide on our color scheme."

"Okay, do you have anything in mind?" the clerk asks.

"We were looking at this—cornflower," Carl says trying to sound like he's a connoisseur of art and color, while giving Melissa a sly smile.

"Ah, cornflower is very popular with weddings lately. A great accent to this will be ivory." The clerk shows them the fabric as Melissa caresses the cloth.

"Ooo, I like this," Melissa says as Carl nods in agreement.

"Have you decided on your flowers yet?"

"Not yet," Melissa admits.

"If I may make a suggestion? Matsumotos are absolutely fabulous with this color scheme."

"Matsumoto? Sounds like a Japanese sushi bar," Carl says.

"They actually belong to the Chinese Aster group, and come in purple, pink or white varieties with a yellow center."

"Oh, okay. We'll look those up, thank you," Melissa says.

"We also offer package deals, which include tablecloths, napkins, chair covers, and runners in both of these colors if you decide to go with this option," the clerk says.

"Okay, we'll come back after we've talked more about it," Melissa replies.

"That's absolutely fine. Let me give you our catalogue so you can page through it." The clerk walks over to the counter and hands them a catalogue from the stack.

"Thank you for all your help," Melissa adds. They give the clerk one last wave before exiting the store and heading back to the car. Melissa holds her phone up in front of Carl's face as soon as they get inside.

"Here are those Matsumotos he was talking about. I kinda like them." Carl glances at the image but notices the cost in much greater detail rather than the appearance of the flower.

"They're two hundred bucks?"

"Don't be cheap on our wedding," Melissa retracts her phone and continues scrolling down the page.

"I have lavender that comes up every year. We can use that," Carl says. Melissa lowers her phone and gives him a long look.

"Was that a joke?" Carl hesitates before responding.

"They're purple."

"Unacceptable," Melissa says before returning her full attention back to her screen.

Later that afternoon, Caleb is leaning heavily on his cane while limping down his walkway towards the mailboxes at the curb. The bright sun glistening off the snowy mounds give a misleading sign of a warm day, but the temperature gauge is closer to the truth with its needle pointing to five. Caleb braves the icy air with a fisherman sweater and a pair of jeans with lounge pants hiding underneath. He retrieves his small stack of mail and then shuts the plastic door.

The park across the street is a vast deserted plot of snow and ice with even the hills void of excited sledders. In the distance gray clouds signify a possible snowstorm and another cold night. Caleb shivers and then turns back to walk back inside. He shuts the door and locks it before skimming through the envelops in his hand. "Junk, junk, bank statement, bill—" he says as he goes through his pile, but the next envelope he studies more in depth. It's a light blue envelope with a floral pattern on the front and the names, Carl & Melissa are listed on the gold embossed return label. He turns it over and reads the words *Save the Date*, on the flap. He keeps his eyes on the envelope for a long moment before gently setting the entire stack on the foyer table without opening any of them.

"Aren't you going to open it?" a voice says. Caleb looks up startled to see a blond-haired girl, about his age, standing in the hallway just ahead of him.

"Who are you? What are you doing in my house?"

"Don't you remember me?" the girl asks.

"How would I know you? You just broke into my house." The girl laughs.

"I'm not a stranger."

"How did you get in here so quick? I just went to get the mail."

"I hear getting the mail is the only time you do leave."

"You don't know anything about me."

"Yes, I do Caleb. I can't believe you've forgotten me. Think back when you were eight. I lived next door to you."

"I don't think much about the past anymore."

"Remember when that tree was cut down in the woods? You tried to make a fort from it. You even invited me over for tea." Caleb drops his eyes to the floor to recall the memory. There was a wooded area in between their homes. The city cut down some of the older trees to eliminate the risk of them falling and potentially causing damage. Most of the trunk and large branches were mulched up, but the rest was left to decompose. Caleb attempted to build a fort from the remaining branches and sticks but gave up after starting three walls. There's only one other person who would know this too.

"Jessica?"

"Hello, old friend," Jessica says with a smile.

"How did you find me?"

"I just answered the call."

"What call?"

"The call to save a life." Jessica holds out her hand and waits for Caleb to finally take it. "C'mon, let's go down memory lane."

Caleb's surroundings become blurred, and a sensation of rushing forward is felt despite his legs remaining firmly in place. Caleb soon discovers he's no longer in his foyer, but in a front yard next to a Dogwood tree. Caleb inspects his surroundings before turning to Jessica beside him.

"This is where I grew up. I almost forgot what it looked like."

"We used to climb this tree," Jessica says as she lays her hand on the trunk of the Dogwood. "I remember you fell flat on your back six feet up," She continues while looking up. "It scared me half to death, but you got up like it was nothing and climbed the tree again. You weren't afraid of anything in those days."

"Many things were different in those days."

"There's no way to stop change. You just find a way to welcome it." Caleb gives Jessica mournful look before lowering his eyes.

"I didn't know you died." Jessica gives him a bewildered glance.

"What makes you think I'm dead?"

"Because you are here. How can you still be alive and use these superpowers?" Jessica chuckles at Caleb's assumption.

"Superpowers, really? Don't make me sound like one of the Avengers. I'm more of Jessica's essence, everything she is, everything she knows, everything she thinks, and everything she would say. The real, flesh and bone, Jessica is home with her family and doing very well, if you must know."

"So, you aren't real," Caleb replies while slowly extending his finger toward her cheek. She swiftly slaps his hand away making him cry out after feeling the lingering sting.

"Of course, I'm real! I'm just a temporary copy, that's all."

"Why is this happening to me?" Caleb says softly.

"Why does anything happen? Chemical reactions, collision of forces, cause, and effect. The physical and the spiritual exist on different planes, but every once in a while, they cross and interact." Caleb looks up the tree with the sun shining through the foliage. There is a peacefulness that his younger self remembers basking in, but as an adult it all seems like a lifetime ago. Caleb has forgotten his childhood and really has no intention of recalling it now, but Jessica has other plans for Caleb and what memories she will force him to relive.

"Do you want to climb the tree again?" Jessica says with some excitement. Caleb shakes his head and returns his gaze to the ground.

"I can't anymore. Not with my legs the way they are."

"You use your disability as an excuse to stop living."

"My legs were crushed, Jessica."

"I know what happened, Caleb. Stop thinking about your misfortunes and consider your blessings. How many people would trade in their wheelchairs for your cane?" Caleb takes a few slow steps away from her. He ignores her question as he's too focused on his own short comings to care where others stand around him. His thoughts primarily, and immediately go to self-pity.

"Why did it have to be me? Why couldn't it be someone else?" Caleb asks after pondering his misfortunes.

"Would you wish what happened to you on someone else?" Jessica responds a little disappointed. Caleb doesn't want to admit right out that he does, but a part of him knows that is not completely true. After a short moment he fails to find which emotion is stronger.

"I don't know."

"You do have some degree of control over your own life, Caleb." He gazes at Jessica admirably. Her smile fills him with a warmth he had not felt for a long time. He always hoped she would stay by his side; he was sure they were meant for each other. In some way she makes him feel like a kid again; with all the wonder the world has to offer, yet to come. An endless land of adventure, treasure, and mysteries to solve. Anything is possible in the mind of a child, but as an adult so many days feel the same. The world becomes darker and smaller; this is especially true for Caleb; his world has been reduced to 1200 sq. ft.

Jessica holds out her hand again. He feels his hand in hers as she closers her fingers around his. Caleb observes a few moments of motion blur, before he and Jessica appear on a woodland trail

"We used to spend the whole day here." Jessica says looking around. Caleb remembers this wooded area between their homes.

"We caught caterpillars," Caleb reminisces. Jessica giggles.

"That's right, you remember." Jessica begins walking down the trail while holding Caleb's hand. "The summer days seemed like they lasted forever," she continued.

"We were never too tired to go to bed, never too hungry to go to supper, never too cold to go inside." Caleb allows Jessica to pull him along the path until she stops.

"Here it is." In the clearing ahead of them is Caleb's makeshift fort he once attempted to build. The walls are constructed of mixed logs, branches, and leaves, both from the felled tree and those from around the area. With only three walls and no roof, it was quite an achievement for an eight-year-old. Caleb advances in the middle of the fort and sits on one of the two stumps that are inside. Jessica follows him and sits on the other one. He admires the partial construction before coming to his conclusion.

"It's not very well built."

"No, you weren't exactly an architect," Jessica laughs. "You just wanted to build it."

"For you. This was supposed to be ours." Jessica smiles at the memory Caleb turned up.

"Oh yeah. This is where you proposed to me. Of course, you didn't know what that meant."

"Your parents let us camp here in their tent."

"And we read ghost stories all night so we couldn't sleep."

Caleb pushes the tip if his cane to draw a series of lines in the soft dirt while thinking to himself.

"And then you left."

"We moved," Jessica confirms. "My dad found another job. We had to go." Caleb continues writing random shapes in the dirt.

"You said you would visit, but you never came back. You just forgot about me."

"I never forgot about you, but there was no way for me to communicate that with you."

"You were my best friend, Jessica. After you left, I had nobody."

"You know it wasn't my choice."

"The past that once was a blanket is now a dagger," Caleb lifts himself back to his feet. "You can take me back now." Jessica stands up and puts her hand on his shoulder to direct him towards her. She then reaches into her pocket and takes out a small flower pressed in plastic before handing it to him.

"Memories never fade completely away," she whispers. Caleb holds the flower in his open palm. "You gave that to me before I left," she says. "I still have it."

"You still have this?" Caleb says while making eye contact. She smiles and nods as he admires the flower further. "It still holds its shape too."

"It's preserved. I gave you something too. Do you remember what it was?" Caleb thinks for a moment and then nods.

"It was an oak leaf." Jessica giggles.

"I didn't know what else to give to a boy." Caleb draws his eyes into hers and extends the flower back to her.

"How would have things turned out if we grew older together?"

"You mean would we have dated?" Jessica questions while reclaiming her flower.

"Would we have?"

"I don't know, but that wasn't meant for us. We were only meant to cross each other's paths for a moment, and when the time came, we went in different directions.

"I wished that was not so."

"Wishing things were different is okay, but refusing to move forward because of them, isn't."

"Now an image of you fades back into my life."

"Why didn't you look me up? Now with Facebook you could have."

"I thought about it, but I was afraid I might find you. You were gone and there was no reason to bring you back."

"No matter what separated us or came in between us. You will always be my friend, Caleb."

"Things are never the same the second time around. What worked once is somehow different when replicated."

"C'mon, there is one last place I need to take you," Jessica says. She takes his arm and the two fade from the woods and then appears on the breakwater next to a sandy beach.

"Do you remember this place?"

"Yeah, this is where we came to swim," Caleb recalls.

"Look, Caleb." Jessica points to their younger selves as they climb on the rocks just ahead. The waves splash over the top of the rocks and then empties back into the water. The slippery rocks cause young Jessica to slip and fall to her stomach. When another wave crashes against the rocks, it washes over Jessica and then recedes with her in toe. The waves pull her out and under before slamming her against the rocks again. She struggles to keep her head above water and yells for help. Young Caleb hurries down towards her as she desperately reaches for him.

"I remember this," Caleb says watching the moment play out. Young Caleb extends his arm out as far he can, but the waves take her away from his reach and submerge her again. Caleb leaves the safely of his position and jumps into the water. He puts his arms around her and pushes her onto the rocks until she finds her footing and climbs out of the water. Suddenly, another wave collides into Caleb and throws him hard against the rocks. He lets out a painful cry before Jessica pulls him up and the two crawl to the top.

"You saved me that day, but the outcome was having your ankle wrapped up for three weeks," Jessica says.

"I sprained it when that last wave hit me," Caleb nods.

"Did you ever regret saving me?" Caleb looks at her stunned with the unthinkable question she dared to ask.

"Of course, not. Why would you ask that?"

"Because life isn't perfect. Things happen, Caleb. Sometimes we have a chance to act and sometimes we do not." Caleb looks down at his leg before looking back up.

"This time my scars won't heal."

"Scars are a sign that the body has healed the best it can." Caleb remains silent for a moment and then glances at Jessica.

"It was nice seeing you again, Jessica."

"You should go to your brother's wedding," she says smiling.

"He doesn't need me there."

"*You* need to be there. Step out of your hiding place."

"I'll think about it."

"I remember that phrase. That's your way of politely saying no. But that's okay. There's still time."

"How many of these experiences will I have?"

"I don't know that answer, but the time has come to say goodbye once again." Caleb feels weightless and his vision begins to blur. "Oh, and one last thing, take a walk in the park on New Year's Day," Jessica says before her image completely blends into the white of the surrounding area. Caleb doesn't get a chance to question her last words to him before he finds himself back in his foyer and Jessica, is once again, only a memory.

Caleb wonders if maybe these occurrences are just hallucinations. Perhaps his mind is suffering from a new ailment with bouts of blacking out. He may not really be talking to anyone or going anywhere after all. He glances at the mail he had placed on the foyer table and notices a folded piece of paper resting on top of Carl's letter. He picks it up and slowly unfolds it.

Take a walk in the park on New Year's Day.

Another unexplainable note that demands Caleb to rethink the belief that there are no reasons behind these visitations.

He stands in front of the foyer table for a few more moments before finally opening the top drawer. On one side of the drawer is a carefully placed oak leaf pressed in plastic. He studies it for a while but refuses to pick it up. He then gently closes the drawer again. Like most of his memories, he finds it best to hide them from view.

While Caleb is left with replaying the latest events, Melissa is visiting Carrie with a handful of wedding catalogs and magazines tucked underneath her arm. Neither of the girls grew up with a sister, so the opportunity to meet up and talk about fashion and the upcoming wedding over a bottle of Moscato brings a new level of elation to them. Melissa begins questioning about Carrie dating again, but her reply turns the focus back towards Melissa, "let's just focus on you getting married first."

Tommy's father wasn't a bad man—he just wasn't a family man. He enjoyed his time, his friends, and his plans too much to compromise. It may have been a mutual decision to call off their engagement, but Carrie had to endure her parents' embarrassment of having an unmarried, pregnant daughter. Her brothers; however, refused to abandon her and took every step needed to ensure she and Tommy was well cared for. Five years later their family bonds were challenged again with a mournful loss and a brother who alienated himself.

Melissa turns one of her catalogs to her desired page and then hands the open book to Carrie.

"This is going to be my wedding dress." Carries sets down her wine glass and admires the white dress and veil.

"That is gorgeous, Mel." Melissa picks up another catalog and flips through it.

"This is where we are renting Carl's tux and everything all the guys will need."

"What's he wearing?"

"I think he's leaning towards a tailcoat."

"He was always difficult when it came to dressing up." Carrie says as she skims through the pages of tuxedos. Melissa grins and hands the cornflower and ivory fabric samples to Carrie.

"We also decided on this cornflower and ivory color scheme." Carrie takes the samples and fans them out in her hand.

"Oh, this is beautiful."

"Carl doesn't understand how flowers can be so expensive, so we haven't decided on those yet," Melissa admits.

"That sounds like him. Did he try to nominate the flowers in his garden yet?"

"Yes!" Melissa answers in an elevated tone while laughing. "If it was up to him our wedding flowers would be lavender and ornamental grass." Carrie and Melissa share in a long laugh.

"Good ol' Carl," Carrie replies.

"He doesn't believe anything that grows in the wild should cost that much."

"But wedding flowers aren't just randomly picked in some forest or meadow."

"That's what I tried telling him. They are specially grown and cared for."

"I would just pick the flowers you like, dear; because to him they all will look like daisies."

"Well, the clerk at the fabric shop made a suggestion that I did like." Melissa scrolls through her saved pictures on her phone and then hands it to Carrie. She studies the Matsumotos shown on the screen and then holds the phone next to the fabric samples.

"Yes, Melissa. Go with these." Melissa accepts her phone back and finishes her glass of wine before working up the nerve to ask her next question.

"There's something else I wanted to ask you. Do you know Caleb's size? Carl doesn't."

"Does Carl still think Caleb will show?" Carrie responds in a hushed tone, even though no one is nearby to eavesdrop.

"I think he's planning on paying him another visit."

"I love Caleb, but he's stubborn. I don't even know if he's the same size anymore." Melissa lowers her eyes in disappointment, but Carrie decides to lift the men's catalogue back up. "What will he need?" Melissa smiles and begins listing the required articles of clothing and accessories Caleb will need. Carrie jots down the approximate sizes she thinks may still apply to her brother near each item.

Later that night, Caleb is watching TV in his recliner when the doorbell chimes. Caleb picks up the remote and mutes the TV before directing his gaze towards the front door. He hesitates for a moment, but then stands up with the aid of his cane.

"The ghosts ring doorbells now?" he questions out loud as he makes his way into the foyer. Carl walks in with his arms full of clothes almost as soon as Caleb opens the doors.

"I know it's a little late, but I saw the light was on. Were you sleeping?"

"No, I was just watching some nature show," Caleb replies, but can't help noticing everything Carl has just brought over. "What's all this?"

"If you decide to come to the wedding, here's everything you will need to wear. I hope it all fits, but if not, let me know." Carl sets the clothes down on the foyer table. "I'll also keep the spot for best man open until the wedding day. That is, if you want it." Carl slides his arms out from underneath the clothes and accidentally knocks the pile of Caleb's mail to the floor. "Oops, sorry." Carl bends over to pick up the mail.

"No, it's alright, I can get it." Caleb quickly announces with his hand out hoping to stop Carl before he lifts the envelopes. Carl picks up the pieces of mail and notices his, *save the date*, notice. He slowly flips it over to see it's still sealed. He carefully places the mail back on the table in a neat pile.

"I was going to look at everything tonight," Caleb says in a soft voice.

"Nah, it's okay," Carl responds with a shake of his head. He's trying to appear as if he's unfazed by the discovery, but Caleb knows this isn't the case.

"I actually haven't looked at any of my mail yet."

"It's no big deal, Caleb."

"It's just that things have been a little odd lately," Caleb says trying to find an excuse to make Carl feel better.

"You don't need to explain, Caleb." Carl glances back at the door. "Look, I gotta run. There's a lot we need to do in the morning," he continues and then steps outside.

"Carl, wait—" Caleb calls after him but he continues walking to his car. Caleb watches him get in and then drive away without ever looking back.

Caleb gently shuts the door. He remains standing in the entryway for a moment before slamming his fist into the wall. He swings his cane at the chair and then brings the cane down on top of the banister with both of his hands. He loses his balance and falls back against the wall. Caleb returns the cane back to his side to prevent him from falling over. He's angry at himself for letting Carl leave in his condition. He can tell his feelings were hurt and that he was doing his best to hide it, but there's nothing Caleb can think of that would make it right. Carl's grief, and knowing that he caused it, burdens him, but telling him that the spirit of their grandfather and a copy of Jessica had visited him recently, couldn't possibly make the situation any better.

3

Past and Future

Shortly after two in the morning the furnace kicks in and warm air begins to swarm around Caleb's bed. He's used to the sounds of his home, but tonight one sound, in particular, has never before echoed through his halls. It begins as a soft tapping while keeping a steady pace. Caleb opens his eyes and listens. As the sounds become louder it becomes clear they are made from a pair of high heels walking on the hardwood floor of the hallway just outside his room.

"Who's there?" Caleb cries out in the darkness. No answer, but the high heeled footsteps continue to advance. "Go back to your coffin and leave me alone," Caleb yells and then pulls the covers over his head. Caleb believes whoever is walking has just entered his room. The footsteps stop and he remains still while listening to the temporary silence. Just then the bedroom light turns on and his covers are yanked down from his face. A beautiful woman named; Miss. Di Cocco is now standing at his bedside.

"Now, is that any way to greet your teacher?" she says.

Miss. Di Cocco was Caleb's third-grade teacher. To him

she was the epitome of beauty, gentleness, and compassion. She always smelled like roses and vanilla caught in a warm summer breeze, and her voice was like a lullaby. She was a patient soul who had left an everlasting impression on Caleb that resonated with him throughout the years. He wasn't the only third grader who loved his teacher, but he was the only one who was *in love* with his teacher. No one had, or since, spent so much of their time and energy to ensure his success. At the very base of it was the feeling of being completely cared for and the knowledge that it was real. What a cruelty to make the two meet at such extreme age gaps. Just as with Jessica, Caleb feels at ease and once again filled with a childlike innocence.

"Miss. Di Cocco? Are you dead?" Caleb asks.

"No, I'm not dead."

"When will these visitations stop? I'm beginning to question my sanity."

"They will stop when they are meant to stop." Miss. Di Cocco says while handing him his robe.

"Time to get out of bed, Caleb. I have to take you someplace you don't want to go." Caleb takes his robe and then slides his feet into his slippers. He then accepts his cane being handed to him and stands to his feet.

"Where must we go now?" Caleb questions.

"To a place you have been, but never seen." Miss. Di Cocco puts her arm inside his and guides him to the doorway, but instead of walking into the hallway they step onto a snowy intersection on a chilly afternoon. Caleb takes in his surroundings trying to place where he is. It isn't until he notices his former car slowly coming to a stop at a red light that he makes the connection. This is the past, and not just some random moment in his past. This is the worst moment of his entire life. He immediately becomes filled with dread as he observes himself stopped in the left lane.

"You're right; I don't want to be here. Take me back." Caleb orders.

"Not yet," Miss Di Cocco responds.

He remembers looking into the rear-view mirror and seeing Tommy smiling in the backseat, but he doesn't want to relive this moment.

"Please, can we leave now?!" Caleb begs with utmost urgency.

"Avoiding something doesn't make it go away."

"I don't need to see this!" Caleb becomes agitated and nervous when he focuses his attention back to Miss. Di Cocco. He feels trapped and unable to escape, as if drowning in a dream.

"Look at the car in the right lane," Miss Di Cocco tells him. "You don't know them. You never saw them. You never met them, but this day, your destinies have become intertwined."

Another car rolls to a slow stop to the right of Caleb's car. Inside are two young girls, one about six and the other about nine, along with their pregnant mother. Caleb never looked over to see who stopped near him and remains focused on the traffic light. Most times no one ever notices who is beside or behind them. The car becomes an inanimate object, a machine taking up a certain amount of space, how many times does one think about the person inside?

The streetlight turns green, and Caleb's car begins accelerating forward.

"No. No! Don't go!" Caleb yells. He begins limping towards his car as fast as his legs will allow it.

"Caleb, get back here. You can't do anything. This is just a replay." Miss. Di Cocco reminds him, but he ignores her and continues.

"Wait, go back! Stop," he continues shouting, but his car takes a small lead ahead of the car that was stopped beside him.

"STOP!" Caleb yells and wishes he could run faster.

The sound of screeching tires enters his ears. He hopes to change the outcome of this moment with every fiber of his being. With all his waving motions and hollering he knows deep down he is helpless in the prevention of what is about to occur. No one can see him and nothing he does will stop something that has already happened.

"Don't drive!"

A red pickup truck slides through the intersection before crashing into Caleb's car. His car flips onto its side and then upside down before coming around and landing back on the tires.

Caleb yells at the top of his lungs while falling to his knees. He continues crying out until he runs out of air. With his head lowered, he stares at the road, in front of his nose, while breathing heavily. Miss. Di Cocco approaches and squats down beside him.

"If it wasn't you, it would have been them."

The pregnant woman gets out of her car and hurries over to Caleb's car while her daughters watch from their windows.

"What made that family better than mine?" Caleb says still looking at the ground. There is a sharp pain in his throat as if it is filled with needles. There is a tightness in his chest and pain around his heart, but he still refuses to sob. Blinding anger is easier to understand and is preferred over immobilizing sorrow. This is how Caleb copes.

"Not better. Is that how you think? Three lives and an unborn child were saved. Isn't that something worth caring about?

"I don't care about anything anymore," he responds softly.

"I know that's not true." Miss. Di Cocco gently places her fingers under his chin and guides his head up. "Look, Caleb. You never saw this."

Other drivers begin to gather around Caleb's mangled car. The pregnant woman drapes a cover around an unconscious Caleb through his broken window. She then opens the back door and sobs as she wipes the blood from Tommy's head.

"Why did it have to be Tommy?"

"These events seldom collide with escaping criminals. They happen to the unsuspecting. Good people who are almost home or sometimes farther away." Caleb puts all his weight on his cane and pulls himself up with the help of Miss. Di Cocco's arms. "You never came back to this spot after the accident. You would have seen Tommy's cross."

In one area of the medium is a small wooden cross surrounded with dozens of flowers, and a picture of Tommy is in the center.

"The family who was beside you contributed these flowers. Tommy's sacrifice did not escape them. The whole community felt sorrow over this incident, but you've been trying to convince yourself it never happened."

"It was the pickup's fault."

"Bad brakes and black ice."

"Don't make excuses for him. He was going too fast and cared not of the red light in front of him. I know his type. Always trying to get one car ahead and still going nowhere. Trying to dart ahead on an ending lane with no regard of who is already in the correct one. Trying to save a second makes everyone lose a minute who trails him. Taking unnecessary risks with flawed logic and no fear of consequences."

"He received his punishment, and the knowledge that his actions took the life of a small child. I can assure you his choice still haunts him."

"My whole life was torn apart, and Tommy was robbed the opportunity to grow up!"

"Stop thinking about Tommy as a victim and more of a hero."

"He trusted me to keep him safe."

"It wasn't your fault, Caleb."

"I should have looked twice. Maybe never have left home that day. I don't know."

"Don't look at ways to change the past. Only look for ways to understand it."

"You don't know what it's like! This didn't happen to you. You don't get to have an opinion on this. I hate this cane. I hate this fucking cane!"

Caleb hits his cane against the road several times with all his strength before hurling it away from him. With his support now missing his knees buckle and he collapses to the pavement. Caleb makes himself the bigger victim in hopes that it takes his mind away from Tommy.

"You check that temper right now," Miss. Di Cocco scolds him. She takes it upon herself to retrieve Caleb's cane and then returns to him. "This cane is not the source of your melancholy. It is your deflection." Miss. Di Cocco extends her hand. "Give me your hand." Caleb inhales and exhales several times trying to calm down before he takes her hand. She lifts him up and allows him to grab his cane. "Do you think you are broken because your legs are not what they used to be? That your life no longer has any value? There are open arms waiting for you, Caleb, but you're always going in the opposite direction."

"What do you want from me?" Caleb says softly.

"I have always wanted the best for you."

Caleb feels ashamed for lashing out at Miss. Di Cocco like he did. Now as an adult she's still there to help him up, and her soothing touch is more longed for now than ever before. It's not due to infatuation, but the sensation of being in the warm embrace of someone who deeply cares about him. Caleb has managed to push everyone away, but Miss. Di Cocco is always willing to forgive his outbursts.

"When you were in my class, I knew you were a good kid, but you thought acting out was the only way to get attention. Sometimes we need to be reminded who we really are underneath it all."

"I'm sorry I lashed out at you," Caleb says. Miss. Di Cocco smiles and puts her arm around his shoulder.

"There's one more place to go."

Before his very eyes, the intersection transitions into the park that's across the street from Caleb's home. The nightly bitter cold wind of winter blows the freshly fallen snow across the field and the swirling flurries glimmer as they pass the amber light of the lampposts that line the park's path.

"You used to walk here," Miss. Di Cocco says.

"That was a lifetime ago. Nowadays this park is nothing more than a deserted frozen tundra."

"Not completely deserted." Miss. Di Cocco turns to face behind them as she guides Caleb's arm to silently instruct him to follow her gaze. In front of them is a fifteen-year-old girl curled up on a park bench. She's shivering but still tries to sleep with only a light windbreaker for a blanket.

"Who is she?" Caleb asks.

"No one knows."

"What do you mean, no one knows?"

"If you were to pass her under normal circumstances, would you care who she was? Would it matter why she's here, or what her name is? Would you offer any help at all, or would you just keep walking?

"She's just a child."

"You didn't answer the question. Would you think about her later when you crawl into your nice warm bed with the flannel quilt?"

"I don't know her."

"She will be dead before morning. If this was your chance to save a life, would you?"

"How can I reach out to someone I don't know?"

"I can't believe I just heard that. Are you saying a life unknown has less value?"

"That's not what I meant."

"Not many knew Tommy, but that didn't stop them from attending his funeral; to acknowledge a life cut short."

"That's different."

"How is that different?"

"She's homeless."

"Maybe she left home or maybe her home left her. Does she deserve to die on a park bench alone?"

"It's not my job. What do you want me to do?"

"I first showed you a past event. One you cannot change, but she is here right now." The girl coughs several times and holds her arms tightly around her chest while shivering with her eyes still closed.

"Is she really going to die?" Caleb asks showing concern.

"If she does not receive help, yes, she will freeze to death. What you do from here is up to you. Who are you, Caleb?"

"I used to be a good person. I once wanted to marry and have a family of my own. Now I'm a hollow shell."

"You can still be that person."

"It's too late now. I cannot see beauty anymore. Nothing amazes me. Nothing impresses me. I see the same walls and hear only my own footsteps day in and day out. I'm too old to have hope for a future."

"You're only thirty-four, Caleb; and it's never too late to save a life. Yours included."

"How can I save her?"

"To save her will require you to leave the familiarity of your home. Can you do that?"

"How do I know this isn't just a dream?"

"There is only one way, but is it worth your time to find out?"

"That's not an answer."

"As an educator my job is not to tell you the answers, but to show you where to find them."

"So where should I look?"

"Inside yourself."

"Typical answer," Caleb sighs, but Miss. Di Cocco only smiles.

"Find Tommy's gift," she says as the park scene begins to fade.

"Where is it?" She remains smiling until Caleb's surrounding morphs back into his bedroom. Yet another experience has ended, and he's once again alone in his room. When he glances at his pillow, he discovers a note had been gently placed and folded with care. He unfolds it to reveal the dainty handwriting that says:

Find Tommy's gift.

Caleb stands in his room silently contemplating his next action. It only takes a glance outside his window and seeing the falling flurries to motivate him to descend the staircase.

He opens the coat closet and tugs on the sleeve of one of the winter coats. He hesitates again before looking out the window near the front door. It's the middle of the night, who goes for a stroll in the early morning freezing temperature of a Wisconsin winter? Maybe that girl won't even be there. What's stopping Caleb from forgetting this whole thing and just going back to bed? After a sigh, he pulls the coat off the hanger and then slides his arms through and zips it up. He then grabs another one and drapes it over his arm. He opens the front door and walks outside with his cane in hand.   The next morning, the girl on the park bench, awakes to find she's wearing more than she was the day before. She touches her head and feels the hat on her head. She looks at her hands and see they had been slid into warm gloves. She also discovers Caleb's coat draped over her like a blanket. She immediately puts the coat on and then puts her hands in the pockets. She slowly lifts one of them back out to find three twenty-dollar bills. She smiles and begins running out of the park.

Meanwhile, across town, there's a small café that offers a welcoming relief for Carl and Melissa after their long day of running errands. They each have ordered the largest coffee available and split an eclair that dwarfs many other pastries at most bakeries. Carl watches the flurries starting to make an appearance, while Melissa jots notes in her floral-pattern wedding notebook.

"We should get home before the roads get bad," Carl says, already worried at the first hint of snow. Melissa glances up from her writing and then shakes her head.

"That's not going to accumulate, hon."

"You called me hon?" Caleb says shyly.

"Yeah, I did," she replies with a smirk. Carl enjoys his coffee and a few bites of his portion of the eclair.

"Did we get everything done?" Carl asks. Melissa turns a

page back and then skims through her lists.

"Let's see, we picked out the cake and planned the color scheme. We still need to get you fitted for a tux, but we can do that tomorrow. We reserved the banquet hall, but we still need to decide on the meal. I think we should do this next." Melissa circles the item and then looks up to notice Carl gazing at her with a slight smile.

"What—" she asks, but Carl just shakes his head.

"Nothing, I just can't stop looking at you," he admits.

"Well, you are going to see a lot more of me in a few months."

"A lot more?" Melissa smirks knowing his reference.

"Yes, a lot more," she agrees with a giggle.

A car suddenly screeches to a halt at the stop light just outside the café. Someone may have second guessed the amount of time they had to make it through the intersection, or noticed the red light too late, either way this event ends without an incident; however, the sound directs Carl's attention to the scene and remains fixated outside. He remembers seeing Caleb's mangled car as the events from that day replay in his head.

"Carl?" Melissa says when noticing his zoned-out expression. Her voice reaches him as a distant whisper and fails to snap him out of his trance-like state. She calls his name again, but still doesn't get his attention. She lays her hand on top of his and tries again. "Carl?" He finally snaps out of his pensiveness and directs his focus back to Melissa. "Are you okay?" she asks concerned.

"I'm sorry," he says while massaging her hand with his thumb. "Caleb's accident just came back to me." He becomes lost in the moment again and drops his eyes to the surface of the table before continuing. "I had to be the one who told him that Tommy didn't make it—"

Caleb has his leg in a cast and a bandage around his head when he begins to stir in the hospital bed. Carl stands up from the bedside chair and leans over him.

"Caleb?" he says softly. Caleb slowly opens his eyes and takes a moment to look around with confusion.

"Where am I? What happened?"

"You were in a car accident." Caleb remains silent trying to recall his last memory. The details surrounding that moment are hazy, but he does remember stopping at a red light. He also remembers glancing into the rear-view mirror and seeing Tommy giggling. He saw the light change to green and then his memory ends. Concern now turns to his nephew.

"Where's Tommy? Is he okay?" Carl holds back his tears as he slowly shakes his head.

"He hit his head. They said it was instant."

"What was?" Caleb asks fearing Carl's response. Tears swell up in Carl's eyes; he swallows and tries to answer without his voice cracking.

"Tommy couldn't be resuscitated. He's with God." Caleb blankly stares at Carl without any indication of an emotion or feeling. No reaction of any kind comes over him. No reply is made.

Carl finishes explaining the moment to Melissa.

"I never saw a single tear. Not that day, not since that day," Carl continues. "I remember seeing just a blank stare, and then nothing. He wasn't there anymore. I was looking at a man who became a shell. He just disappeared."

"Oh-my-God," Melissa says. "You're right; he did shut down and then shut everyone out. I feel so sorry for him."

"He buried Tommy in his own way—out of his memory."

"I wish we could help him."

"When he didn't show up at the funeral, we took it as an insult. We didn't know how serious his condition was. We ostracized him. We let him build his own prison. We may have even locked his cage."

"I think it's time everyone stops blaming themselves. You miss him and Carrie misses him. We all could go over there and talk to him."

"I don't think an intervention is going to work in his case. He's just going to shy away from us." Carl pauses and adverts his eyes outside. "What hope does a broken man have who lost his faith?" Melissa squeezes his hand to bring his focus back on her.

"The lost and broken are first to receive God's loving embrace."

Carl and Melissa stand up and put on their coats. The flurries have stopped, but a Wisconsin winter's forecast can never be trusted. An overnight report can call for ten inches and only becomes one, while a zero chance of snow can become a blizzard.

That evening, Caleb is sitting at the kitchen table with a piece of toast on his plate. His meals are usually easy to make and something he can't mess up. Toast and eggs, grilled cheese, spaghetti, Swedish meatballs, and macaroni and cheese are his staples. Caleb looks down at his single piece of toast and becomes caught in a sudden daydream.

It is a time when his home was decorated with a plethora of Christmas string lights. The sealed-up memory escapes through his defenses and rushes into his thoughts. Tommy excitedly walks in through the front door and becomes amazed at the fully lit hallway and living room.

Caleb quickly blinks and shakes his head to push the unwanted thought back into submission. He has attuned himself to a dull surrounding and any kind of change fills him with an uneasy feeling. He turns his attention back to his piece of toast, but a woman's voice disturbs him before he can take his first bite.

"How long are you going to sit there?" Caleb jolts his head up to find his ex-girlfriend standing with folded arms just before the kitchen.

"Christy?" Caleb asks with surprise. Christina unfolds her arms and advances toward the table.

"Can I sit down?"

"I suppose," he replies, not sure if he can refuse her request.

"The house looks good," she begins after taking her seat. "Not as colorful as I remembered it, but at least you can keep it clean," she says while glancing around.

"You are an essence of Christina, aren't you?"

"I am," she confirms. Caleb nods with acceptance.

"I knew the real you would never come back." She ignores his comment and continues with her question.

"Is this how you spend your days now? Living off disability in your slippers, and eating toast and jam?"

"What does it matter how I spend my days?"

"Don't take that tone with me."

"You don't care about me anymore. Why are you here?"

"You just want to be hated by everyone so you can continue feeling sorry for yourself."

"I don't care what people think about me."

"Where are all your lights, Caleb?"

"I don't need to be questioned by an apparition."

"In this crypt there are many ghosts, but they're all yours." Caleb sighs and lets a moment of silence pass.

"There's no one to see the lights anymore."

"Tommy loved your lights. Maybe if you put them up, he will see them."

"Christmas is over anyway." Christina remains focused on Caleb, but he pretends not to notice her gaze.

"Just because someone leaves your life doesn't mean they didn't play a part in it," she says. Caleb turns to glare at her.

"Are you talking about Tommy or yourself?"

"We both had a part in your life, did we not?"

"Yeah, but you left by choice."

"I left because you were too complex for me. I knew I couldn't be the woman you needed."

"That's what everyone else did too."

"Don't start that."

"What do you expect? You can't just walk back into my life after abandoning me."

"I felt you drift farther and farther away from me. I thought some time away might help us both, but then I didn't know how to come back."

"My dream always included you. Weekend cookouts with the family and late-night movies when it was just us. What was wrong with that?"

"It was your dream. Mine was to leave Wisconsin, and I knew I could not beg you to follow. We were in the same book, but always on different pages."

"I could have followed you."

"But then you couldn't be who you are.

"Some people ask for everything. I ask for the bare minimum, and it gets ripped out of my hands," Caleb says with frustration.

"Our paths crossed for a moment in our lives, but it was always meant to go in different directions."

"Is that all I was to you? A passing moment?"

"Don't twist my words around." Caleb sighs and ponders his next question.

"So, where are you living now?"

"New York." Caleb lets a retired laugh exit his lips while nodding his head.

"You knew my career was going to lead me away." Caleb stands up from the table without a word and grabs his cane to help him to the sink. Christina stands up and follows to meet him.

"You need to move on too. Do you like being alone?"

"You never like it, but you do get used to it."

"I'm sorry it didn't work out between us, but your dreams are still ahead of you."

"I've forgotten how to be a part of this world."

"Look," Christina says while pointing back to his chair.

Sitting at the table is an old man having a coughing fit.

"Is that me?"

"You are dying. In this cold, lonely house is where you will someday fall, and you won't be found for many days afterwards. You have been living in your own coffin, Caleb."

"I'm afraid of this future," he admits.

"It's not too late, Caleb. It doesn't have to be this way." Christina guides him to look into the living room. A future Caleb is handing presents out to a little boy and girl.

"Who are the children?"

"They are yours."

"I have a family?" The futuristic Caleb smiles as a pair of arms embrace him, but the identity of this person is hidden behind the corner of the wall.

"Who is she? I cannot see," he says as he stretches his neck to look.

"That's for you to find out, Caleb."

"How?"

"In order to find love, your mind must be brave enough to look for the answers your heart is asking." Caleb whiffs the air around him.

"What's that smell?"

"Honey baked ham."

"I can't remember the last time I've had honey baked ham."

"There's still a life here for you. Look outside."

It's a summer afternoon and the futuristic versions of Caleb, Carl, Carrie, and Melissa are in the backyard sitting at a picnic table with hamburgers and hot-dogs on a smoking grill."

"Isn't this your dream, Caleb? Summer cookouts?" Caleb points to Melissa, who he still has not met.

"Who's that woman?"

"Her name is Melissa. You haven't met her yet, but she will be your sister-in-law." Caleb admires the scene in front of him before shaking his head and turning away.

"These images are not real. Mere hallucinations," he says a little upset.

"They can be, but you must attend Carl's wedding, or the old man you first saw will be your fate."

"It's too late now. Carl will assume I won't be there. Even if I do show up, they will reject me."

"You created that lie. Let me show you the truth."

Christina takes hold of Caleb's arm as a blur effect forces him to shut his eyes and blink. When he reopens them, he finds them standing in a banquet hall instead of his kitchen.

Carl and Melissa are sitting at one of the tables while looking at a leather-bound menu; neither of them can see Christina or Caleb standing directly in front of them.

"We have a choice for two meats," Melissa begins.

"The beef looks good, but Caleb likes pork," Carl points out.

"Okay, so we can do one pork and one beef."

"Carl hates pork," Caleb says after hearing him. "Why would he have it at his own wedding just for me?"

"Despite everything, he still has hope you will make it," Christina reminds Caleb. Melissa and Carl continue their conversation with no knowledge that Caleb is observing.

"Did you ask Caleb about being the best man?" Melissa asks.

"I may have mentioned it, but I didn't wait for him to answer."

"I suppose we still have time."

"I have someone as a backup, but I want to give Caleb as much time as possible."

"I know," Melissa agrees.

"You are at a crossroads, Caleb," Christina begins. "What you do now will determine the rest of your life. You can have a family and be loved or be the old man who dies alone on his kitchen floor."

"How can going to Carl's wedding impact my entire future?"

"Haven't you learned anything yet?" Christina grins. "We know more than you." Caleb inhales and then exhales deeply. "I must return you home now, but before we depart, I leave you with my clue. Look for the symbol of the archer," Christina concludes.

"Why does everybody give me a riddle? I don't understand any of them."

"When the time is right, you will."

In that moment Caleb finds himself standing back in his kitchen without Christina. He sighs and puts a hand into his pocket and makes a dumbfounded look when his fingers brush against something. He curiously withdraws a folded piece of paper and then unfolds it to discover Christina's message:

Look for the symbol of the archer.

Caleb takes his time to advance to the pantry door to open it. On the inside panel of the door is a pinned cork board with all the previous messages he had received. Caleb tacks his newest clue in an orderly list just below Miss Di Cocco's. He may not know the meaning of these messages or why he's receiving them, but these occurrences cannot be ruled out as some bizarre coincidence. The fact that they are continuing to occur, hints they serve a greater purpose; even though it may seem like pure fantasy. He studies the board like a detective recalling the clues to an open case. One side of him wants to disregard everything he has experienced; this also includes these mysterious notes that seem to lack in any clear meaning, whatsoever. The other side of him; however, advises him not to ignore events that prove to be constant by pretending they are random.

4

The Girl

Tommy is ripping the wrapper off a present with enthusiasm as Carl and Caleb sit on either side of him. The gift is revealed to be a superhero puzzle and action figure set.

"Cool!" Tommy shouts and holds the puzzle up. "Can you help me put this together later?"

"Of course, I can," Carl agrees. Caleb hands Tommy another present.

"Here's one I ordered directly from Santa's website."

"Santa has a website?" Tommy asks surprised.

"Yeah, he takes orders all year 'round. You didn't know that?" Caleb says smiling.

"Ah, no, I didn't." Carrie, Caleb, and Carl laugh at his reaction.

"Everyone, get close," Carrie says while holding up her phone to snap a picture.

Carl and Caleb close around Tommy and all three smile just as the picture is taken. It will become Carrie's most cherished picture.

Caleb is rummaging through several totes on the top shelf of his coat closet when he uncovers one labeled, *Pictures*. He focuses on the small clear box for several moments debating if he really wants to look inside. He cradles it in his arms while tapping his fingers on top of the cover. He ultimately decides to place it back on the shelf without investigating the memories locked inside. He gently closes the door before letting his forehead lightly press against it. He closes his eyes and sighs to help him get over his recent discovery. A sudden tapping on the kitchen door leading to his backyard interrupts his thoughts. Most visitors usually go to the front door; who would go through his yard to arrive at the back? The rapping on the door continues again. Caleb cautiously strolls toward the door and peaks through the blinds to notice a man wearing a peacoat. He stands still and silent with both hands in his pockets and a good distance away from the door. It is no one that he recognizes, but he also wonders how someone can knock on his door without being near it.

Caleb gives in to his curiosities and opens the door. An unnatural fog creeps across the ground and around the man's feet. This must be another visitation experience, but unlike those before, this one is a stranger. Caleb navigates through the thickening haze as he carefully approaches the stranger who waits patiently for him to arrive.

"I don't know you," Caleb admits.

"No, you don't, but I know you. My name is Henry."

"How many more are to disturb me?"

"I don't know who came before or who will come after. I just know my part."

"And what would that be?"

"Let's go for a drive, Caleb."

Before Caleb can protest, he's suddenly sitting in the passenger seat with Henry driving. He snaps the seatbelt that's strapped across his chest and feels the rise and fall of the car traversing the hills of the road. Can this be an elaborate illusion; is he really riding in a car?

"It's been four years since you've been in a car, hasn't it?" Henry asks.

"The last time I had a bad experience," Caleb answers softly while gazing out his window at the snow-capped tree branches whizzing past his viewpoint.

"Will you ever drive again?"

"I don't think so."

"There are many things that defeat us, Caleb. But when we refuse to try again, we defeat ourselves."

"That might apply to forgetting your lines in a school play or having your manuscript turned down, but other things leave a deeper scar."

"A scar means an open wound has healed." Caleb lets the conversation end there as the next few moments are driven in silence. Henry pulls over to the side of the road and parks the car in front of a building. "Do you know this place?"

Caleb studies the complex before nodding his head. "It's an elderly home."

"It's a place for those who have no one to take care of them. Some have disabilities, some are ill, and some no longer have a home or a family." Henry turns off the engine and opens the car door.

"Why are we getting out here?" Caleb questions.

"Because we have reached our destination. There's someone here I want you to meet."

"Is it someone I know?" Caleb asks as he unbuckles his seatbelt and then opens the door.

"No, and he doesn't know you either."

"I don't know how this can possibly be relevant then." Caleb puts his cane in front of him and then steps onto the sidewalk.

"It's more relevant than you know," Henry replies, and then begins walking up the pathway towards the automatic double doors. Caleb sighs and reluctantly follows his guide.

The lobby is furnished with several loveseats and waiting chairs surrounding a crackling double-sided fireplace. Henry continues past the unmanned reception desk and then heads down one of the corridors. The room, at the end of the hallway, is a gathering place for the occupants to socialize and play boardgames or cards. Only a few tables are occupied at this time as Henry leads Caleb towards the windows where an elderly man sits quietly in his wheelchair while looking out.

"Good day, Oliver," Henry greets him when he gets close. Oliver spins his chair around and reveals the fact that he had lost one of his legs earlier. He appears to be overjoyed by his visitor and smiles wide to show a grin with three missing top teeth. He shakes Henry's hand energetically while chuckling.

"Henry, my boy. How are you?"

"Very good. Very good," Henry repeats, and then waves his hand towards Caleb. "I brought a friend with me today, this is Caleb." Oliver extends his hand out to Caleb and the two shake politely.

"Nice to meet you, Caleb."

"Likewise," he replies.

Henry brings two chairs over and places them facing Oliver.

"What happened to your leg, lad?" Oliver asks after observing Caleb's cane and his limp before taking his seat.

"Car accident," Caleb responds, but chooses not to go into any further details.

"I'm sorry to hear that," Oliver responds with empathy.

"Why don't you share one of your stories with Caleb," Henry suggests.

"My story began on the day I was born. My father said it was the champagne, my mother said it was the fireplace. In any case I was conceived in front of a roaring fire on New Year's Eve." Henry begins laughing, but Caleb keeps a relative straight face.

"You can skip ahead a little bit," Henry says chuckling. Oliver smiles his iconic partially toothless grin before continuing.

"If you insist. What is your earliest memory?"

"I don't know how far back I can go. I have trouble remembering last night's dinner," Henry answers.

"Nobody remembers last night's dinner. It's too trivial." Oliver turns to face Caleb. "How about you, Caleb?"

"I never tried to think about it," Caleb admits with a shake of his head.

"It may sound like an odd question coming from an old man." Oliver pauses to gather his thoughts and then continues. "My earliest memory is of a long black-haired girl with an Italian complexion. She was the daughter of one of my mother's friends who used to babysit me. I remember being in a tub looking up at her. She was fourteen, I was three."

"You remembered being bathed?" Caleb asks.

"Oh, yes. She was a pretty sight to behold. I never told my wife my memory, however. She might have thought I would track her down. But she never had to worry. Once I met my Vadanya she became the only woman I will ever love.

"Vadanya, that's a unique name," Caleb says.

"The first time she told me her name, I thought she was swearing at me in Russian."

"That's why you're so cheerful," Henry says smiling.

"It's hard to be in a bad mood with such a great woman in your life."

"Where is she?" Caleb says glancing around the room to see if she will be joining them soon.

"She's in heaven." Caleb turns back to face Oliver.

"My condolences, I thought she was still here"

"She is," Oliver answers. "When someone goes to heaven they aren't taken out of your life." Oliver spins his chair around to face the window. "That's why I always sit here. So, I can see her throwing acorns at me." He spins his wheelchair back around to face his guests.

"Acorns?" Caleb questions with a bewildered expression. Oliver points behind him at the tree just outside the window. Its large branches extend the entire length of the window and provides a shady patch for him in summer.

"Yes, see this tree out here? She knows I sit here, so she shakes the branches to make the acorns fall on the windowsill. Of course, in winter it's tiny little snowballs. That's how I know she's always with me." Caleb figures it's more likely the wind or the squirrels causing the acorns to fall but decides to keep these thoughts to himself.

"Where did the two of you meet?" Henry asks.

"She was a registered nurse at the VA hospital I was recuperating in."

"You were a soldier?" Caleb asks.

"Yes, I was. Desert Storm, in the battle of Khafji, January thirty-first, nineteen ninety-one. Our mission was to recapture the city from Iraqi forces, which we finally did on February first. I left my leg in that city along with twenty-five others who lost much more."

"I'm sorry you went through that horror," Caleb says sincerely. He never had to be in a war and cannot comprehend what that must be like, or suffering being wounded in battle. In comparison, his injury is far less cumbersome. Oliver continues explaining the rest of the incident as Caleb and Henry listen respectfully.

"When that mortar exploded nearby, I remembered lying there half alive, in a daze and numb. I saw those brave twenty-five men trying to climb a hill towards a lantern in the sky. I told them to take my leg so they may use it to pull themselves up."

"You wanted to lose your leg?" Caleb asks.

"Nobody wants to lose any of their limbs, Caleb. But when I married Vadanya I was so grateful I still had both my arms to hold her. What need of a leg when you have someone to hold you up?" Caleb looks at his leg and gently rubs his knee—his condition no longer feels all that crippling, but he's still not ready to fully adopt it.

"Did you have any children?" Henry asks.

"I always wanted to be a father, but as it turns out, Vadanya was barren. We thought about adopting, but the agency frowned upon my disability. She took it pretty hard; she always wanted to be a mother. Knowing her dream could never come true was disheartening, but we still had each other." Oliver reaches into his pocket and takes out a leather case. He opens it up and hands a picture to Caleb. "That's us on our wedding day."

Caleb takes the wedding picture of Oliver and Vadanya and admires it. She's standing under a trellis wearing a beautiful white gown and holding Oliver's hand as he's wearing a tux and sitting in his wheelchair. Both are smiling happily, and it appears Oliver still has all his teeth in this photo. He must have lost them in his elderly years. Caleb studies the picture before handing it over to Henry.

"It's a beautiful picture," Caleb says.

"Thank you," Oliver says proudly.

"How long were you married?" Henry asks as he observes the photo.

"Thirty-six years, and I wouldn't trade a second of it for anything else. Not the moment when we discovered she had a brain tumor. Not the moment when the doctors gave her five years to live. Not even the night, three years later, when she visited me in my dreams. She told me she had to take care of twenty-five injured men. I thanked her for looking after me for as long as she did and told her to go do her work."

"How could you accept that so easily?" Caleb says.

"It's never easy. I wish I could have another thirty years with her, but sometimes a few good memories can make all the bad ones bearable."

"I don't understand. How can you be happy being abandoned here alone?" Caleb says feeling sorry for Oliver and somewhat puzzled that he was never defeated by all the pain he had to endure throughout his life.

"It's true that I will spend the last of my days here, but I'm not abandoned or alone." Oliver wheels his chair around to look back out the window. "This is my Garden of Eden."

Caleb slowly comes to a stand in bewilderment. The desolate tundra landscape outside the window is now a flowering garden with several water fountains, and the bare branches of the oak tree are now in full bloom.

"How did that happen? It was all snow a moment ago," Caleb asks softly. Oliver remains looking outside with a huge smile while observing Vadanya walking among the flowers.

"There she is, and she has a child with her," Oliver says.

Caleb continues looking but does not see Vadanya or the child that Oliver just mentioned.

"I don't see anyone," Caleb admits.

"Let's take a closer look," Henry says.

Caleb is now standing in the flower garden next to Henry instead of in the room with Oliver. The sweet smells from the flowers and the tranquil flowing water from the fountains make this a calming environment that would attract any who set foot on this hallowed earth; however, this place doesn't occupy a place in reality, it belongs to Vadanya and Oliver has the luxury of seeing it.

"How can all of this just appear?" Caleb asks admiring his surroundings.

"You are looking through Oliver's eyes now," Henry answers.

"You mean, we're in his head?"

"Yes," Henry responds with a nod.

"How do you know Oliver anyway?" After a moment's hesitation Henry answers somberly while lowing his head.

"I met him at the funeral."

"Vadanya's?"

"No." Henry takes a few steps ahead of Caleb and then stops. He avoids direct eye contact as he explains. "I was late coming home from work when my wife called to tell me she witnessed a horrible accident; she was pregnant with our third at the time.

When I arrived at the scene, I was relieved to see they were okay, but that's when I found out a little boy was not so lucky." Henry turns around to face Caleb's imposing glare.

"It was my family who was parked in that lane next to you, Caleb." Henry reveals. "We went to the funeral to pay our respects. Oliver's shuttle passed through that intersection the light right before yours. He was one moment away from being part of it. That's why he wanted to be at the funeral too."

"But he was a complete stranger."

"A lot of complete strangers were there."

"Why?"

"Because we don't just feel for those we know. We are all connected in much deeper ways. I'm sorry this happened to you, but it doesn't mean your life is over." Caleb becomes aggravated and turns away from Henry.

"That's easy for you to say. You lost nothing." Henry steps around Caleb to look him in the face.

"That's not fair. I brought you to see Oliver so you could learn from him. He had many moments in his life that knocked him down, but he found a way to endure with joy in his heart. You and Tommy saved my family."

"What do you want me to say, you're welcomed? Do you find comfort in my sacrifice?" Caleb argues. The gently flowing water hardens into ice and the green flowering garden returns to being buried under snow.

"No, I want you to see that it's not all despair," Henry tries to explain a way to change Caleb's one-track perspective. Caleb begins his slow departure from Henry with a flick of his wrist.

"Go home to your family. I'll just stay here until this spell ends." Henry chases after him refusing to give up.

"It's not a spell. Do you think all these visitations are a coincidence? Someone is trying to give you a message."

"I don't need any more messages."

"If you could just have a little faith—"

"Faith in what?" Caleb interrupts. "An invisible God who trades lives like baseball cards? I was never greedy, I never harmed anyone, yet I was the one who was abandoned. I hate God! I hate everything which he stands for!" Henry waits for Caleb to calm down before responding.

"Oliver saw war, lost his leg, watched his fellow soldiers

perished, and then lost the love of his life. Why is he happy?"

"He must be a better man than me."

"He healed himself by keeping Vadanya alive in his heart. You can heal yourself as well by keeping a memory of Tommy."

"It won't change anything."

"It'll change everything about you."

"I can't change." Caleb drops his eyes to the ground.

"When our son was born, we named him, Jacob Thomas. That's how we kept Tommy alive." Caleb lifts his head to look at Henry. "Think about all these experiences, Caleb. Tomorrow is New Year's Eve. How will you bring it in?"

The snowy garden fades into his kitchen and this experience ends.

Caleb remains standing in silence for a long moment. He isn't so bull-headed to ignore every person who has appeared before him or the sights he's seen and the words he's heard, but this also means accepting the greatest pain his heart has ever felt. This thought turns to fear and then becomes anger so fast that Caleb doesn't realize it's happening. Rejecting it all together gives him a sense of normalcy, which he accepts as comforting and safe; however, his mental block is slowly starting to break down.

Caleb strolls back to the coat closet and carefully retrieves the tote containing his photographs. The first picture he pulls out is the one Carrie took of Tommy, Carl, and himself in front of the Christmas tree. He gives it a short moment and then drops it back inside and snaps the lid back on. He returns the tote to its place, and then shuts the door. It's been four years since he saw his nephew's face and he's trying to convince himself that he's not bothered by it. *What chance do I have at a normal life?* he thinks to himself. *I have nothing to contribute. I live to never be seen, and no one is looking.*

At this coincidental moment, the doorbell interrupts his thoughts. He turns to the door confident that he's not expecting anyone, and Carl has no reason to stop by. Caleb leans on his cane and advances toward the door. Curiosity turns into surprise when his sights discover the same girl who was sleeping on the park bench.

"Hi, are you Caleb?" she asks.

"Yes, but how did you know where I lived?" The girl lifts her arm to show Caleb's coat draping over it.

"It's on your coat." Caleb takes the coat from her and notices a sewn patch with his name and address on the inside flap.

"My sister, she had to tag everything. I forgot about that," he recalls.

Carrie believed in some older traditions of labeling certain personal possessions just in case they should become misplaced or forgotten. She gambles on the honor of others to return what had been lost and refuses to acknowledge that these acts of kindness were lost a generation ago. She argues that from time to time she will still walk a block to drop off a misdelivered letter. While many others would rather just make a note on the envelope and then stick it back into the mailbox. Carl says that Carrie is a sweet and caring person, but Caleb thinks she's being naive. Does one stop being righteous for fear of betrayal, and if so, is the outcome the development of a better person, or another egotistical clone lost in the crowd? Brave are those who will take a chance on another, foolish is the opinion of them from those who will never try.

"I just wanted to thank you for helping me, and also to return your coat," the girl continues.

"Thank you. Do you want to come inside?" Caleb asks.

"I can," the girl replies and then walks in. Caleb lets the storm door gently close behind her, and then heads into the kitchen as the girl follows.

"Do you like tea?"

"Yes, I drink tea." The girl takes a seat at the table while focusing intensively on Caleb's cane as he moves around to prepare two cups of tea. Caleb brings one cup to the table and hands it to the girl.

"Thanks," she says with a smile and takes it with both hands. Caleb then retrieves his cup from the counter and returns to sit down across from her.

"What's your name?"

"Megan," she replies after taking a small sip of the hot tea.

"Did you go home, Megan?"

"Yes, I was stupid to leave."

"We all run away from home at one point or another. Sometimes it's for an hour. Sometimes it's a lot longer."

"Did you ever fight with your parents?"

"Of course, everyone does."

"Why?"

"Well, it's two sides of the same coin. On one side are your parents who are trying to keep you safe and raise you right. On the other side you're trying to fight for independence and searching for an identity." Megan thinks about Caleb's answer for a moment before nodding in agreement.

"Sounds about right." Megan continues sipping her tea while watching Caleb with deep consideration. He notices her intense focus and wonders why he's the subject of this attention.

"What is it?" Megan drops her eyes before responding.

"Does your leg still hurt?" She says in a somber tone.

"No, it's fine. Just not as strong as it used to be," Caleb answers, but only after responding does he question why Megan had asked him the way she did. "What do you mean by, still?" Megan pushes her cup of tea away and stands up.

"I'm sorry, I should not have come here," she says, and then begins to leave the kitchen. "I should go." Caleb stands up bewildered at her sudden change in demeanor.

"Why, what's wrong?" Megan stops walking but avoids making eye contact.

"I had to see if it was really you."

"I don't know what you mean," Caleb says calmly. Megan forces herself to look up.

"I knew your name when I read it."

"How?" Megan's eyes become filled with tears; she guides her hands over them and then up through her long hair while taking her tears with them. She sniffles and recomposes herself before continuing.

"My dad was a good man," Megan returns to the table and sits back down. Caleb takes his seat and listens to what she has to say. "He was good to both my mom and I. He worked, he cooked, he never drank too much or raised a hand at me. His friends would say he was good for a laugh and my mom said he was very smart. He only had one flaw. He had a temper. When his blood boiled it always overflowed. He would punch the walls or throw things across the room. That was how he dealt with it. One day, after an argument, he sped off. I don't know what it was about. I wasn't there. He slammed that door a hundred times before, but he always came back. He should have known his brakes weren't good and neither were the roads."

Caleb was about to take a sip of his tea but sets his cup gently down and glares at Megan instead.

"Anger always blinded his judgment." Megan's tears begin to stream down her face and her next words come out as a whisper. "When that light turned red, he couldn't stop in time." Caleb pushes down on his cane and slowly comes to a stand.

"What was he driving?" Megan keeps her eyes glued to the table; she can't bring herself to look up or answer right away. "What was it?" Caleb repeats assertively.

"It was a red pickup," she squeals out.

"No! It was him? Your father did this to me?!" Caleb shouts while slamming his cane against the floor.

"He's sorry. I'm sorry!" Megan screams while crying.

"Sorry? Sorry doesn't mean anything to me!" Megan cowers while looking at Caleb. He realizes he's just talking to a child and forces himself to calm down. After a strong huff and a moment to regulate his breathing, he sits back down.

That ill-fated moment, three days after Christmas, four years ago, disaster was looming. A good man made a bad mistake and paid dearly for it, while an innocent family dealt with the aftermath. Today, Caleb is faced with a connection to the man who was responsible.

"I'm sorry about Tommy," Megan sobs.

"I never dealt with the accident or losing him. I didn't have to go into his bedroom. I didn't have to go through his toys and clothes. I don't know what that must have been like for Carrie to do it; for her to move his things. It was just easier for me to lock myself up in here and forget." Megan wipes her tears away with her fingers.

"Nothing will ever be the same again," she says.

"No, it won't. None of us will be how we were before it."

"Both of our lives are ruined," she concludes. Caleb thinks to himself for a moment. The advice from those who have visited him over these last few days are starting to change his state of mind.

"Nothing is ruined. Some lessons are hard learned for the guilty, and hard teachings for innocent observers."

"I thought if I ran away, I could start over. A girl with no family and no past sounded better in my head."

"Why did you run away?"

"I did the same thing he did. I got into a fight with my mom, and I left. I told her it was all her fault. I put all that blame on her. Everything he did; everything that happened. I said she started that. I was afraid to go home. How could anyone take me back after a thing like that?"

"I'm told a mother's love and forgiveness is everlasting. I doubt there is very little a child can do to change that." Caleb considers Megan's explanation and understands a common fear of rejection. "I haven't talked to my sister in four years. Now my brother wants me to attend his wedding. I can't just show up like nothing has happened."

"I was wrong thinking my mom wouldn't want me back. Maybe your worries are for nothing too."

"Yeah, but you ran away for a day. I've been away for four years. How do I go back? Besides, I think the bond between mother and daughter might be stronger than siblings."

"I think you are wrong," Megan says while grinning. Caleb almost laughs, but it comes out as a small grunt. "What happened to your father?" Caleb asks after a short pause and a sip of tea.

"He never came home. He went from the hospital bed to a jail cell. He received ten years on the charge of vehicular manslaughter. Although, I'm told he could be released in eight with good behavior. But I don't think my mom forgives him. She wants a divorce. I don't think I can fully forgive him either. He threw everything away over nothing."

"I'm afraid I cannot advise you in that department," Caleb admits. Understanding and acceptance is hard enough for him, but forgiveness can't even be considered at this moment.

"Do you regret helping me?" Megan asks, "Now that you know who I am?" This question may have once been hard to comprehend, but Caleb doesn't need to put any thought into it now. He knows she has suffered in other ways from this event and admires her for coming to him knowing what she knew.

"No, a child should not be held accountable for a parent's mistake."

"I'm not a child."

"You're younger than me so you're a child."

"A lot of people are younger than you." Caleb remains looking at Megan without responding until she drops her eyes back down. "Sorry."

"Your mother must be a strong woman," he begins calmly.

"She raised a very audacious daughter."

"What does that mean?"

"Brave." Megan smiles at his remark.

"You will be a good dad someday."

"You think so?"

"Yes."

"Thank you, Megan." She finishes the last sip of her tea and then stands up.

"My mom doesn't know I'm here. I should get going."

"Okay," Caleb responds. He stands up and follows her back to the front door.

"Thanks for the tea," she says as she steps out onto the stoop.

"Thank you for the talk."

Megan grins and then heads to the sidewalk. She turns around, and the two exchange waves before she begins her walk home.

5

Auld Lang Syne

Carl and Melissa arrive at Carrie's home with a pie and two bottles of champaign. She gives them a warm welcome and take their coats as Carl takes a whiff of the air.

"Ah, something smells good." Carrie chuckles knowing that her whole afternoon cooking wouldn't be for nothing.
New Year's Eve dinners were always a time to come together for lively conversation, a hearty meal, and a few drinks to lighten the mood. The holiday table is set for three and the feast consists of a seafood smorgasbord, crab legs, lobster tails, shrimp cocktail, grilled mussels, stuffed clams, and scallops. Carrie, Carl, and Melissa serve themselves and then pass the dishes and a bottle of wine around the table until everyone has a full plate.

"Everything looks so good," Melissa points out.

"Food has always been a passion in our family," Carl says.

"Yes, everybody cooks; that's a house rule," Carrie chimes in.

"We all have our specialties," Carl adds.

"Mine are vegetable and seafood dishes," Carrie explains. "And Carl's soups and pasta dishes are unbelievable."

"I make my own sauces too," Carl admits proudly.

"I'm lucky to be marrying such a great home chef," Melissa says while rubbing Carl's upper arm.

"My culinary arts degree finally paid off," Carl jokes.

"And baking will be my contribution then," Melisa says.

"I can't wait to try the pie you brought. That alone may have earned your place amongst us," Carrie announces.

"You make it sound like a knight's code of honor." Carl deepens his voice. "You may now dine with us." Melissa and Carrie laugh at his impression. Next, they hold hands and Carl begins saying grace.

"Thank you, Lord for presenting this bounty before us and keeping us happy and healthy."

"And allow these two to present me a nephew or niece so I may spoil," Carrie adds. In between the giggles Melissa adds her prayer.

"And please help Caleb through his troubles." They exchange smiles and then collectively say, "Amen." After the first few bites Melissa turns the attention back to Caleb.

"What's Caleb's culinary specialty, if I may ask?"

"Grilling," Carl answers. "He can grill anything. Steaks, burgers, ribs, chicken, kabobs, you name it."

"I never knew how long to keep anything on for," Carrie admits. "But with Caleb all that was innate."

"The table feels incomplete without him. I tried calling him, but he didn't pick up," Carl says.

"I think this new year he'll come around," Melissa says.

"You are very hopeful," Carl points out.

"I truly think he wants to come home. He just doesn't know how," Melissa continues.

"I don't understand what happened to him," Carrie argues as Melissa further explains.

"I've been doing some research. Those who develop agoraphobia feel unsafe in social settings."

"But we aren't strangers," Carrie responds. "I just don't know how his condition became so severe."

"I read that when someone makes a connection between a negative feeling and where it occurred, they will avoid similar places. In his case it may be your connection to Tommy and the fear that he would be reminded of him when seeing you or being back in your home."

"So, is it a safety concern or a fear of not having control?" Carl asks.

"A little bit of both, actually. In his mind, his home is safe, and outside is where bad things happen."

"Will he ever move past that?" Carrie asks.

"There is therapy for his condition, but generally he needs to be immersed into a situation in order for him to get used to it."

"You mean, literally facing his fear?" Carl inquires.

"Right, such as starting out in a less crowded place and slowly working him into larger crowds; typically, with a trusted companion this treatment can help him overcome his fear."

"I don't think he has a trusted companion," Carl woefully admits.

"If he acknowledges his condition as an issue, he could cure himself," Melissa replies. "There are relaxing and calming techniques he can practice to introduce himself back into society."

"I think your wedding is a good motivation for him," Carrie says. "Maybe it's forcing him to at least think about it now."

Caleb is sitting in his recliner under a dim light; in the silence he waits patiently for something to happen. He lifts his cell phone and taps the screen to illuminate the time, 11:08PM; nearly one more hour until New Year's Day. Normally he would be in bed by now, but the belief that he will be awaken by some unknown visitor has kept him from retiring. Caleb taps his fingers on the armrest wondering if anything will happen at all. He tries to recall all who had visited him prior, and what their messages were.

His grandfather was the first. He passed away when Caleb was still a child, and he did not know him as well as he wanted to. He felt robbed for not having that bond or the ability to learn from a man who his younger self adored so much. Caleb reaches over to the side table and picks up the pile of notes that mysteriously appeared after every encounter. He reads his grandfather's message again, *sometimes we are heroes without even knowing it.*

His next visitor was a childhood friend from long ago. Jessica was someone Caleb didn't want to let go; he regrets not being able to continue their friendship as they grew older. More than that; however, was the fact that after her moving away a void was left inside him that made him feel alone. It is another moment in his life where he was unable to hold onto someone who was special to him. He reads her message to him next, *take a walk in the park on New Year's Day*. That will be tomorrow, but how can a walk in a snowy park on New Year's Day have any impact on his life?

The third visitor was his third-grade teacher, Miss Di Cocco. Not just a caring and patient soul who always knew Caleb was a good person inside, but also an inspiration and fascination to his younger mind. Her presence allowed him to develop a sense of self-worth and the longing to feel the love he always desired. It was something he had forgotten, but a segment of that idea resonates within him once more. She showed him a memory he wanted to forget, something he could not change, but she also showed him something he could do. He made a choice that night to save Megan's life. Even after finding out who she was, he never regretted it. Miss Di Cocco also left Caleb a message as he reads it one more time, *find Tommy's gift*. This one, like all the others still baffles him. What could Tommy's gift be?

Christina, his ex-girlfriend became his fourth visitor, she showed him a grim future, but also a bright one. She was another person that didn't remain in Caleb's life for long, but she showed him that he was not forgotten by his family and that his life will go on if he truly desires it to. Caleb rotates the next piece of paper in his hand and recites Christina's message to him, *look for the symbol of the archer*. Another riddle, one that he can't even begin to decipher. How could something that belongs in an Indiana Jones movie possibly apply to him?

His latest visitor was Henry, not counting Megan, who was the only real person that had interacted with him. Henry is the father of the girls, and unborn child that was in the car next to him on that fateful day. In hindsight he feels ashamed for being angry with him. Caleb doesn't even want to consider the pain Henry would have gone through if he had lost his wife and children all at once. For four years Caleb has been asking, *why me?* But now knowing what the alternative could have been, he is left with a vicarious relief for Henry. Also, during this time, he was introduced to Oliver, a man who suffered much more than him in his lifetime, yet he remained hopeful and joyful.

It is now nearly midnight. How will Caleb welcome the new year?

The last thing on the table is Carl's unopened envelope. He reaches for it and slowly opens it to read the card. At the bottom

Carl has written: *Will you be my best man?* Caleb gently lowers the card and stares at the floor as if he's lost in thought. How can he accept it? How can he refuse it?

Just then, the melody of an Irish flute begins to fill his home. He lifts his head in bewilderment and continues to listen to the jig. It is not unfamiliar to him, but also has not been heard for many years. He finally places his mother's favorite tune of *Swallowtail*. He kicks the footrest down and gets up from the chair to investigate.

Caleb enters the kitchen to discover an elderly woman sitting at the table while playing her flute. When she notices him, she stops playing and sets down the flute to greet him with a heavy Irish accent.

"G'day, Mr. Caleb. Have a seat, please." Caleb sits down across from her still in surprise.

"Are you another ghost?" he asks in an exhausted tone.

"Ghost? Now don't be believing in such tales, Mr. Caleb. My name is Mary Flynn, your great, great, great grandmother." Caleb knew he was part Irish, but never heard stories or seen pictures concerning these relatives or his Irish roots.

"You're from Ireland then?

"Yes, Cork, Ireland. We left for New York in 1844, right before the potato famine of 1845," Mary explains.

"I wish I lived back in the 1800's."

"Why is that?"

"Times were simpler, people were better to one another, and all the problems of today were not around then."

"No, we had completely different problems, young Caleb. Life was never easy, not now, not back in 1844. Drunken factory workers prowled the alleyways looking for young girls. Rather they were receptive to their advances or not rarely mattered. At just seven months, my sister died from a fever. And to make matters worse, not a week later, a man with a knife thought a bag of flour was worth more than my grandfather's life when he stabbed him for it. But we endured, none-the-less. What choice did we have?"

"I'm sorry. I didn't know any of that," Caleb says while lowering his gaze. He may have thought life used to be easier with better family values and manners toward strangers. This was just an image of a glorified past romanticized by fictional movies and books. The truth is mankind was always plagued with weakness, imperfections, the degenerates, and their ilk.

"Tragedy was just a part of life," Mary continues. "My mother had to bury three of her children, my sister and two brothers. One was kicked in the head by a horse, and the other paid a gambling debt with a bullet to the chest. Neither of them saw thirty. When I asked why I must say goodbye, my mother answered, siúil a rúin; which means walk, my love. We all had to keep walking forward."

"I never said goodbye to Tommy. He was gone before I woke up," Caleb finally admits.

"What is it about the accident that pains you the most?" Mary asks. "You need a cane, but you can still walk. Tommy isn't in pain." Mary rises from her chair. "It's time, Caleb."

"Time for what?" Caleb asks while shooting her a glance.

"Siúil a rúin."

Caleb's kitchen flashes back and forth from itself to that of a pub until the pub setting takes over as the new location. Caleb and Mary are sitting at a booth, inside a crowded Irish pub, as an Irish band plays on the stage. The guests are drinking their beers and eating their fish and chips and fried cheese curds, while talking and laughing loquaciously. Irish flag tablecloths drape over the tables and Irish pennants hang down from the rafters.

"Are we in Ireland?" Caleb asks as he looks around seemly impressed with his surroundings.

"No Caleb, this pub is two blocks from your house." Caleb focuses back to Mary a little stunned a place like this was so close without him knowing.

"Why did you bring me here?"

"Because you need to get out more. The last thing you celebrated was Christmas, four years ago." Caleb rubs the tablecloth gently without responding.

"Everyone here has faced something hard, but tonight they sit here with a smile on their face." Caleb takes a glance around the pub once more as Mary continues. "You aren't meant to brave everything alone, Caleb. You have an opportunity now to take back your life. You are a fool if you do not take it."

"I don't know how to change. I don't know what to believe in," Caleb confides in Mary.

"I was brought up catholic. My husband was protestant.

I had to choose between him, or my previous life. My decision ostracized me from my side of the family. Sometimes you just have to go with your heart."

"Did you ever regret it?"

"No, never. I had a good life. He was a good man. If I didn't choose him, I may have never felt real love. The man you are today would not exist. I had to accept my losses and cherish my gains; just as you must."

"But I didn't gain a thing. I just lost everything."

"Hush now. You've gained more than you know. Your experience will make you a mentor to others."

"Why would it matter?"

"Maybe it's in the form of advice you will give or a lesson you would teach. Maybe it's a memory you need to remember to prevent making a mistake. What you say could save a life or overpower a bad influence. Sometimes your actions can be seen in the same lifetime, or sometimes over several generations. In any case what you do and why you do it, will connect and interact with other people. And that, just may be something to believe in. You were not forgotten, you were chosen."

"How can I start over?"

"Do you feel uncomfortable right now?"

"No, why?"

"Look around, Caleb. You're sitting in a room full of people and you don't know a single one of them." Caleb takes quick glances around himself and realizes he isn't nervous or feels out of place.

"So, I am."

"When you suppress an emotion, you don't want to feel, it becomes a disease. When you fear that emotion it will consume you. When that happens, it will always be felt."

"I remember the day before the accident. Tommy wanted to go out for a burger and malt, but Carrie had already made his lunch. He asked me to take him the next day. It was supposed to be fun—not a disaster."

"Some events cannot be avoided."

"I feel like my life was put on pause. I never left that intersection. In my mind Tommy is still waiting to arrive at the restaurant."

"No, he has moved on, and he's waiting for you to catch up.

Only those who are capable of dealing with the hardest of times are chosen to endure them."

"Someone has chosen poorly; I am not him. I have failed that task."

"That is still to be determined."

"What do you mean?"

"Hope tends to be the last thing that's discovered. What is your hope?"

"I want to be free. Please, is it not too late? I don't want to be alone anymore," Caleb cries out while grasping her hands. She squeezes his hands with hers and smiles.

"Open your eyes, Caleb. Broaden your view. Let the music explore freely within your mind." Caleb looks toward the band. All the mixture of incoherent chatter and gossip suddenly stop. Just the Celtic music and Mary's voice is heard by Caleb.

"Believe in love—" Mary says. Caleb sees himself at another table across the room. He can see the back of an unknown woman setting across from him. He believes her to be the same woman he saw when Christina visited him.

"Remember your dreams—" Caleb remembers the summer cookout vision he saw with his family.

"Trust your family—" Caleb notices Carrie, Carl and Melissa at the bar smiling at him.

"Now, reach for it."

The pub becomes completely silent and then fades from view. Only the table, underneath the hanging lamp, is in view of an otherwise pitch-black surrounding. Caleb and Mary stand up from their table.

"What happened?" Caleb asks.

"The time has come for you to make your choice."

Three illuminated doors suddenly appear. The first is right next to Caleb. The second is on his opposite side but it's separated by three suspended steppingstones. The third appears in front of him on top of a cliff that is impossible to leap or scale.

"Choose your door, Caleb. The one near you is simple. All you have to do is reach for it. The one on your right takes a little more work and finesse to get to. The third door looks impossible to arrive at."

"How do I know which one is right?" he asks.

"Doesn't matter. They all lead to the same place." Caleb looks at Mary confused.

"If all the doors lead to the same place, then why are two harder to reach?"

"That's just how you see them," Mary smiles. "Your destination doesn't change; the complication is in the path you have chosen to take." Mary sighs. "Sometimes people just make things harder for themselves." Caleb thinks about his decision for a moment before deciding to reach for the simple door on his left.

A bright light fills the dark abyss and forces Caleb to close his eyes. After it has dissipated, he reopens them to observe Mary and him are in the snowy residential park across from his home.

"The right path doesn't have to be the hardest one," Mary points out.

Thousands of Christmas lights suddenly illuminate on all the trees and bushes throughout the entire park, and a large group of carolers appear, while singing Auld Lang Syne.

Caleb's grandfather, Jessica, Miss. Di Cocco, Christina, Henry, Vadanya and Oliver make their way from within the crowd and line up in front so Caleb can see them. When the singing ends Caleb's attention turns to his impeccable guides.

"We've been waiting for you, Caleb. I always knew you would find your way," Christina begins. Caleb's grandfather is next to speak.

"When a message needs to find its way to someone; the rules are bent ever so slightly to bring it to them."

"We had an obligation not only to deliver our messages, but also to bring you where you needed to be," Jessica points out.

"In the last few minutes of the year; we all gather to cherish those we love," Miss Di Cocco continues. "You are not excluded from our grace. You are here to know you are loved."

"They say people come together in tragic times, but we've always been a social species. We learned a long time ago we cannot survive on our own," Henry says.

"When your heart is safe, your mind is free," Oliver advises."

Vadanya steps forward to inspect Caleb's leg. She lightly places her hand on his knee and for a moment Caleb's pain subsides.

"Don't use your cane as a crutch; use it as a third leg; an extension of yourself." Caleb nods and she returns to stand next to Oliver. She puts her arm around his shoulders as he happily reaches up to hold it.

Mary leaves Caleb's side and joins the others.

"You've come a long way, Caleb, but there is one last person who will conclude your journey."

Someone begins to advance through the crowd, Caleb spots the top of his head as this person gets closer to the front of the line. Caleb can't believe his eyes when Tommy finally steps out into view with a huge grin on his face.

"Happy New Year, uncle," he says.

"Tommy—" Overcome with emotion Caleb falls to his knees as Tommy runs to meet him. They throw their arms around each other and squeeze each other tightly.

"I've missed you," Tommy says in Caleb's ear.

"I've missed you too. Oh, how I've missed you." Tommy pulls away still smiling. He looks around the park before turning back to Caleb.

"I like all the lights. Where are yours?"

"I thought you couldn't see them anymore." Tommy rests his hands on Caleb's shoulders while looking at him.

"I can always see you."

"I'm so sorry. I really am. About everything."

"I'm not sad, uncle. I want you to be happy."

"I will be. I promise." Tommy holds his hand out and with the help of his cane and Tommy he rises to his feet again.

"Come with me," Tommy says.

Tommy holds Caleb's hand as the two walk a few paces until the park transitions into a church hallway. The two continue walking down the long corridor before turning into a room full of flowers. In the front of the room is a small, opened coffin.

Caleb immediately stops in his tracks and looks ahead in complete horror.

"Why did you bring me here?" he says in a loud whisper.

"This is what you are running away from. This is how you move forward." Tommy drops his hand and looks up at him waiting for his response. Caleb slowly shakes his head.

"No."

"It was me. I asked everyone to find you. And through them, you found me. I wanted to save the baby. And now, I want to save you."

"I still can't do this."

"Yes, you can." Caleb turns to face Tommy. His hidden grief is starting to show.

"You're asking me to do the hardest thing imaginable."

"I know, but everything gets easier once you stop avoiding it."

Caleb reluctantly begins to walk forward. His heart is heavy, and a pit makes a home in his throat. His cane falls heavily on the floor as he proceeds closer to the coffin. His eyes begin to water, but he doesn't stop or look away from his point of travel. He takes the last step toward the tiny coffin with tears running down his cheeks. It's the first time since the accident that he has shown his sorrow.

He places his hand on top of the open side and peers inside to see Tommy's lifeless body. He completely breaks down and cries uncontrollably. He lets his hand slide down the side and lowers himself to the floor continuing to sob.

"I'm sorry I left you, Tommy. I was afraid."

Tommy is standing behind him, and gently glides his arms around his shoulders.

"Don't cry. I love you."

"I love you too. I'm sorry it took so long."

A pastor approaches the nearby podium while Caleb weeps beside his nephew's coffin.

"There is a calm surrender following tragedy; a mournful send-off, but also a peaceful embrace of things to come. For rarely do events occur without reason," the pastor begins. "May the road rise to meet you, may the wind be always at your back. May the sun shine warm upon your face, the rains fall soft upon your fields and, until we meet again, may God hold you in the palm of His hand."

Tommy begins walking back towards the hallway. Caleb turns around to watch him while still sitting on the floor. Tommy smiles while looking at Caleb from the hallway.

"I can see you every time you remember me," Tommy says. Caleb wipes away his tears, but new ones always seem to be taking their place.

Vadanya appear beside Tommy and takes his hand into hers, as a mother usually does. Tommy makes one last motion to wave with his other hand before a bright cascading light surrounds them. In a moment the light, and those within it, vanish from Caleb's view.

The pastor steps down and offers his hand to Caleb. He accepts it and is pulled up.

"You aren't broken. You aren't abandoned. Because I have lifted you up." The pastor then hands Caleb his cane.

Caleb closes his eyes and feels lightened, as if a great burden has finally been lifted from his soul. He is weightless and has a sensation of floating. He cannot see anything but feels as if he is surrounded by light, warmth, and loving arms carrying him to another location. He can still hear the pastor's voice in his head.

"I will never turn away one of mine from my home, despite how long they may have been away. Claim your place beside me and live your life freely, and full of hope and joy. For you are healed. You are now returned to your home, Caleb. The memories from your experiences are yours to keep. Do with them as you wish."

Caleb opens his eyes to find himself in his own bed. He blinks several times and looks around. The morning sun is trying to squeeze through the closed blinds of his bedroom window, and he has a sudden urge to open them. Caleb throws the covers off and reaches for his cane. After a few short steps he pulls the blinds up as high as they will go. The sun blinds him for a moment, but when he reopens them, he sees a bright sunny day welcoming him. He unlocks the window and then lifts it up to let the unseasonal warm air into his home. It is the first day of a new year. It may look exactly the same as the day before, but nothing about it feels the same.

6

A Gift of Acorns

Thirty-eight degrees is a welcome relief from the single digits of the last few weeks, and cabin fever forces a few to venture outside. Just after mid-day Caleb becomes one who seeks a stroll in the park. He's not sure if his appearance will hold any significance like Jessica's message had claimed; regardless, today feels like a good time to get some fresh air. Caleb zips up his coat and takes hold of his cane before taking his first step out the door. He stands on his stoop for a moment and then begins his walk towards his mailbox. This is usually as far as he goes and that thought stops him again. He glances back at his house and with a sigh, steps off the curb and continues across the street.

He observes the snow-covered trees and bushes and soon makes it half-way around the perimeter with ease. The walk seems to make his legs feel better as they stretch and feel the pressure of his weight pressing them down against the path. His cramps and tight muscles loosen and relax the further he advances. A family of five is seen gradually heading toward him. At first, Caleb doesn't put much thought into it; this could just be a random encounter or chance meeting. The family consists of a man, woman, two girls and a younger boy. The man gives in to a common habit of giving strangers a smile and single nod while his wife audible says her hello. Except this isn't an ordinary meeting of strangers. Caleb recognizes the man as Henry.

"Henry?" Caleb says as he and the family stop to converse. "And this must be Jacob," he recalls after glancing at the young boy.

This version of Henry never met or spoke to Caleb, and his wife doesn't remember him by appearance alone.

"Yes, it is," Henry responds, but after a curious look from his wife continues with uncovering a clue to who Caleb is. "I must apologize, but I can't place how we know each other." Caleb rests both hands on top of his cane with it in front of him.

"That's quite alright. We never actually met. Four years ago, your wife witnessed a car accident where she covered an unconscious man. That was me, and Tommy was my nephew." In a split-second Henry's wife covers her mouth in shock.

"Oh-my-God," she says and picks up one of Caleb's hands into hers. "I'm so sorry."

"I never got the chance to thank you for looking after us," Caleb says sincerely.

"I wished I could have done more," she somberly replies. Caleb smiles while shaking his head.

"No, you did more for us than you know," Caleb admits.

"You have our deepest sympathies," Henry adds. Caleb directs his gaze to each family member before returning it to Henry.

"For the longest time I wished I was never there," Caleb begins sympathetically. "I'm sorry I ever wished that."

With tears pooling in their eyes, they extend their hands and shake. No further words are needed between the two men. How close can bonds be among those we've never met? Caleb's New Year's Day walk answered just that, and one other. Sometimes we are heroes without even knowing it.

Caleb's peruses through the Christmas clearance shelves of a local hardware store and grabs as many of the boxes of colored lights as he can load into his cart. When he arrives at the checkout the cashier gives him a warm smile.

"You must be preparing to set some kind of record."

"I just want to make sure everyone can see them this time," he replies.

On the drive home Caleb passes the elderly home that Henry had taken him to meet Oliver. He pulls alongside the curb and stops the car. He sits in silence while observing the building, but the urge to visit an old man doesn't subside. Caleb enters the front doors and looks around the lobby. It's uncanny how similar this area is to his experience with Henry, despite never seeing it before. This rules out any chance of it being recovered from a memory. The lady behind the reception desk tries to get Caleb's attention while he admires his surroundings.

"Sir? May I help you?" Caleb snaps out of his bewilderment and advances toward the desk.

"May I see Oliver."

"Are you a friend or family?

"Both," he says after a short pause.

Caleb enters the room and looks to the spot by the large window and spots Oliver in his wheelchair looking outside. Caleb carefully makes his way across the room with the aid of his cane until he reaches behind Oliver. He spins his chair around and reveals his missing leg and the same three teeth. Oliver appears to be somewhat surprised to see Caleb standing in front of him.

"I saw you in my dream," he says.

"I too shared the same experience," Caleb admits and sits down next to him.

"What brings you here, my boy?"

"I wanted to thank you. I was a broken man, but I learned from your wisdom."

Oliver looks at Caleb's leg and must have remembered the moment in his dream. "Car accident?"

"Yes, the one you know. Tommy was my nephew." Oliver reaches his hand out and gently grasps Caleb's.

"I didn't see you at the funeral."

"I wasn't there. It took me four years to say goodbye to Tommy."

"My wife told me the exact moment she was leaving, but I never stopped thinking about her."

"I know." Caleb smiles. "You said you saw her with a child."

"Yes, I see her with a small boy and I'm happy that she is now a mother."

"She's a very good one."

"Thank you," Oliver grins. "One day I will walk beside her, and one day, much later, so will you. That's why some people have to go when they do. We may think it's unfair or untimely, but they are the bridge; they find and connect souls. We are never alone."

The winter months gradually turn into spring; however, at times, Wisconsin springs can appear to be identical to their winters. On the days that tease the locals with warm weather, Caleb will venture to the park or walk around his block, but he never ran into Henry again and hasn't experienced any further visitations. There are still two messages he was never able to resolve, and the time to do so may have long passed. Finding Tommy's gift and the symbol of the archer have eluded him; perhaps some mysteries are beyond the comprehension of those who seek to uncover their secrets.

The day of Carl's and Melissa's wedding arrives. The church is decorated with Matsumoto floral arrangements and cornflower-colored cloths and runner. The guests are starting to take their seats in the pews while others are still standing around talking. Almost everyone on the guest list have arrived as Carl remains focused on the entry doors hoping to see Caleb walking through. He glances down the corridor, but on one is behind him either. The door stoppers are pulled out and the wooden doors begin to shut. The ceremony is about to begin. Carl lets out a disappointed sigh and starts to make his way toward the alter.

Friends and family reach out to shake his hand and give him their blessings as he smiles and thanks them. He clasps his hands in front of him and waits beside his groomsmen with his head down until the bride is signaled. The sparse conversing continues as well, before suddenly falling to a hush. The pews creak as the entire congregation turns in their seats. Carl lifts his head to see what the disturbance could be.

Caleb remains standing in the doorway dressed in his tux and resting his hands on top of his cane. Carl takes a moment to make sure he didn't force his thoughts into reality. He takes several slow steps forward before picking up the pace to meet his brother at the entrance to the hall.

"Am I late," Caleb asks. Carl shakes his head while laughing.

"No."

"I forgot the card," Caleb admits. Carl chuckles and throws his arms around him while patting him on the back.

"This is better."

"Is the spot for best man still open?"

"Yes."

Caleb glances over Carl's shoulder to notice Carrie staring at them from the front of the church. Carl turns to see where Caleb's focus went and then turns back to him.

"Go talk to her," Carl advises softly.

The room follows Caleb as he advances down the aisle toward his sister. They exchange silent looks until Caleb lowers his eyes.

"I'm sorry, Carrie," Caleb says with tears in his eyes. "I'm sorry I took so long." Carrie immediately throws her arms around him and begins to cry.

"I love you," she says.

"Can you forgive me?"

"You always were. I just wanted you back." They embrace each other for several more moments before she pulls away and dries her eyes.

"Come on, we need to get you in place," she smiles.

Carrie takes him by the arm and leads him back as smiles from the guests ensures Caleb others are also happy to see him.

Melissa and her maid of honor are waiting in another room when Carrie and Caleb enter.

"Look who I found, Mel," Carrie says. Melissa grins and then kisses Caleb on the cheek.

"I knew you would make it, Caleb."

"How could I not?" Melissa turns to the woman beside her.

"This is Tanya, she's my maid of honor. Tanya, this is the best man." Caleb and Tanya exchange smiles while shaking hands.

"Please to meet you," Caleb starts.

"You too," She replies. Caleb notices the cross on Tanya's necklace, but it appears to be leaning and has a point at the top."

"Your cross looks like it's falling," he says while pointing." Tanya lightly touches the necklace with her fingertips.

"Oh, it's not a cross, although you aren't alone in thinking that," she giggles. "It's my zodiac sign for Sagittarius."

"Which one is the Sagittarius?"

"He's the archer."

"The archer—" Caleb softly says out loud.

Some say they just know when they find the one that they are destined for. Caleb was given the biggest clue anyone could be given. Wedding music begins playing from the hall signifying the ceremony is starting. Caleb gives Tanya a smirk while holding his arm out.

"I think we're walking together." Tanya nods and smiles as she holds onto his arm.

Caleb takes his place next to Carl as Tanya strolls over beside Carrie. The wedding march begins, and everyone stands up as Melissa slowly paces herself down the aisle.

Caleb cannot fathom how he almost wanted to skip coming to his brother's wedding. He had forgotten what it felt like to be part of a family, and today it just got bigger. As the pastor speaks his words to Carl and Melissa, Caleb can't help but glance over at Tanya. She shyly smiles but pretends not to see him.

"Now for the rings," the pastor says. Caleb obeys his cue and hands a ring to Carl and then one to Melissa before returning to his spot behind Carl. The couple slides their rings onto each other while saying their, I do's.

"I now pronounce you husband, and wife. You may kiss the bride." Everyone applauds as the two kiss and then begin to lead the wedding party back up the aisle. Caleb and Tanya rejoin arms while beaming as they follow the bride and groom.

The banquet hall fills up fast with guests, as the wedding party advances to their row of tables at the front of the room. Cornflower and ivory tablecloths, chair covers, and drapes litter the hall elegantly with centerpieces of Matsumotos on all the tables. Someone clings their glass and the room falls silent. Caleb stands up from his chair and accepts the microphone being handed to him. A massive gathering, of mostly strangers, look up and wait for him to give his speech. Speaking in front of a crowd would never have been possible just a few short months ago.

"I know it's been a long time since some of you have seen me, and for many it was never expected. I've learned to believe that every wound, no matter how it's inflicted, heals with love; however, it takes a degree of bravery to open your heart to receive it. Sometimes all it takes is a helping hand or a push in the right direction." Caleb turns to Carl sitting beside him and gives him a cheeky smile and a pat on the back. "In some ways marriage operates in the same way. You offer her a hand, and she pushes you around." The room bursts into laughter and claps as Carl stands up to hug him. Caleb allowed himself to embrace his visitors' advice and have come to realize how important their tutelage and notes were to him. With their help he was able to overcome his fears and find what's been missing in his life. Caleb and Tanya are often seen talking or dancing together as the night carries on into the wee hours of the morning. Oliver once said, what need for a leg when you have someone to hold you up? With Tanya by his side, Caleb can leave his cane at his chair. Her arms are all he needs.

Caleb hasn't been in Carrie's house since the accident, but he finally works up the will to visit. He paces around the living room and finds the framed picture of him, Carl, and Tommy at Christmas. He picks it up and studies it before gently setting it back down. He turns back around to find Carrie watching him with a small flat present still wrapped in Christmas paper.

"I've been keeping this for you," she says and hands him the gift.

"This is for me?" Caleb takes the gift and gently admires the wrapping with his fingers.

"I found it in Tommy's closet. He must have forgotten to give it to you."

"This is from Tommy?" Caleb says shocked. He turns it over and notices the tag that reads, To Uncle Caleb, in different sized letters with no baseline. "Why have you never opened it?"

"It was the last thing he wanted you to have. I wasn't going to take that away."

"He wrapped this himself?"

"Yes."

Caleb sits down in the nearby chair while still admiring the present in his hands. He almost doesn't want to unwrap it; he wants to preserve the last thing Tommy did. All the clues have been given and every mystery has been solved, except for this last one. In order to conclude his journey, he needs to discover Tommy's gift.

Caleb lifts the flaps while tugging gently at the taped edges. With each unfolded side the gift reveals more of itself until a framed portrait of Tommy, with his iconic wide grin, is in full view. Tears stream down as cheeks as he reads the words, *I'm Fine, love Tommy* written in the white margin. He can't bring himself to form words, but none are needed. He holds the picture against his chest and sobs as Carrie holds him in her arms.

Caleb places Tommy's portrait on the foyer table, so it will always be seen. Every morning, and every night he will pass it, everyone who comes over will notice it; Caleb isn't hiding Tommy's memory any longer.

This almost concludes our story about one man's journey into the depths of his soul to find peace, acceptance, forgiveness, and love. Do you believe his tale I just told? I must admit it does sound too fantastical at times to be true. Not even I had believed it when I first heard it. After all, a child always expects his father to tell him extravagant stories. I cannot deny the fact that he always walked with a cane as far back as I can remember. I've seen Tommy's picture and read the notes my father had kept. Who am I to prove or disprove what is possible in this world?

Is the man who helps push your car out of a snowy ditch, in the early morning hours, just a man going for a walk, or a divine being? When someone falls from a great height and walks away with almost no injury, is it happenstance or divine intervention? Maybe the answer solely lies in the hearts of those who live it, and of those who hear of it. That is the best way I can explain it.

The following year, Caleb takes a job as a creative writing teacher in a local high school. It is the last day of class before summer vacation, and his students are getting anxious to leave. He hears them talking about partying and taking road trips or racing their new cars. He does not condone celebrating or even moderate alcohol consumption, but teenagers are seldom thinking beyond the moment they are currently in. He makes his way to the front of the desk and then sits on top of it before leaning his cane beside him. His students never asked him why he needed a cane, but most of them talked about it amongst themselves. He heard some of their hypothesizes over the past few months ranging from being a soldier to belonging to a bank heist gone wrong. Though some of them were amusing he decides to set the record straight.

"I heard some of you question why I needed a cane." Some of his students quiet down and look up at him. "I was on the receiving end of an angry driver who broadsided me. My leg was smashed, but more importantly than that, the accident took the life of my five-year-old nephew who was in the backseat." His classroom now falls completely silent as everyone listens to him. "I lived the following four years of my life as a hermit. I didn't know how to deal with the aftermath of the accident, and I soon developed a condition where I became afraid to leave my home. I was afraid to be around other people, and just the thought of being outside filled me with anxiety. Worst of all, I kept finding ways to pretend the accident never happened. I refused to mourn the passing of my nephew and blamed anyone I could for my disability. One day, my brother stopped by to ask me if I could be in his wedding, I didn't think I would be able too, but luckily some visiting friends took the time to slowly reintroduce me back into the world. That's how I got past my phobias. It took me four years to accept this cane and bury my nephew." Caleb pauses and looks around the room. "I know some of you like to race, when I was in high school, we did the same thing, but my point is, when you get behind that wheel, you are no longer responsible just for yourself."

The school bell rings, but the end of the day doesn't motivate his students to rush up and run out of the room. Caleb looks up at the clock and then slides off the desk to walk behind it. He waits for a moment when he observes no one is rushing to the door. "Class dismissed." His students begin to get up and head for the door while giving him small smiles. "Enjoy your summer," he says after them. He leaves them with a greater understanding of who he is and where he came from, but also words that will remain in the back of their minds. Who knows if it will change anyone's mind? Maybe when the school year starts up again someone will admit, I remembered what you said.

Caleb and Tanya are holding hands while walking in the park at the peak of its summer bloom. They find a vacant park bench in the shade of a tree and decide to sit down. They keep their hands interlocked and kiss before Tanya lays her head on Caleb's shoulder.

Several acorns fall near Caleb's feet.
Caleb looks down—
and smiles.

"Big action with explosions and car chases are always fun, but sometimes it's good just to tell a character-driven, dialogue supported story about someone's life."

About the Author

Jerry J.C. Veit was born in the spring of 1983 to a German and Portuguese family. He developed a love for writing at a young age and a fondness for classic literary works by Charles Dickens, Mark Twain, Edgar Allen Poe, and others.

His introduction into writing began with screenwriting in 2008. After making it to many of the finals in several screenplay contests and writing countless query letters to literary agencies, he ultimately decided to abandon this form of writing. In 2016 he explored self-publishing and transformed all six of his screenplays into novelized scripts that resembled a play. It wasn't until 2021 that he decided to rewrite, reformat, and extend all his titles once again—this time into traditional novels starting with his debut novel, Apocalypsia, and a two-volume anthology of his novellas containing five stories total.

He currently resides in southeastern Wisconsin working by day as a graphic designer at an ad agency, but by night he's a builder of worlds who enjoys writing character-driven stories that inspire, entertain, and hopefully leave an everlasting impression on his audience. He's passionate about writing in the genres of fantasy, dystopias and paranormal, but also penned an inspirational story as well.

www.ingramcontent.com/pod-product-compliance
Lightning Source LLC
Chambersburg PA
CBHW072114300726
48975CB00003B/803